QUEEN
OF HIS HEART

NATIONAL BESTSELLING AUTHOR

ADRIANNE BYRD

QUEEN
OF HIS HEART

ARABESQUE®

Recycling programs
for this product may
not exist in your area.

QUEEN OF HIS HEART

ISBN-13: 978-0-373-83166-1

© 2009 by Adrianne Byrd

www.kimanipress.com

Printed in U.S.A.

To Eliot
My Rock

Acknowledgments

To my family and friends, thanks for all the support and love that you've given me. To my editor, Evette Porter, thanks for loving my stories. To my wonderful fans and readers, thank you for allowing me to do what I do. It's always a pleasure to entertain you.

I wish you all the best of love,

Adrianne

Chapter 1

"All a single girl needs to be happy is a strong vibrator and a lifetime supply of Energizer batteries."

Keenan lurched forward and nearly spit out his drink as the voices of a group of women at another table floated over a wall of fake foliage at Las Brisas restaurant in downtown Los Angeles.

"Girl, you ain't never lied." Another woman chimed in. "The last time I had a man do right by me, I was wearing a training bra."

A chorus of giggles followed while Keenan dabbed water from the front of his shirt. Normally he didn't make a habit of eavesdropping, but as it was he'd been anxiously waiting for his afternoon appointment for more than forty-five minutes, and the women's conversation had him cracking up.

"I don't know, girls," the one with the sexiest voice spoke up. "I'm not ready to give up on men just yet. Despite all the drama they've put me through I still want that pie in the sky. The ring, the house, the children—"

"The heartbreak, the drama, the divorce, the custody battle," another woman cut in. "Jalila, your problem is that you don't recognize the world has changed. There's no more Mr. Rights out there. There's only Mr. Right-Nows."

"And your problem, Martina, is that you keep choosing to listen to your body and not your heart."

"You damn right. I'm all about the pleasure and satisfaction. Wham-bam, thank you, sir. And if he's real good, I'll leave him a tip on the nightstand."

"You're incorrigible," the voice he recognized as Jalila's chided.

"Whatever. Deep down you girls know I'm right," Martina continued. "Especially you, Jalila. All that pining away you do on the Internet. You just need to face facts. Men ain't no good. Particularly in *this* town. You either use or get used."

"Jalila, don't pay this chick any attention. She ain't right. I'm happily married and I want the same for you, girl."

"Thank you, Fantasia," Jalila said. "I need all the positive vibes I can get."

"Oh, that's right," Fantasia continued. "You have a date tonight."

"With who?" Martina demanded.

"With Richard," Jalila claimed. "Remember, I told you about him Monday?"

"Rich— You mean that guy that picked you up at the gas station? Ha!"

Keenan smiled as Martina's laugh echoed off the walls like a starter pistol.

"Girl, *that's* your problem. You just can't say no. You let all these geeks and freaks pick you up whenever wherever. It don't make no sense."

"There's nothing wrong with meeting a man at a gas station. Besides he was really sweet," Jalila reasoned. "At least I know he has a car—unlike Keith. I had to drive over fifty miles *one way* to pick him up for our dates, and then he'd always either lost or forgotten his wallet. Then, to top it all off, he insisted on calling me Kulula."

"Humph. That tells me he's used to dating strippers with liquor names like Alize, Dom, Moët and Cristal," Martina sassed. "You should have just installed a stripper pole and made you a few dollars on the side."

Keenan noticed that Jalila's laugh was different from the other women's. It was light, lyrical and contagious. So much so that Keenan turned and tried to take a peek at her through the fake plants.

"It wasn't *that* funny," Martina said when Jalila's laughter continued.

"Well, Keith…uhm…*did* have a stripper pole in the middle of *his* living room."

The table erupted with loud shrieks and laughter. Other diners looked around but the women were too deep into their conversation to notice.

"Did you give the pole the old college try?" Fantasia inquired.

There was a long pause and then, "Just once."

More shrieks and laughter.

"And I almost broke my damn neck," Jalila added.

Keenan spotted a sizable hole with a view through to the other side, and his gaze immediately landed on a face that was so poetically beautiful that for a few seconds he found it hard to believe that he wasn't dreaming. Big doe-brown eyes, flawless skin and a smile so breathtakingly beautiful that he instantly reached for his business card. Surely, being in this town, the beauty was either a model or an actress.

"I'm so sorry to have kept you waiting," a low steely baritone said.

Keenan jerked around as if he'd just been caught with his hand inside the cookie jar. When he recognized his afternoon appointment, he relaxed and forced a smile. "Steven." He stood up and hovered above the other man's six-foot-one frame. "I'm glad that you could meet me this afternoon."

"Not a problem. It was great being able to get away from the studio for a little while. I hope that I didn't keep you waiting long."

"Not at all." They shook hands just as the table behind them erupted with laughter again. Keenan glanced over his shoulder, longing for another look at the beauty.

"Sounds like they're having a great time," Steven commented, taking his seat.

"Looks that way." Keenan sat back down and signaled for his waiter. "So what's the verdict from the focus group? Is *The Royals* going to make the fall lineup?"

Before Steven could answer, the giggling women rounded the corner, adjusting their purse straps and huddling together as they headed out of the restaurant.

Keenan's eyes found Jalila just as she glanced in his direction. Her gaze raked over him and a soft smile touched her lips. While she and her friends walked past his table, he was vaguely aware that Steven was prattling on about the television pilot his company, A.M. Production, had produced, but damn if he could force himself to listen. Despite the fact that it had taken him weeks to nail down this luncheon, and that he'd had to wait over an hour for Steven to show up, all he could think about right now was stopping this gorgeous woman from walking out the door and never seeing her again.

His gaze followed the curvy beauty. He guessed her height to be about five foot ten. Her thick hips and plump backside were usually seen only on red-beans-and-rice sistahs from the Deep South and were, quite frankly, hypnotizing.

"Keenan." Steven snapped his fingers and cut into Keenan's thoughts.

"What?" He jerked his head back toward Steven and blinked.

"I was telling you about how I don't think *The Royals* is a good fit for the network at this moment."

"Great!" He slapped Steven on the back. "Can you excuse me for a minute?"

"I, uh—"

"I'll be right back." Keenan launched from his chair and performed a sort of walk-run out of the restaurant.

Hurry. Hurry. His heart pounded wildly in his chest and his stomach looped into knots. When he rushed past the hostess stand and out the front door, he made it just in time to see Jalila pull out of a parking spot in a champagne-colored Mercedes.

"Hey! Hold up!" He raced over, risking being run over.

Jalila frowned and rolled down her window. "May I help you?"

"Yes— Uhm…hey. How are you?"

Her brows stretched up. "Fine."

"Uhm. I know this may sound strange but, uhm… are you a model or an actress?"

She rolled her eyes at what was clearly one of the most clichéd lines in this town. "Are you for real?"

"Look. I'm a producer." He pulled out his business card and passed it to her. "I have plenty of connections in this town and I'd love to work with you."

Jalila reluctantly took the card so she could be on her way. "Thanks. I'll keep it in mind," she lied and pressed the power-window button.

"Wait. I'm serious—"

She hit the accelerator and sped off.

Keenan jumped back in time to avoid injury. "Damn."

Jalila shook her head. If she had a dime for every time she'd heard that line, she'd be rich. She glanced in her rearview mirror and stole another look at Mr. Producer. Too bad, she thought. This guy was really good-looking. He was extremely tall, physically fit, and he was wearing the hell out of that suit.

A horn blared and Jalila slammed on her brakes before plowing into Martina's convertible at the parking lot's entrance. She placed a hand over her heart and drew in a deep breath. "Damn. Pay attention, girl."

Chapter 2

"I had a nice time," Jalila Goodwyn whispered, smiling.

Richard, the latest Friday-night adventure, stepped up onto the low-lit porch. He slid his arms around her waist and then splayed his hands over the high end of her curvy butt. "How about you invite me in for a little nightcap?" he asked, flashing his blindingly white teeth.

Jalila closed her eyes, mainly because his halitosis, mixed with her date's overindulgence in garlic this evening, was practically singeing her nose hairs. Too bad, because the guy wasn't *that* bad-looking. He was a little over six feet tall with a peanut-butter-brown complexion, but he was also proof positive that if you have a little head fat you can't pull off the whole black-Kojak look.

Still, bad breath and head fat aside, Jalila's body responded to Richard's touch because of one overriding and important factor: she hadn't had sex in two years.

Two years.

Twenty-four months.

Seven hundred and thirty days.

"What do you say?" Richard asked, pulling her close so she could feel his arousal. All three inches of it—but it would have to do in a pinch.

What the hell, she could give him some Listerine and turn out the lights, right? Standards be damned. Her body was hypersensitive and starved for sex. A deadly combination when wading through L.A.'s shallow dating pool. Her body didn't care that Richard didn't have a *good* job, that he was a music manager without any clients or even that he didn't have his own place. At forty-two, he still lived at home with his parents. He blamed the bad economy. Jalila suspected it was his lack of ambition. But hell, she didn't have to tell anyone about tonight. Right? Even if her best friend Martina pressed her for details, she could lie. Why couldn't she, for once, be one of those women who just did a wham, bam, thank you, sir and then kick him to the curb?

"One drink," she said and then whipped out her house keys. Her libido practically gave her a high five and then performed a victory dance while she fumbled with the front-door lock.

Just get him upstairs and turn out all the lights. Maybe if she was lucky she could convince herself that she was making love to Idris Elba. *Whoo. Now*

*that's a fine brotha I wouldn't mind knocking dents into
the headboard with.*

She slipped her key into the lock and because it
tended to stick, she gave the door a good shove and
nearly tripped over her own feet.

"Easy now. Easy." Richard's hot breath seemed to
curl the tiny hairs at the back of Jalila's neck. "There's
no rush. We've got all night."

*Pleeze. You have thirty minutes tops before I shove
you back out of the door and pretend that the whole
date never happened.*

"I sure hope that you got plenty of baby oil, girl,"
Richard hummed into her ear. "I wanna show you how
I play slip and slide."

Jalila's plastic smile dropped and her hyperesca-
lated libido took a major hit over that crude remark.

"When I finish rocking you with this ten-inch pole,
you'll be screaming my name, ma."

10 inches? Had she misjudged? Her smile returned.

Woof! Woof!

Richard jumped. His hands shot straight up into the
air.

Woof! Woof! Grrr!

Jalila rolled her eyes. "Cujo, it's all right. He's with
me."

Her usually friendly two-hundred-pound Great
Dane Cujo's growl deepened. He hunched down low
and even flashed Richard his pearly-white canine teeth.

"Whoo. Damn, girl. What are you doing with such
a big dog?"

"Oh, he's not *that* big." Jalila grabbed Cujo by the

collar and attempted to pull him away. Cujo refused to budge and continued to growl.

Richard's hands remained in the air while a look of pure terror covered his face. "I don't think she likes me."

"She is a he." Jalila tugged again. "Come on, boy. Let's go out in the yard."

Richard dropped his hands.

Cujo barked and moved forward, pulling Jalila a few feet with him.

Richard's hands shot back up as he fell back against the door.

"Cujo!" Jalila offered Richard an apologetic smile. "I'm so sorry about this." She pulled the dog again, this time successfully getting him to come along.

"Sure. Sure. No problem." This time, Richard slowly lowered his hands and then expelled a breath when it looked as if he was actually going to survive this encounter.

Jalila rushed Cujo toward the back door. "I'm not going to let you ruin this for me," she hissed. "I'm getting laid tonight and that's that!"

Cujo barked, and she could've sworn that he was calling her crazy.

"You don't get a say in this," she told the dog, opening the back door and ushering him out. After shutting the door, she turned around and forced herself to relax. After working seventy-hour weeks for the past two years to get her spa and cosmetic line up and running, she deserved this one, didn't she? She just hoped that this joker was at least half as good as he claimed. Even as she hoped, doubt crept up her spine.

Richard strolled into the living room. "Is the coast clear?"

"Yeah." She chuckled. "Sorry about that." She removed her sweater and tried to steal a sneak peek at the man's inseam. There was nothing that even hinted at ten inches—or five for that matter. Was it too late to fake a headache and give him the heave-ho?

"Ah, checking out the goods," Richard snickered, catching Jalila in the act.

Jalila rolled her eyes. How did her life come down to this? She was supposed to be married by now, with a house filled with children and an adoring husband who made her breakfast in bed every Mother's Day. She had made such meticulous plans ever since Santa had brought her a Barbie Dream house when she was eight years old. Living happily ever after wasn't just the last line in some fairy tale for Jalila. She saw true love every day by watching her parents. Their constant kissing and touching and laughing was an inspiration to all her childhood friends.

She couldn't wait to find her own Prince Charming. Once, back in junior high, she'd thought she'd found him. Jeffrey Becker. Hands-down the flyest boy in school. Every girl bent over backward to get his attention. Some slipped notes in his books and in his locker, others baked brownies and tried to pass off Rice Krispies treats as generations-old family recipes.

But it was Jalila who had caught Jeffrey's eye and had kept it all through junior high and high school. The trouble had come when Jeffrey was accepted at NYU while she had elected to attend UCLA. It had been a bittersweet separation. The young couple had vowed they would alternate visits on holidays and spring and summer breaks. Jalila's plan was for them to get their degrees and then walk down the aisle six months later for a beautiful Christmas wedding.

Jalila hadn't counted on someone else catching Jeffrey's eye.

And she certainly hadn't considered the possibility of that other person being another man.

Not until she received *that* devastating news did Jeffrey's insistence on waiting until they were married to make love make sense. Before that, she'd chalked it up to Jeffrey being a true gentleman. He respected her. He adored her.

Nope. He was gay. His tear-filled confession included detailing how he'd used their relationship to ward off any suspicions about his sexuality.

Ouch.

So there went all Jalila's plans. When she was unceremoniously dumped back into the dating pool, Jalila discovered that she was ill-equipped to navigate through the seemingly endless line of misogynists, momma's boys and downright losers. And now that she'd just passed her thirtieth birthday, she was no better off or closer to landing a husband than when she'd first started.

"Now, what does a brotha have to do to get that drank, gurl?" Richard asked, pulling Jalila back to the here and now. His long arms returned to encircle her waist.

It didn't go past Jalila's notice that as the night wore

on, Richard's country roots were showing. He was twanging left, right and center now.

"Maybe we can even put on a little Teddy P." He chuckled and started singing. "Turn off the lights…and light a candle."

Jalila rolled her eyes. The brotha couldn't even sing.

"How about a couple of mojitos?" she offered, peeling herself out of his arms. At least there were mint leaves in those.

"Sounds good to me," Richard said, swatting her on the butt.

Jalila jumped, but clamped her teeth together as she waltzed over to the bar.

"Damn, gurl," Richard said, glancing around. "This all you?"

"It's all me." She boasted. She loved her Mediterranean villa with its sweeping canyon view. It was spacious and elegant and dotted with colorful paintings by her favorite artists.

"What do you do again?" He pivoted around on the hardwood floor.

Figures. He didn't hear a word I said all night. She drew in a deep breath. She really needed that drink now. "I own and operate a day spa off Rodeo."

"How much you pulling down to afford something like this?"

What the hell? "Oh, I do all right."

"Sheeeeit," he continued, touching the leather couch and picking up expensive knickknacks around the room. "I know this place gotta be costing you a pretty penny in this town." He glanced back at her. "Where do I submit my application for a sugar momma?" Clearly, he was trying to pass the comment off as a joke, but there was an unmistakable glint of seriousness in his eyes.

She chuckled but didn't find the question the least bit funny. A few minutes later, she handed him his drink.

"Thanks, baby," he said, accepting the glass with a wink.

Jalila gulped down her liquid courage and then returned to the bar for a second round. This time she doubled up on the rum.

"Where's your bathroom?" Richard asked, setting his own empty glass down and removing his jacket.

"You'll have to use the one upstairs," Jalila informed him as she moved toward the stereo. "The one downstairs is being renovated. Once you get to the top floor, just go straight down the hallway. It's the last door on your right."

"Be right back." He winked.

"I can hardly wait." She plastered on a fake smile. Jalila watched as he jogged up the stairs and once he was out of sight, she picked up the rum bottle and took a couple of chugs straight. "Idris Elba. Idris Elba," she chanted, but her usually active imagination was having a hard time fitting the handsome actor's face onto Richard's shoulders.

Instead of selecting Teddy Pendergrass as Richard had suggested, Jalila had to go with her magic man, Maxwell. If his *Urban Hang Suite* couldn't close this deal, then she would just need to hang it up. The bass line of the opening track instantly put a smile on her face. At the same time, the rum started to hum oh so nicely through her veins. She was definitely back in action.

But by the time the intro to the third song poured through the speakers, she wondered what was taking Richard so long. On the fourth song, she got up from the couch and decided to go upstairs to check on him. The bathroom door was open, but Richard was nowhere to be seen.

Jalila frowned. What did the guy do—jump out of the window?

Thump.

She turned. The sound was coming out of her bedroom. Stealthily, Jalila followed the sound. Her heart hammered inside her chest. Seriously, how well did she know this guy? What if she caught him trying to steal her blind? What was she going to do—wave a finger at him? Maybe she should go for backup?

But of all the scenarios that played in Jalila's head, she was totally unprepared to find Richard's grown butt sitting in the center of her walk-in closet, taking long, deep sniffs of her beloved Prada shoes.

"What in the hell?"

Richard's head snapped up. Guilt changed his face from dark brown to damn near cranberry-red. "I, uh—"

She blinked, trying to process what she was seeing.

He tried again. "I was just, uh—"

"Out," she thundered, pointing in the direction he needed to take.

"Whoa, hold up." He jumped to his feet. "I know this looks bad."

"You're sniffing my shoes!"

"Okay." He shrugged. "So a brotha got a little thing for women's feet. And c'mon. You've been teasing me all night in those pretty scandals with your red-tip toes peeking out."

Jalila looked down at her neatly pedicured feet.

"Woman, the things I want to do to those toes," he said, practically salivating.

"Out!" She tried to suppress a shudder of disgust.

"C'mon now. It's not like I'm a freak or nuthin'. Don't knock it until you try it. Let me just wash your feet and—"

"I said get out—or is all that head fat making you hard of hearing?"

"H-hold up now," he stuttered.

"Now your funky breath makes perfect sense. You've been running around sucking on people's toes." She stormed off. "Ughhh!"

"Yo, baby. Wait up." He charged after her.

Downstairs, Jalila grabbed his jacket and shoved it at him.

"Aww, baby. It's no big deal. Let me stay and show you what you're missing."

Jalila marched to the back door. "How about you take your big butt home and suck your momma's toes?"

"Damn, baby. That's cold."

She opened the door. "What the hell ever. Kick bricks!"

Woof! Woof! Grrr! Cujo rushed into the house, his long legs galloping straight toward Richard.

Richard took off running. "Aw, hell!"

Jalila folded her arms and watched the comedy unfold. Unfortunately, Richard escaped the house, but not without Cujo tearing the seat out of his pants. Surely that was worth a doggy biscuit.

Chapter 3

"I hate this town!" Keenan Armstrong swore and slammed down his office phone. "Hack actors, whiney writers and crazy directors with God complexes are running this business into the ground."

Nitara Murphy, Keenan's longtime coproducer and business partner, laughed as she dropped into the leather chair before his desk and crossed her jeans-clad legs. "You're starting to sound like a scratched DVD. You love this town and you know it. We both do." She snatched the hair clip from the back of her hair and allowed her rich ink-black hair to tumble free, hanging past her shoulders like an exotic curtain. "We'd be lost if we couldn't tie a knot in someone's chain on a daily basis or suffer from a bleeding ulcer at least twice a year."

A brief smile spread across Keenan's thick sexy lips but then disappeared the next second when he groaned and plopped his head back against his large leather chair. "I don't know, Nitara," he huffed. "We're in for a rough season. Network TV ratings are tanking across the board. The three pilots we shot over the summer all crashed and burned, and now I'm having a hard time getting the suits over at ABC even to take my calls." He shook his head and exhaled slowly. "At this rate we might actually go into the season without a show in the lineup. I can't remember the last time that happened."

"Five years ago," Nitara stated, giving her nails a quick glance-over.

Keenan's glare cut across the table.

"What can I say? I keep tabs on things like that. Besides, I told you, scripted drama is out. Scripted reality TV is *in*. Reality shows are the new programming of choice and they're cheap to make."

"Trash," he sneered flippantly.

"One man's trash is another man's treasure," she sing-songed.

Unaccustomed to sitting for long periods of time, Keenan unfolded his six-foot-six frame and pushed himself out of his chair and began pacing the office. It was an old habit that often annoyed his partner. "Maybe it's time to get out of television," he pondered aloud.

"And do what—movies?" Nitara asked with a lilting laugh. "The movie industry is having a tougher time than we are. Outrageous budgets that directors ignore, high-maintenance actors and even more whiney writers.

Hell, it only takes one bomb to land you in bankruptcy court."

"Unlike television where you just die a slow death." Keenan grunted.

"Exactly. I'd rather live on life support than die prematurely." She rewarded him with a sarcastic smile. "If you were honest with yourself you'd admit that you agree with me."

"Humph!" Keenan continued pacing.

Nitara smiled as she allowed her gaze to drink in her partner's profile. Even dressed in his casual black slacks and sky-blue button-down shirt, he could give the hottest male models in the business a run for their money.

Despite their twenty-five-year friendship, Nitara sometimes still reacted to Keenan's muscular chocolate body the same way that every warm-blooded female did: with her nipples hard and at attention and her aching clit thumping against her panties. It was shameful really.

At times like this, when she was horny as hell, Nitara couldn't remember exactly why she and Keenan had never been more than just friends. They'd known each other since high school, both were crazy about football (go '49ers!) and they both held the firm belief that *Armageddon* was the best movie ever made.

Of course, there was that little snafu of him dating and then marrying her sister Tenetria. The marriage didn't last long. Once Keenan made it as a big-time television producer, Tenetria had indulged in the shady side of Hollywood: too many parties, drugs, too much alcohol, and she'd capped it all off with an affair or two that had left Keenan a broken and jaded man as far as relationships were concerned.

Too bad.

The divorce was nasty, but Keenan had gladly written the check for half his net worth just to be able to put the whole episode behind him. Once—just once—Keenan had made the careless remark that he had married the wrong sister. Of course, it was at some glitz party and it was questionable as to whether he was sober at the time. Nitara pretended she hadn't heard the comment, but a part of her secretly agreed.

She and Keenan would have been perfect together. She should have grabbed him before her sister had ever gotten the chance. Instead of waiting for the inevitable disaster to hit so she could scoop Keenan up on the rebound, Nitara had impulsively proposed to her then boyfriend of two weeks, Martin. Now, Keenan was a free agent and she was the married one.

Never let it be said that God didn't have a wicked sense of humor.

Keenan absently licked his lips and heat rushed up the column of her neck. Belatedly, her gaze dropped to the sparkling five-carat diamond on her finger and she was suddenly pulled back down to reality. *Good Lord, I need to get my hot tail home before I do something I'll regret.* "I'm out of here." Nitara reluctantly climbed out of her chair. "If I'm lucky I can battle my way through traffic and make it home in about two hours to start dinner."

Keenan laughed, causing his mountainous shoulders to quake. "Start dinner? Still passing off the local pizza parlor as DiGiorno's?"

"Ha-ha. Very funny." Nitara cocked her head and massaged the side of her neck. "I'm cooking. I can cook, you know."

"Since when?" Keenan countered, his dark eyes dancing with mischief.

"I've been loading up on episodes of *Top Chef* and *Hell's Kitchen*. I've been inspired. Tonight I'm taking on my mom's lasagna. I think I can give her a run for her money."

"Only if she gave you the recipe." Keenan chuckled. "If not, you're just going to embarrass yourself. Tenetria tried for years to get the recipe. Your momma wasn't having it."

"Gee. Thanks for the vote of confidence."

"A woman should know her limitations," he said. "And yours is anything having to do with a pot or a pan."

Nitara rolled her eyes. "That's what you think."

"Poor Martin." Keenan shook his head, waltzed over to his desk and pulled a bottle out of the top drawer and tossed it to her.

Nitara's reflexes kicked in just in time and she caught the bottle. "Pepto-Bismol? Very funny."

"I'm just looking out for a brotha," he said, flashing her his winsome smile.

"You're supposed to be *my* friend," she reminded him with a pout.

"Then as your friend I advise you to hire a cook.

Mama Maria's lasagna ain't nothing to be messed with. Hell, to this day I still have dreams about her cooking. Tell your old man he better watch his back. I might scoop in and steal his woman."

Irritated, Nitara's spine stiffened. "C'mon, how hard can it be? I've been eating her lasagna for thirty years."

Keenan crossed his arms and stared at her.

"Thanks for the support." She rolled her eyes.

Keenan's hands shot up in surrender. "My bad, my bad. If you think that you're up for the challenge then I'm standing behind you one hundred percent. Knock him dead, girl."

Nitara beamed. "Great. Then I'll bring you back a plate."

"Actually, I'm, uh…sort of watching my weight."

Her glare returned. "Go to hell," she said, rolling her eyes.

"Aww." He walked over and gave her a much-needed hug. "I didn't mean to hurt your itty-bitty feelings." He planted a kiss in the center of her forehead. "There. That should make it *aaall* better."

"Get off me." She squirmed out of his muscled cocoon. "With friends like you, I don't need enemies."

Keenan's laughter deepened and Nitara's annoyance melted away. It was hard staying mad when he launched his charm offensive. She sighed as she headed toward the door. "I don't care what you think. I'm going to make this damn lasagna and my husband is going to eat it and he's going to love it or he can just fix himself a bowl of Captain Crunch."

Keenan cleared his throat.

"And not another damn word from you!"

"What? I didn't say anything," he said, unable to keep the amusement out of his voice.

Nitara snatched open the door. "If Martin likes my mother's cooking so much, then he should have married her."

"I don't suggest you tell him that," Keenan warned. "He might take you up on it."

"Great. I'm thirty-four years old and competing with my mother for my husband's affection." She sighed. "I thought the whole point of my being a successful businesswoman meant that I didn't have to be a traditional housewife. Turns out you don't have the choice of one or the other. The more you do the more you add to your to-do list."

"Wait until you have children."

Nitara arched one delicate brow at him. "Is there something you want to tell me? You got a rug rat running around here or something?"

"Not hardly," he laughed, his dimples flashing, and transforming his handsomely chiseled face into something even more adorable and mischievous. "Unfortunately, you know all there is to know about me. Warts and all."

"Lucky me." Nitara jumped to her feet and headed toward the door. "I'm out."

"If you come up with any ideas for the fall lineup, please feel free to share them with me," he said.

"If I do that, what will you stay up all night thinking about?" she asked sweetly and opened the door.

"Contrary to popular opinion I do sleep."

Nitara glanced back over her shoulder.

He shrugged. "Sometimes."

Making an about-face, Nitara tossed up her arms. "I already told you, scripted reality. Stop fighting it. They're cheap and people love them."

Walking back to his chair, Keenan dropped down into it and proceeded to rub his temples. From Nitara's viewpoint it looked more like he was trying to squeeze out another idea. She didn't see the point. They'd been having this same conversation for the past six years. The world of entertainment had changed drastically since they had gotten into the business. People no longer held movie and television stars in the same regard. In fact, it had become more of a sport, in recent years, to tear them down.

"I got nothing," he finally admitted. "Maybe I should go home, too," he said wearily.

"You're just fighting the inevitable." Nitara started out of the door again, but Keenan's quick bark stopped her in her tracks.

"*If* we were to do this…reality thing…" he shrugged his shoulders as if this was a vague possibility "…what kind of show would it be?"

Nitara twirled around, not sure she should trust her hearing.

He glanced up. "I'm not saying that I'm interested. Just…hypothetically."

A slow smile spread across Nitara's face. "It's all about romance, baby."

Chapter 4

"Ladies, where have all the good men gone?" A frustrated Jalila sat cross-legged on the edge of her bed while she ranted in front of her camcorder. Her weekly chat session on YouTube was like e-therapy: a way to vent her frustrations about navigating the L.A. dating scene. Over the past year, she'd grown accustomed to the camaraderie of her subscribers. Their frequent comments and questions lifted her spirits and gave her hope and courage to keep plugging away.

One bad date at a time.

"The guy was in my closet, *sniffing my shoes!* Ugh!" Jalila squeezed her eyes shut and tried to erase the image from her head. It didn't work. Chances were she was doomed to relive that horrible moment for the rest of her life. Then it occurred to her. "Do you know that means my shoes have seen more action than I have in two years?" Jalila lowered the camera and screamed up at the ceiling.

Cujo padded his way into the bedroom, parked himself next to the bed and cocked his head.

Jalila glanced over and met her loyal friend's questioning gaze. "Don't mind me. Momma is just horny as hell." She picked up the camera again and flashed a smile. "Now where was I? Oh, yeah—men." She shook her head. "I know, ladies, that we've talked about all this before and I totally appreciate the whole thing about bonding and singing 'Kumbaya' but…damn, ladies. I gotta tell you. I want a man." She laughed at herself and then waved a finger at the lens. "And I don't mean just any man. I need a real man. You all know what I'm talking about."

Cujo barked and swished his tail across the hardwood floor.

Jalila rolled her eyes. "Hush, you got out of the yard last week and got you a little sumpthin' sumpthin' with that German Shepherd down the street."

Woof!

"Anyway…I know I said last week that I was just going to embrace my singlehood and be happy. Hell, I even treated myself to a dinner and a movie Wednesday night. Turns out I'm not exactly a cheap date." She winked. "But that's not the point. Look, I know that women can do a lot for themselves. We have careers and our own money. But like Billie Dee Williams said in *Mahogany*, 'Success means nothing without someone you love to share it with,' and he ain't never lied."

Jalila rolled over onto her belly and panned the camera around the bedroom. "I'm tired of the other side of the bed being empty. I want to cook for more than one person. I even want to argue with someone to take the garbage out." She turned the camera back on herself. "Ladies, I have to believe that my soul mate is out there. He just has to be."

"True love," Keenan mumbled as he strode through the door of his homey Beverly Hills mansion. What the heck did he know about love? Yeah, he loved his small close-knit family, his best friend Nitara and of course his nine-year-old dog, Chips. But that other stuff—that deep, cosmic soul-mate stuff—he was just as lost as the average Joe.

That sounded bad since he'd been married once. Looking back on it now, one could say that he'd married Tenetria more out of loyalty than anything else. And, quite frankly, he wasn't too keen about ever doing it again. In college, Tenetria had been the perfect girlfriend—pretty and fun-loving. She'd stuck by him while he struggled to make a name for himself in this crazy town. However, it was during the transition from kids to grown-ups that their problems came to light. Suddenly, Keenan didn't know the woman who carried his last name. With new eyes, he saw that his wife was petty and spoiled. And when he caught her cheating…it destroyed him.

Despite being in business with his ex-sister-in-law, Keenan didn't know what Tenetria was doing now. He never asked and was thankful that Nitara never mentioned it. He'd dated from time to time in the five years since his divorce. Nothing serious, mainly because L.A. seemed to produce only petty and spoiled women, code for aspiring actresses and singers.

No, thank you.

So how was he going to come up with an idea for a reality show about true love?

For the past two days Nitara had hounded him about going into reality television. She'd covered his desk with budgets, profit margins, focus groups—anything and everything she could get her hands on to convince him.

In the office, he resisted the whole idea, but during his drives home and while pacing his bedroom floor, he was actually caving in to the whole idea. They could just give it a try this one season—see if they liked it. Tonight, he'd come home with his arms full of DVDs—footage of different reality shows over the past ten years. That's why he had in his other arm a cold six-pack.

Woof! From his comfortable spot on a red velveteen doggy pillow in the den, Chips, Keenan's Great Dane, raced to the door to greet him.

"Hey, Chips." He shifted the DVDs and gave his best friend an awkward pat on the head. "You've been good, boy?"

Woof! Chips pivoted in a quick circle and sat back on his haunches in hopes of a quick rub behind the ears. Of course, he got his wish.

In the kitchen, Keenan dumped the DVDs on the kitchen counter, stashed the beer in the refrigerator and poured some dog food into Chips's bowl. Without preamble, Chips attacked the food like he hadn't eaten in a week. A few times, he sounded as if he was choking.

"Slow down," Keenan warned with a stern frown. "The food isn't going anywhere."

Chips ignored him.

"Fine. Suit yourself." Keenan stood and washed his hands at the sink before looking into the fridge to see what Jenny, his personal chef, had prepared for him for dinner. He was in luck: fried chicken, whipped potatoes and green beans. The first time Jenny had made him fried chicken, he'd thought he'd died and gone to heaven. The old wives' tale was true when it came to him. The fastest way to his heart was through his stomach.

Before he kicked back and did his "research," Keenan washed away the day's stress with a scorching-hot shower. He had been teased before about how he could stand such hot water, but he found it soothing.

When he shut off the water, thick clouds of steam rose out of the shower stall as he exited. In the distance, he could just barely hear the phone ringing in the bedroom. He rushed out of the bathroom, wrapping his bath towel around his hips.

"Hello?"

"Well, if it isn't the world's most elusive Holly-wood producer."

Keenan smiled. "Keisha, I've been meaning to call."

"And I still believe in Santa Claus."

"You never believed in Santa Claus," he reminded her as he headed back to the bathroom for his robe.

"No thanks to you." She chuckled. "When I was little you told me that someone shot Santa because they thought he was a burglar coming into the house."

Keenan rocked back, laughing at the memory. "Oh, God. I can't believe you fell for that."

"I was five…and foolishly looked up to my big brother."

He refused to feel guilty. "I remember you running into Mom and Dad's room, yelling for them to call the police."

"I was hysterical, you jerk."

"You were adorable." His laugh deepened.

"I swear. Sometimes I don't know why I bother calling you."

"C'mon, you know you love me," he coaxed.

"You'll do." Keisha sighed.

"So what are you doing calling me on a Friday night?" He glanced around for a clock. "Shouldn't you be out on a hot date or something?"

Keisha clucked her tongue. "Please. I'm giving up on men."

"You decided to come out of the closet over the phone?" Keenan laughed and shook his head. "Tacky. And you can forget about me telling Mom and Dad. You'll have to do that on your own."

"You're not funny," Keisha deadpanned. "And I'm not coming out of a closet. I'm just not having any luck finding a man that's worth my time. Most of these knuckleheads out here either wanna turn me into their mommas or their checkbook, and I ain't havin' it."

Keenan rolled his eyes as he pulled on a pair of

black silk pajamas and headed back downstairs. "Is this going to be another man-bashing phone call? You do realize that I'm the so-called enemy?"

"Then you need to get your team to act right," she sassed.

Keenan had no trouble picturing his sister rolling her eyes and swiveling her neck, which she was prone to do whenever she got pissed off. Still he couldn't resist goading her. "Have you ever considered that maybe *your* team is the problem?"

Her voice jumped an octave. "Do what?"

He snatched the phone from his ear and then gave Chips a conspiratorial wink. When he felt it was safe, he put the phone back up to his ear. His sister was still going off.

"And another thing," she ranted. "If I can invest in myself—a good education, a good job—and take care of myself, then why can't a brother? I'm supposed to give him the bizness just because…what? He looks aight?"

Keenan just smiled as he held the phone. It was an older brother's birth right to push his baby sister's easily accessible buttons.

"Humph. Please," Keisha said. "I'd rather curl up in my bed with a bowl of popcorn and make it a Netflix night."

"Sounds like fun."

"And what about you?" she challenged. "What makes you any different than me?"

She did have a point. "I'm not the one perched on a soapbox." He removed his dinner from the microwave and grabbed a beer. But before he headed out of the kitchen, his eyes landed on the DVDs on top of the counter. If he needed some type of show about true love or romance, then maybe he had the perfect person on the phone.

"Keisha, do you watch any reality shows?"

"Now, you know I do." Her tone instantly turned more cheerful. "I don't miss an episode of *The Bachelor, The Bachelorette, Rock of Love, Flava of Love...*"

Keenan frowned. "All right. I get the picture."

"Why do you ask?"

He huffed as he tucked a few DVDs under his arms. "Nitara thinks it's the way to go for next season. I have my doubts."

Keisha squealed and Keenan almost dropped the phone. "Oh, this is great. What are you going to do? Are you going to do something with millionaires? Can I be on the show?"

"Calm down. Calm down." He chuckled. "I haven't agreed to anything yet."

"Yet?" she repeated and then squealed again. "When you say *yet* that means a *yes* is just around the corner."

"Since when?" He set his plate and beer down on the coffee table and went to his sixty-inch flat-screen and DVD player.

"Since forever." She laughed. "Do you need any help vetting the applicants?"

"Didn't you just say that you were giving up on men?"

"That was *so* twenty minutes ago."

Laughing, Keenan turned around and caught Chips devouring his dinner. "Hey! Get away from there."

Chips grabbed the chicken leg and took off running.

"Scoot—aw, man." Keenan huffed at the sight of his nearly empty plate. Why on earth had he set his food down like that?

"What happened?"

"I don't want to talk about it." He returned to the kitchen. Looked like it was going to be another night of sandwiches and chips.

"You know that I'm not the only woman that feels this way about this shortage of good men. My girl, JalilaG1000, is constantly talking about the *real* state of the black union on a weekly basis."

"Jalila—who?"

"Oh, it's this chick I subscribe to on YouTube. She's hilarious. Whenever I watch her weekly vlog, I feel like I'm sitting in church."

Keenan laughed. "Oookay."

"Naw, I'm serious. You should check her out. It's JalilaG1000."

"Yeah, I'll put it on the top of my to-do list."

Keisha instantly caught an attitude. "Fine. Whatever. I was just trying to help *you* out."

He put his foot in this time. "I'll check it out."

"Naw, naw. Don't do me any favors."

Frustrated, but also knowing just how long his sister could balance a chip on her shoulder, Keenan abandoned the contents for the sub he was making on the counter and left the kitchen. "I'll do it now," he told her.

"Well, don't do it for me."

"Keisha, I'm two seconds from hanging this phone up," he warned. "I said I was going to check it out so that's what I'm doing."

She didn't respond, but Keenan knew that she was wearing a smile as big as Texas. In his home office, he quickly booted up his computer and zipped over to YouTube. "Now what was her name again?"

"JalilaG1000." Excitement crept back into Keisha's voice. "My girl be spitting the truth about these men running around here in Cali."

Keenan rolled his eyes.

"And stop rolling your eyes at me."

"Then stop trying to sound like you're straight out of Oakland when you were born and raised in the suburbs."

"Whatever."

He chuckled as he clicked onto JalilaG1000's YouTube channel. The beautiful woman who popped up on his screen was definitely a stunning surprise. "Hey, I know her."

"You do?" Keisha asked, surprised.

"Well, kind of." He stared into those hypnotizing deep-brown eyes that were surrounded by a fan of long, curly lashes. Her flawless, oval chocolate face and full, plump and kissable lips caused something to stir within him.

"Keenan! Are you still there?" Keisha barked.

He blinked and successfully broke the strange spell he'd fallen under. "Uh, yeah. Who is she—some kind of actress?" Even as he asked the question, his eyes scanned the left column for her stats. There wasn't much there. Her name, of course, and age. She warned viewers that this was the space where she'd like to opine about life and love as a single woman in L.A.

"I don't think so. From time to time, she talks about owning some spa."

Keenan stared at her picture again and couldn't stop the soft smile that crept across his lips. The camera loved her. He clicked the play button on her recent vlog.

"Ladies, where have all the good men gone?" she asked in a soft, honeyed voice.

Keenan's smile inched higher. He found this Jalila woman adorable in her pink, flannel pajamas with her black hair pulled back in a ponytail. "Did she just say some guy was *sniffing* her shoes?" he asked, certain he'd heard wrong.

Keisha cracked up. "Ain't that some crazy mess? Ha! You should watch some of her other videos. One time she was set up on a blind date with a guy who showed up with boobs. Boobs! Ha! He was taking hormones and was three months away from having a sex-change operation."

"Say what?" His eyes remained locked on the beauty before him. He couldn't believe that someone as beautiful as she was would have problems in the men department.

"That's not all. Here was a guy wanting to become a woman, but not because he wanted to date men. He still wanted to date women—but as a lesbian. Ha!"

Keenan laughed as well. "And here I thought you were the only magnet for losers."

"Now I'm about to hang up on you."

On the screen, Jalila rolled over onto her belly and panned the camera around the bedroom. "I'm tired of the other side of the bed being empty. I want to cook for more than one person. I even want to argue with someone to take the garbage out." She turned the camera back on herself. "Ladies, I have to believe that my soul mate is out there. He just has to be."

The footage stopped, freezing Jalila's solemn but angelic face on his computer. "Keisha, let me call you back." He didn't wait for an answer and hit the end button on his cordless phone. He replayed the video.

"Ladies, I have to believe that my soul mate is out there. He just has to be."

An idea began to form, and Keenan spent the rest of the night watching every video JalilaG1000 had uploaded to her channel. They weren't all about the trials of dating. Her best friend Martina, her father, James, and her beloved dog, Cujo, made frequent cameo appearances.

She openly shared her opinions about politics, books and movies. She was an intelligent woman who knew what she wanted—all that was missing was her Mr. Right, and Keenan was just the man to help her out.

Chapter 5

Rodeo Drive had long been the premier shopping area for the Hollywood elite. It was one of the few places where old and new money mingled. Despite the shaky economy there were still plenty of Mercedeses and Bentleys lining the sidewalks. All along the pearly, pristine strip a fresh batch of starry-eyed actresses wandered, with their traveling posses and paparazzi.

Keenan pulled up to Body by Jalila shortly after eleven. He had called earlier and spoken with the receptionist and had been told that the best time to catch the owner was between the hours of eleven and three. Now that he was here, he wasn't quite sure just how to go about doing this. First of all, there was no reason in the world this Jalila would accept his offer this time either, and second, he hadn't run his idea by Nitara. He was flying solo on this one.

Keenan killed the engine and hopped out of his cobalt-blue Bentley Continental GTC. A group of leggy women strolled toward him. Each lowered her shades and flashed him a flirtatious smile.

"Ladies," he greeted them, tilting his head in a slight nod. After their smattering of giggles, Keenan smiled and slid on his Hugo Boss sunglasses. He loved this town.

The moment he entered the day spa he was instantly greeted by the welcoming scent of jasmine and orange blossoms. He smiled, drew in a deep breath and immediately relaxed. The place was much bigger than it looked from the outside. The décor of white and silver gave the place a modern chic feel, while the music pouring through the speakers was an odd combination of nature sounds and classical piano.

"Good morning."

Keenan glanced toward the receptionist's desk and smiled at a beautiful, full-figured woman with a mammoth afro. He approached the desk and read her name tag. "Good morning, Tracee."

"Welcome to Body by Jalila," she chirped. "May I help you?"

Removing his shades, Keenan flashed his best smile. "Yes. I'm here to see Jalila Goodwyn."

She frowned and glanced down at the calendar in front of her. "Do you have an appointment?"

"Uh, no. Not exactly," he admitted, still trying to charm her with his smile.

Tracee smiled back. "Your name?"

He hesitated. It wasn't like Jalila was going to recognize the name unless she'd actually read his business card.

Tracee arched a pencil-thin brow at him. "Sir?"

"Uh, it's Keenan Armstrong," he answered, taking a chance.

"And is this personal or business?" she queried.

"It's personal…no, it's business—make that personal."

Tracee's expression turned dubious. "Well, which one is it?"

"Both." He chuckled. "It's complicated."

The receptionist looked him up and down, probably trying to decide whether to call her boss or 911.

"Look, I promise you. I'm on the up-and-up."

Tracee picked up the phone. "Ms. Goodwyn, there is a gentleman here to see you." Pause. "A Keenan Armstrong." Pause. "He said it was both."

Keenan smiled. He was getting closer to his goal. He thought about the beauty whose videos he'd spent all night watching and felt a little flutter in the pit of his stomach.

"Yes, ma'am. I'll tell him," Tracee said and then hung up the phone.

"Ms. Goodwyn is in a meeting but she'll be right out in a few minutes."

"Thank you." He rewarded Tracee with another smile and then turned away from her. He faced a long display wall with neatly arranged lemon-colored bottles. He leaned in and read the labels on the different bottles of cleansers, lotions and moisturizers.

"Have you ever tried our products before?" Tracee asked, picking up on his interest.

"Uhm, no." Before he knew it, Tracee had popped out of her seat and rushed around the desk.

"You know, there are plenty of men who use our products," she said, opening the display cases.

"Really?"

"Oh, of course. It's just as important for men to take care of their skin as women." She grabbed a bottle and took his hand. "Especially in this town," she added cheekily as she squeezed out a dollop of cream onto the back of his hand and began rubbing it in. "Feel how light that is?"

"Uh, yes." He cleared his throat. "That's very nice."

"That's because we use all-natural ingredients. And this particular formula cleans and moisturizes at the same time."

"I guess that would be…beneficial," he said, trying to add to the conversation.

Tracee bobbed her head. "Mind if I ask what products you use to clean your face?"

Keenan blinked. It was the first time he'd found himself discussing his "beauty regime." "Soap and water."

Tracee's sunny disposition collapsed. "Oh, my God. Do you know how harsh soap is to your skin?"

If he hadn't been there to see it with his own eyes, he would never have believed that this woman actually pulled out a large magnifying glass from her white jacket and began inspecting his face. Keenan held his breath and stood perfectly still while she carried on with her inspection.

"You know what you need?" she asked. The magnifying glass made her look like a huge Cyclops.

"What's that?"

"A deep exfoliating seaweed facial mask."

"An ex-what?"

"Exfoliating mask. Knock off all that dead skin."

Dead skin. What on earth is she talking about? He glanced toward a mirror. No one had ever told him that there was something wrong with his skin.

"C'mon." She grabbed his hand again. "I'm gonna hook you up." She marched back to her desk and picked up the phone.

"Wait. What about Ms. Goodwyn?"

"Don't worry. When she's done with her meeting, I'll bring her over to your chair. Right now, you need an emergency intervention."

Keenan touched his face. *Is it that bad?* "But— but—"

"Trust me. You'll thank me later."

"I knew it!" Martina howled. "I told you that his big butt was a freak, didn't I? Ha!" An even five feet tall plus-size woman with a penchant for wearing her clothes a few sizes too small, Martina was larger than life. Her boisterous voice and her constantly changing hair color (this week a frosted honey blond) made sure that everyone within a three-mile radius knew whenever she was near.

"All right. All right," Jalila conceded. She struggled to prevent a smile from easing onto her face.

"*Never* pick up men at a gas station." Martina slapped her hand down on Jalila's desk and continued to laugh her butt off.

"Hey, he picked me up," Jalila stressed. "I was just giving a brother a chance. Men are always claiming that sistahs are just too picky."

"The men that say that ain't about nothing." Martina's hands settled on her hips as her neck swiveled around. "They want the total package in a woman while they roam the streets looking like whodunit and what for."

Jalila conceded the point.

"Ain't nothing wrong with being picky, girl. The last thing you want to do is end up spending the rest of your life with the wrong man. Settling is for losers."

"Yeah, I hear you." Jalila folded her arms and leaned back in her chair.

Martina snapped her fingers. "I know what we need to do."

"What's that?"

"Go on vacation."

Jalila finally laughed. "Girl, there is too much work around here."

"You always say that."

"That's because it's always true. Maybe next year."

Martina clucked her tongue and rolled her eyes. "I'm telling you, you need to go away so you can get your groove back."

"Please. You know what happened to the last sistah that did that. She got played."

"True. True. But what about—"

"You know, Martina. I just need to take a break right now."

"A break? Girl, you haven't had sex in two years. If you break any longer you're going to forget what to do with a good stiff dick."

"Martina!"

"What? I'm just keeping it real. Don't you miss it?"

"Hell, yeah, I miss it. Damn, I was just minutes away from jumping that shoe-sniffing freak the other night. But there's got to be a better way of going about doing this." Jalila turned in her chair and stared out of her office window. "Finding love shouldn't be this difficult."

"Says who?"

Jalila didn't have an answer. She just knew that she was tired of club-hopping, online dating and speed dating. After a long silence she stood up from her desk and said, "I'd better get back out on the floor. There's somebody out there waiting to see me."

Martina took pity on her solemn expression. "Chin up, girl. We're going to find you a husband one day."

"Yeah. Maybe."

Keenan struggled to move his face. It felt like a block of concrete had cemented everything in place. *Is this normal?* He reached up from beneath his smock to try to touch his face but his hand was quickly smacked away.

"No. Don't touch," his clinician, Fantasia, warned. "You just have a couple more minutes and then we will wash it off."

Wash it off or chisel it off?

Reclining in a large leather chair, Keenan tilted his head toward the mirror on the wall to get a good look at himself. The mint-colored goo made him look like something out of one of his favorite old horror movies. Thank God that nobody he knew could see him right now.

"If you could just close your eyes, I can put these chilled cucumbers in place."

Cucumbers?

"Now these little babies are just going to do wonders for the tiny lines under your eyes."

Lines? I don't have any lines under my eyes.

Instead of arguing, he allowed Fantasia to place the cold vegetable slices on his eyes. He sighed. It did kinda feel pretty good.

"So. What is it that you do?" Fantasia asked.

Keenan licked his lips and tried to talk, but it was difficult given that he could hardly move his face. "I'm a television producer."

"Come again?"

"Television producer," he tried again, this time kicking up the volume.

"Oooh. Reeeally?" Fantasia's voice spiked with interest. "You know I used to do a little acting."

Keenan was grateful that cucumber masked his eye-rolling at the standard response people gave him.

"My high-school theater teacher used to tell me that I was a natural," she added.

"Is that right?" How much longer did he have to sit like this?

"I can even cry on demand." Keenan bobbed his head, though his patience was starting to thin.

The soft clicking of high heels caught his attention. When it was clear that they were heading his way, his heart sped up in anticipation. He started to reach up and remove the cucumber slices, but stopped, fearing another smack on the hand.

"Mr. Armstrong?"

Recognizing Jalila's lyrical voice, Keenan tried to smile. He sat up in the chair and risked the abuse of Fantasia by removing the cucumbers.

Jalila smiled and offered her hand. "Hello."

Keenan had thought he was prepared for Jalila's beauty, but he quickly found out that he was dead wrong. Her glowing skin and plump lips had him salivating. However, it was her eyes, dark and vibrant, that pulled and tried to hypnotize him. Finally, he realized that she was waiting for him to speak. "Hello, Ms. Goodwyn. Nice to meet you…again." Of course, his words didn't quite sound right, but she took mercy and smiled at him.

"Have we met?"

"Oh, yeah. I, uh wanted to talk to about…uh, a personal proposition."

"I'm not quite sure that I know what that means," she said.

Keenan suddenly felt frantic to scrape the cement off his face.

She laughed. "Here. Let me help you." She moved up behind him and swirled his chair back to face the wall mirror. "Just lean back. I'll finish you up."

He followed her instructions and was rewarded when he caught her soft scent—Chanel No. 5.

"Oh, I can do that for you, Ms. Goodwyn," Fantasia offered.

"That's all right. I got him. Can you bring over some steamed towels?"

"Yes, ma'am."

Jalila returned her attention to Keenan. He felt that strange beating sensation in his heart again.

"Sooo. You have some personal-slash-business proposition you want to discuss with me?"

He nodded, his gaze still drinking her in.

"You know in some circles that sounds a little lurid."

Fantasia returned with a stack of hot towels. Keenan watched as Jalila's slender fingers unrolled a couple of the towels.

"Okay. Are you ready to experience what heaven feels like?"

An image of her nude body lying hot and sweaty beneath him flashed in his mind and he blinked in surprise.

Still smiling, Jalila lowered the hot towel over his face. The warm steam instantly loosened the hardened seaweed mask.

Keenan could actually feel his facial muscles again. "Ahhh," he sighed.

"Feels good, huh?" Her nimble fingers began massaging his skin. "I told you. This is one of my favorite treatments. Trust me. You're going to feel like a million bucks when you walk out of here."

"Mission accomplished," he mumbled.

"Is this your first time here, Mr. Armstrong?" she inquired.

"Mmm-hmm." His eyes drifted closed. "This really does feel divine."

"Mind if I asked how you heard about us?"

"Online," he mumbled. Did this woman have magic hands or what?

"Oh. So you visited our Web site?"

He stiffened. "Yeah." He had visited the Body by Jalila Web site—after watching hours of her YouTube videos—so it wasn't a lie. "Actually, my, uhm, sister sort of told me about you."

"Ah. Your sister is a client then?" She removed the towel and then stopped and stared at him.

"Not exactly. She's a fan of your YouTube channel."

Jalila blinked. She hadn't heard a word he'd said once she'd removed his towel and found herself looking at the gorgeous man from Las Brisas the other day. Smooth, even chocolate skin, LL Cool J lips and an adorable cleft chin. She couldn't have chiseled out a better fantasy if she tried. Only—wasn't he like some creepy Hollywood something or another?

When Jalila didn't respond, Keenan took it as his cue to hurry up with his explanation.

"You see, I'm a television producer," he continued. "The name of my company is A.M. Production— Armstrong-Murphy. Anyway, my business partner and I were interested in doing a reality show this coming season."

Still silence.

"I know this is…unusual, but after watching your

YouTube videos, I felt that you would be the ideal woman for the show."

Jalila finally emerged from her stupor. "Show? What show?"

He misunderstood her confusion. "See, uhm, the show would be about us, the producers, helping you find your perfect match. A soul mate."

"A soul mate?" she parroted, still struggling to connect the dots. But it was hard. It wasn't every day that some outrageously handsome man showed up in her spa to tell her that he wanted to be her fairy god-father and poof—find her a soul mate. As far as she was concerned she would never fantasize about Idris Elba again. True to form, her body was going haywire. Without looking, she knew her nipples were perking up and stretching against her bra and shirt.

However, he wasn't saying that *he* was her soul mate. Only that he wanted to help her find him. This was definitely a blow to her ego.

"Let me get this straight," she finally said. "You want me to do a reality show?"

"Yes."

"Because you want to help me find my soul mate?"

"Correct."

Off to their right, Fantasia and Martina stood listening to their whole conversation. Jalila glanced over at them.

"Do it," her girls whispered.

"I don't know. TV?"

"Is it any different than YouTube? You're still broadcasting to the entire world."

She hesitated. He did have a point, and hadn't she tried everything else? Her gaze skimmed over his amazing body. *Well, I haven't tried everything.*

"How do I know you're legit?"

He handed her another business card. "Maybe you should look me up on the Web."

She smiled. "Okay," she said, drawing a deep breath. "Why not? If you check out, then I'll do it."

Chapter 6

It was just a little past noon and Nitara was concerned. Keenan had yet to call into the office, and he'd completely blown his conference call with the ABC executives this morning. After working so hard to get on their schedule, it just wasn't like him not to show or at least to call to say what was up. She told herself to give him another hour. After that, she was going to go all Lojack on him.

This would, of course, screw up her own schedule for the day.

Dee Dee, the company's script reader/receptionist, poked her head into the office. "Got a minute?"

"Sure, come on in."

Dee Dee pushed her way through the door, carrying a huge stack of telescripts.

"Wow. You did *all* of those already?"

"Yes, ma'am. Coversheet and overview are stapled on top of all of them."

"Any of them good?" Nitara inquired, wanting to cut to the chase.

Dee Dee scrunched up her face.

"'Nuff said."

"Seems all the writers in this town want to do is a spec script of *The Office* or *Grey's Anatomy*." Dee Dee glanced around. "Keenan hasn't made it in yet?"

"No. I'm starting to worry about him."

As if having some sixth sense that he was being talked about, Keenan strode into the office. "Good morning, ladies!"

"It's after noon," Nitara informed him. "Why the hell are you so happy?"

He shrugged as he plopped into his chair. "Can't a man be happy?"

Nitara and Dee Dee glanced at each other.

"Well, maybe *I* want to be in a good mood, too. How about sharing your secrets?"

"I'm not in a good mood," he corrected with a faux sternness.

"You're happy but you're not in a good mood," she said, trying to follow him.

"Right. I'm not in a good mood, I'm in a *great* mood."

"Oh, really?" Nitara eased back in her chair and crossed her arms.

"Sounds like a woman to me," Dee Dee said.

Nitara shifted in her chair. "Oooh."

"It's not a woman," he said.

"Then what is it?"

"Well, it is a woman—but not in the traditional sense," Keenan explained.

"What—she used to be a man?"

"Ha!" Dee Dee snorted and then remembered her place. "Ah, sorry."

"Are you going to spit this out any time soon?" Nitara glanced at her watch. "I have a pretty busy schedule."

Keenan laughed and propped his heels onto the corner of his desk. "What would you say if I told you I've found the star of our next fall show?"

"I'd ask 'What fall show?'"

"I've decided that we *will* do a reality show."

A smile bloomed across Nitara's face. "Ah, you finally saw the light, did you?"

"I guess you can say that. But more important, I found our star."

"Uh-huh." Doubt crept into Nitara's face and tone. "Now what kind of reality show are we supposedly doing?"

Keenan popped back out of his chair. "Remember you told me that the best or most-watched reality shows are those about romance—single-man-finds-single-woman kind of shows, right?"

"Right."

"Except for *The Amazing Race,*" Dee Dee interjected. "I love that show."

"Well, we're not doing a knockoff of that show. We're going to do a different version of a matchmaking show."

"It's not going to involve a man wearing a Viking hat, is it?" Nitara asked.

"No."

"Then I love it already."

"What I want to do is a sort of *Real World* meets *The Bachelorette*. We're not going to rent a mansion for a few weeks and have the couple do these big corporate-sponsored dates that end after the show's finished taping. What you have there is people falling in love with a mirage."

Nitara and Dee Dee nodded in agreement.

"What *we'll* do is have one big party of say twenty-five male candidates vying for the chance to date one woman. She'll work the room and then narrow it down to three candidates. From there we follow the bachelorette around in her real-world habitat. Meet her friends, her family. Same for the men. We see where they're coming from. But the whole dating process is totally on the guys. They plan the dates, they spend their money. This gives them and the audience a chance to see the real people and not a script. At the end of the show, the woman will pick one of the men she'd like to continue dating."

"Or marry," Dee Dee said. "You can't have a show like this and not have a ring at the end. Women tune in for the ring."

Keenan glanced at Nitara. "I agree with Dee Dee. There needs to be a ring at the end."

"We'll leave that up to the men." His gaze bounced between the women. "So—what do you think?"

The women looked at each other, nodded their heads and then finally Nitara spoke. "I like it."

"What are you going to call the show?" Dee Dee asked.

Keenan paused as he thought about Jalila. Parts of him responded instantly. "How about *Queen of Hearts?*"

"Sounds like a poker show," Nitara quipped.

Dee Dee shrugged. "I kind of like it."

"That makes it two against one." Keenan cocked a smile at his partner.

"Whatever." Nitara tossed up her hands. "Now tell me about our 'star.'" She noticed how Keenan's face lit up.

"I can't wait for you to meet her," he practically gushed. "The camera is going to love her. She's perfect!"

"Perfect?" Nitara found his choice of words interesting.

"Yeah," he continued, pacing the office. "She's beautiful, funny and charming. There're going to be fan clubs popping up everywhere."

"Sounds to me like she already has her first fan." Nitara braided her fingers. "Where exactly did you meet Ms. Perfect?"

"Technically I met her this morning," Keenan confessed. "But Keisha turned me on to her YouTube page."

This time Nitara sprang out of her chair. "Come again?"

"I know. I know. But let me explain. I was talking to Keisha last night and somehow we ended up talking about her trials and tribulations in trying to navigate the L.A. dating scene—"

"Hell, I have a few horror stories myself," Dee Dee chirped.

Keenan chuckled. "Anyway, at some point she started telling me about Jalila's YouTube channel that she subscribes to."

"I take it that Jalila is this star?"

"Right." He stopped pacing and leaned back against his desk. "So anyway, she—Keisha—was telling me how much she related to Jalila's vlogs. Of course, you know Keisha, she practically guilt-tripped me into checking out the channel myself. So I did. And I was hooked. She was engaging, charming and—"

"Beautiful," Nitara filled in. "Yeah. I get the picture."

"I was about to say funny. Oh, and let's not forget her dog, Cujo."

"She named her dog after a rabid, terrorizing Saint Bernard?"

"We both love horror movies." He gave Nitara the thumbs-up.

But you're not going to be one of the bachelors, Nitara wanted to say. "So you skipped out of your conference call with ABC this morning to go meet this 'star'?"

"ABC!" Keenan slapped his palm against his forehead. "I forgot."

"Clearly."

"Don't worry. I'll call them." He walked around his desk. "In fact, I'm going to work a treatment for the show."

Nitara watched her business partner, amazed at the change she saw in him. There was something more to this than met the eye.

* * *

"What do you mean that you're going to find a man on television?" James Goodwyn asked, staring at his daughter.

"Please say that you're not going on that show *Blind Date,*" Jalila's mother chimed in. "I know Sister Mabel watches that every week. She's convinced everybody that goes on that show is going straight to hell."

"No, Momma. I'm not going on *Blind Date.*" Jalila laughed and took a bite of her mother's signature meatloaf. Dinner at her parents' was a Monday-night tradition. It was the only time Jalila could carve out so they could play catch-up with what was going on in their lives. Her parents weren't pleased with this latest bit of news.

"What exactly are you going to be doing on TV?" her father asked. "Do you keep your clothes on?"

"What?" Jalila almost choked. "Of course I'm keeping my clothes on." Well, she hadn't exactly run that particular question by Mr. Armstrong. Actually, she had asked him hardly any questions.

"Well, as long as you keep your clothes on," her father said. "Hey, pass me the cornbread."

Jalila reached over and handed him the basket of cornbread muffins.

"Wait a minute. Wait a minute," her mom said. "I have a few more questions. Who all is going to be watching this?"

Jalila shrugged. "I guess anyone who wants to tune in."

"What channel is it going to be on?"

"I don't know, Mom." She laughed. "Far as I know, it's all in its beginning stages." That answer only made her mother's face go sour even more.

"I don't know if I like this dating-on-TV stuff. How come you can't find dates the old-fashion way—church or some social dance somewhere?"

"Social dances are clubs and there's nothing but losers there. I've tried churches and all the good men are already married and the ones that aren't are looking for a second mother."

"I still don't like it."

Jalila took her mother's hand and gave it a reassuring squeeze. "Don't worry, Mom. Everything is going to be fine. In fact, I think it might even be fun. Heck, I've tried everything else at this point."

"As beautiful as you are? I don't understand why it's so hard for you to get a date."

"I can get dates," Jalila corrected. "I just can't seem to get them with any quality men. Please don't worry. I'm not going to do anything that's going to embarrass the family."

"It may be out of your hands. I've heard stories of how television producers like to cut and paste things to make them look more scandalous than they really are."

"Mr. Armstrong wouldn't do that."

"How do you know?" she challenged.

She didn't know. "He just didn't strike me as that kind of man."

"No offense, baby girl," her father said, catching her eye. "But if he's part of that crazy Hollywood crowd,

I wouldn't trust him any further than you can throw him."

That was food for thought.

"Plus," her mother continued. "Has anyone ever gone on to get married on one of those shows? Or is it just that—a show?"

"I believe there was one."

"One?" Her mother laughed. "One out of how many? C'mon, Jalila. If you like those odds then you might as well keep doing what you been doing."

Jalila's spirits started to plummet.

Her father came to the rescue. "Now, Bettye. If this is something that Jalila wants to do, then I think we should support her."

Bettye Goodwyn didn't respond.

This whole scene had Jalila feeling like a ten-year-old trying to get her parents' permission to go on a school field trip.

By the time Jalila returned home from her parents', she had all but convinced herself to back out of the television show. It wasn't like she had signed a contract or anything. How hard would it be to find another woman to take her place?

Still, it would have been fun.

Cujo barked excitedly as she entered the door.

"Hey, boy," she cooed, patting his broad side. "Have you been a good boy?"

Woof! Woof! He ran around in a tight circle.

"C'mon. Let me get you something to eat." As she marched toward the kitchen, her mind wandered to

how she was going to tell Mr. Armstrong that she
needed to back out of the show.

She scooped dog food into Cujo's bowl and then
washed her hands at the sink. The phone rang, and
Jalila picked up the cordless without looking at the
caller ID. "Hello."

"Ms. Goodwyn?"

She stiffened at the sound of the velvety smooth
voice. She knew exactly who was on the other line.
"Oh, hello, Mr. Armstrong."

"Please. My friends call me Keenan."

"All right, *Keenan*. What can I do for you?"

"Well, I hope I didn't call you at a bad time."

"No. No. I'm just getting in from my parents'." She
folded her arms and leaned back against the sink. How
was she going to do this? *Just tell him.*

"Actually, I was just calling you to tell you that I ran
everything by my business partner and she's on board."

Jalila didn't know exactly what that meant.

"First thing tomorrow I'm going to make some calls.
We're going to pitch the idea to a couple of studios next
week, but I just wanted to tell you that I have a positive
vibe about this whole thing. I'm sure that we can get
picked up by ABC."

Jalila tried to digest all the information he was un-
loading. *ABC? The ABC?*

"Of course, we'll be racing to make the fall schedule. Nitara—that's my business partner—she's going
to post an open casting call in all the trade papers
tomorrow. Plus, she'll reach out to a few casting directors."

"Casting call." Jalila frowned. "Are you just lining up actors?"

Keenan laughed. "No. I wouldn't curse you like that."

She sighed in relief. "Oh, thank God."

"Been down that road?"

"I got a T-shirt around here somewhere."

His laughter deepened and sent a wave of delicious tingles throughout her body.

"Are you nervous?" he asked suddenly.

She weighed whether she should lie. "A little bit."

"Good. I would've been worried about you if you weren't. But don't worry, I'm going to take good care of you."

Something about the way he said those words warmed Jalila's heart and strung a wide smile across her lips.

"So you can trust me. I'm not going to let any crazies or stalkers anywhere near you."

If he's part of that crazy Hollywood crowd, I wouldn't trust him any further than you can throw him.

Jalila tried to push her father's words to the back of her head. "How do you know what kind of men to screen for? Surely you haven't figured out my type just by scanning my YouTube videos."

"You could always tell me your type."

Was it just her imagination or had his voice dipped lower? It was incredibly sexy and was turning her knees into Jell-O. "Well." She cleared her throat. "Ideally?"

Keenan chuckled. "Yes. Pretend you have a blank canvas. What kind of man can win your heart, Jalila?"

Jalila mulled over the question as she left the kitchen and headed upstairs.

"Do you even know what you want?" he teased.

She smiled. "I've always dreamed that my future husband would be tall, dark and handsome." *You sort of fit the bill.*

His laughter continued to rumble through the line. "All women say that. What about personality?"

"Of course, he would have to be kind, funny, generous and thoughtful."

Woof!

"Oh, and he would have to be a dog lover."

"All right. Sounds simple enough," Keenan said, glancing over at the table to see Chips inching toward his plate holding the discarded bones. "I see you, Chips."

Chips glanced around as if to say, "Who me?"

"Oh. I didn't know that you had company. I'm just chatting away."

"No. No one is here. Chips is my always-starving dog." He laughed and handed over another bone— nearly taking off one of Keenan's fingers.

"Aww. What kind of dog do you have?"

He smiled. "Great Dane."

Jalila's excitement exploded. "Get out of here! And you named him Chips? You know there was another dog in a great horror movie named Chips?"

Keenan bobbed his head. "Yeah. I named him after the dog in *Dawn of the Damned.*"

"So you love horror movies, too?"

"When I was younger it was always a great excuse to curl up with a date."

Jalila rolled her eyes. "I should have known." 'Course, she suspected that women didn't need much of an excuse to cuddle with him. She suspected that broad chest of his was actually one hell of a security blanket. And here she was in her bedroom, pulling off her clothes to get ready for bed! "Can I ask you a question?"

"Shoot." Keenan rinsed off his plate and set it in the dishwasher.

"Why me? I mean, there are millions of women with my story and plenty of them are on YouTube, a lot of them a lot more popular than I am. I don't think I even have a thousand subscribers."

Keenan entered his bedroom, sat on the edge of the bed and removed his shoes. "You have what we call in the business a certain je ne sais quoi. The camera loves you and I think what you have to say is relevant to the state of what women—heck, men and women—go through trying to find that special someone."

Even you? Now that she thought about it, what was *his* story? She had noticed at the spa that he didn't have a ring on his finger, but that didn't mean anything in this town. Now they had been talking for nearly an hour and it was edging close to midnight. Should she ask?

"I haven't been out in the dating scene too long myself," he admitted, during the silence. "I've been divorced for five years."

Jalila relaxed at being spared from asking the question herself. "I'm sorry."

"Don't be." He sighed and leaned back against the row of pillows along the headboard. "Truth be told, we simply outgrew each other. We were high-school sweethearts and probably should have broken up after the prom like everyone else."

After thinking about her own romantic missteps, Jalila had to agree with him. "So are you from L.A.?"

"Born and bred. My father used to own the number two GM dealership in the whole state of California a few years back. Now he and Mom are spending their retirement traveling the states in a fancy-schmancy RV, which means they call me and my sister often. Each week they alternate who wants to kill whom." He chuckled. "It's usually my mom wanting to throttle my father for either getting lost or for refusing to ask for directions. But they're crazy about each. I wish I knew their secret."

"Yeah. Sometimes I wonder if my parents' obscene lovey-doviness spoiled me," Jalila said.

"I doubt that." Keenan yawned. "There's nothing wrong with wanting what our parents have. Honestly, I'm a little jealous of them sometimes. I doubt it will ever be me. I may be a bit jaded now."

Jalila yawned as she snuggled under her comforter. "Maybe you should search for your soul mate on TV?"

Keenan climbed into bed. "Nah. I belong behind the camera, not in front of it."

"Who knows, maybe one day you'll change your mind."

"Yeah. Who knows?" He heard her yawning again and fought his reluctance to hang up. "I'd better let you get some sleep."

"I'm not tired." Her words probably would have

been more convincing if she hadn't yawned at the same time. "Okay. Maybe I'm a *little* tired."

Keenan's now-familiar laugh rumbled through the line. "G'night, Jalila."

"Night." She disconnected the call and smiled against her pillow. It was no surprise that she dreamed about a certain handsome Hollywood producer whose only interest in her was to help her find another man.

Just her luck.

Chapter 7

For the next two weeks Keenan was a man on a mission. He shopped the treatment for his reality show, *Queen of Hearts,* to every studio in town. So far he had received two No's and three Maybe's. Up until now, Nitara, Dee Dee and Jalila's best friend Martina had handled the interviewing and eliminations. Thanks to Excedrin and Pepto-Bismol, they'd whittled the twenty thousand applicants down to a hundred. It hadn't come without cost. Every day, Nitara complained that she was close to pulling her hair out, and that she'd forgotten just how many self-absorbed losers lived in L.A.

When his meeting with possible financers wrapped early, Keenan decided that he would help in cutting down the one hundred remaining contestants to twenty-five.

"Wow. How generous of you," Nitara mumbled, rolling her eyes. In her mind most of the hard work was already done. "I thought that you wanted to leave the tedious work to us."

"I never used the word *tedious.* I believe I said *the most important work,* but only because of your superior—"

"You're making me nauseous."

Keenan leveled his dazzling smile on Nitara and her irritation melted away almost instantly.

"At least I come bearing your favorite treat—cupcakes," he said, winking.

Dee Dee and Martina popped up from their chairs and raced toward the tray of desserts.

"Oh, thank God. I'm sooo starving." Martina moaned and in one bite reduced the cupcake by half.

"My, what a big appetite you have," Keenan joked while staring at the woman's fire-engine-red hair.

Martina leveled him a look that almost devoured him. "You have no idea." Slowly, she licked the icing off the rest of her cupcake, leaving no doubt to what she was referring to.

Keenan cleared his throat and returned his attention to Nitara and Dee Dee, who were busy choking back their own laughter.

The office door opened and a handsome, well-dressed gentleman strolled through the door.

"Hello." Dee Dee moved toward him. "Are you here for the casting call?"

"Yes. I'm Dr. Englehart." He jutted out his hand with a nervous smile.

Keenan looked him over, thinking he was in pretty good shape, but he took an instant dislike to the guy. Maybe it was the guy's shifty eyes, Keenan thought, or maybe it was because if the lights were turned off, he was sure the man's teeth would glow in the dark.

"Yes. Yes," Nitara said, stepping forward. "Just go down the hall there and then take the first door on your right."

"Thank you," Dr. Englehart said, his voice deepening perhaps for Keenan's benefit.

Once the *doctor* strolled away, Keenan turned his disapproving frown toward the three women who'd checked out the guy's butt and were busy fanning themselves.

"What's wrong with him?" Nitara and Martina challenged.

"He's a little…short, don't you think?"

Nitara rolled her eyes and said flippantly, "Everyone's short next to you."

Keenan frowned and glanced over at Dee Dee. "What do you think?"

Dee Dee finally jerked her head away from the hallway. "Huh? What?" Her gaze swung between her two bosses. "What did I miss?"

"See?" Nitara thrust up her chin. "He's good eye candy."

Keenan's incredulity quadrupled. "Is that all we're screening for—eye candy?"

Nitara's hands flew to her hips. "What are you talking about? The man is a doctor and he makes great money."

That wasn't good enough. "Oh, yeah, right. A doctor. What kind of doctor?"

Dee Dee scanned her clipboard. "A pediatrician. Says he loves children. He even has full custody of his two daughters."

"Custody? He was married before?"

Another glance at the clipboard. "Yep. Lasted four years."

"No divorcés," he ordered.

"What?" Nitara glanced at the other two women, who were watching their fight with great fascination. "Why would *you* have a problem with divorcés?"

Okay. He didn't have an answer for that. "I mean…" He bit his lips for a moment, but no ready explanation came.

All three women crossed their arms.

"I'm waiting," Nitara said.

"Well, we have a bachelorette who's never been married and I just think that, uhm, maybe we should fix her up with someone who hasn't been married as well. Less baggage."

"I kinda see where he's going," Dee Dee said, rescuing him.

"Yeah." Martina bobbed her head in agreement. "Who wants someone's leftovers?"

"Thank you." Keenan puffed up his chest.

Nitara rolled her eyes, signaling that she wasn't buying it. "All right. All right. We'll cross out all the divorcés. Anything else, your highness?"

He reached for Dee Dee's clipboard. "Well, let's see who else you have on the list." He scanned the forms.

"First of all, we can cut out all these short dudes. Five-five, five-seven... What is this? Most of these guys wouldn't be allowed to ride half the rides at Disneyland."

"Are you serious?" Nitara snapped.

Keenan tried to ease the tension by softening his tone. "I'm just saying that Jalila is what—five-ten, six feet in heels? It doesn't seem right to match her up with some jerk that might have a Napoleon complex."

Nitara stared at him—hard.

He shrugged his shoulders. "I'm just saying."

"Then I'm just saying that you're working my last nerve."

"Actually, I think he makes another good point," Martina interjected.

"What?" Nitara turned on the woman as if she'd just planted a knife in her back.

"Welll..." Martina glanced over at Dee Dee for backup, but saw that the woman was content to let her bosses duke it out. "Jalila does tend to date more tall losers than short ones. I personally don't date short men. It's too much like dating a little brother or something."

"Then why didn't you say something before now?"

"I didn't think about it until he brought it up," Martina said simply.

Nitara gave them all a mutinous look. "Fine! No short guys."

"See?" Keenan threw his arm around Nitara's shoulder. "I'm already helping. Now let's go see who else we got."

Nitara groaned. "Something tells me that this is going to be interesting."

An hour later, Keenan had pared their hundred potential candidates down to twenty-five. The three women sitting around him at the makeshift interview table had long ago tossed up their hands and folded their arms at Keenan's seemingly incomprehensible reasons for eliminating candidates. Most were either too tall, shifty-eyed, too nerdy, too muscular, too lean and Nitara's personal favorite—Keenan's insistence that one of the guys he'd seen on *America's Most Wanted.*

"Great. That wasn't so hard," Keenan said, handing Nitara her marked-up list.

"Piece of cake," she agreed sarcastically.

Martina was the only one who perked up and smiled adoringly at him. "I, for one, am impressed with your instincts."

Nitara glanced at her watch. "It's five o'clock and I'm calling it a day." She jumped out of her seat.

"Going home to *cook?*"

"Don't start with me. I'm not in the mood."

Martina stood and forced her way into Keenan's personal space to the point that he had to take a step back. "You know I'm a good cook?"

His eyebrows arched in amusement. "Is that right?"

"Yeah." She closed the distance between them again. "Maybe I can make you a nice home-cooked meal?"

"Uhm, er…" He stole a glance over at his business

partner, who looked on the verge of cracking up. "I'm going to have to take a rain check on that."

Martina twirled a finger through her bright red hair. "All right. But I'm going to hold you to it."

Keenan's cell phone rang, rescuing him from this awkward conversation. When he answered the call, he received the news that he'd been waiting for.

It was never a good idea to feed dogs table scraps. It could spoil the dog so that he'd refuse to eat dog food and constantly beg for yours. But once a year, Jalila broke her own rule, on Cujo's birthday. She fired up the grill and threw on a big, fat, juicy steak.

Just the smell of the grilling meat excited Cujo to the point that he ran around the yard like a frantic jack rabbit. "I bet you know what day it is," Jalila sang while capturing Cujo's reaction on video.

Woof! Woof!

Minutes later, he returned to her side, carrying his large metal bowl between his huge teeth.

"Are you a little impatient, boy?" She took the bowl from his mouth and then lifted the large steak from the grill.

Cujo leaped into the air in an almost perfect pirouette. Jalila laughed and served Cujo his birthday dinner, singing, "Happy birthday to you. Happy birthday to you. Happy birthday, dear Cujo. Happy birthday to you."

Woof!

"Good boy!" As she leaned down and rubbed the side of his belly, a sound caught her ear. Jalila stood still until she heard it again. The doorbell, she deduced, and headed back into the house. "Coming!" She wasn't expecting anyone, and when she opened the door, she was rendered speechless.

"Hello. I hope I didn't catch you at a bad time," Keenan said, smiling.

Chapter 8

Jalila blinked and tried to get her bearings. "No. No. Come on in," she said, stepping back and allowing him to enter.

Keenan's smile broadened as he crossed the threshold into the foyer. His gaze swept around the room while he nodded appreciatively. "Nice place."

"Thanks." Jalila closed the door and stood before him, waiting. His brief inspection completed, Keenan's dark gaze finally landed on her. Instantly, her body temperature rose a couple of degrees. Nervous, she cleared her throat. "So, what brings you by?" she asked.

Keenan lifted his arms to indicate the gifts he carried. "Came to celebrate."

"Celebrate?" Had she told him about her dog's

birthday? She glanced down and noticed the bouquet of flowers and bottle of champagne. Cujo didn't drink champagne. "What are we celebrating?"

"*Queen of Hearts* has been green-lighted. ABC bought thirteen episodes. Filming starts in two weeks."

"Wow." Her eyes bulged. "That was…fast." This was really going to happen. Suddenly it was hard for her to wrap her brain around actually going on national television to find a man. This would either be one of the best things to ever happen to her or the worst. Judging by the track record of most reality shows, she was beginning to think that it was probably leaning toward the latter.

Having expected a bigger or even better response, Keenan rocked on his feet, searching for something to say. "You wouldn't happen to have a couple of champagne glasses, would you?"

"Uh, what?" She snapped out of her reverie.

"Or we could just drink it straight out of the bottle. I'm game if you are," he joked.

"Oooh." She shook her head and cleared her muddled thoughts. "Let me take those." She reached for the flowers. The bouquet was a carnival of color: orange day lilies, purple asters and blue irises. "They're beautiful. Thank you."

Without thinking, she stepped forward and placed a kiss against his left cheek. The moment her lips touched his face, a spark flared between them and she quickly stepped back in surprise. To her amazement, his warm gaze darkened. Was it her imagination or had she seen desire?

Definitely your imagination.

"I guess I'd better go put these in some water." She turned to head for the kitchen, but she hadn't taken more than a few steps when she looked up and saw Cujo rounding the corner at a full gallop.

Jalila panicked. "Cujo, no! Cujo, stop!"

Cujo paid her absolutely no attention as he continued his race toward them—more specifically toward Keenan.

"*Cujo,*" she shouted one last time before she watched her two-hundred-pound Great Dane launch into the air. "Nooo."

Time crawled as Jalila witnessed Cujo's full-body tackle, his front paws hitting Keenan squarely in the center of his chest.

Keenan reeled backward. His feet were swept up in the air as total shock covered his face. Dog and man hit the hard wooden floor with a loud and resounding thump.

Jalila watched as the air exploded from Keenan's chest, but miraculously he managed not to bang his head or drop the champagne bottle. She couldn't say the same thing for the flowers. She immediately dropped them and rushed over to the scene of the crime, praying that Cujo wouldn't emulate his fictitious namesake and maul the Hollywood producer's face off.

Just as she reached for her dog's collar, miracle of miracles, Cujo began *licking* Keenan's face as though he was his favorite lollipop.

Keenan laughed while trying his level best to ward off the dog's impromptu spit shine. "Well, aren't you a rambunctious boy? Good boy. Good boy."

Confused, Jalila finally pulled her dog away. "Cujo, stop. Get off him."

Woof!

"I'm sooo sorry," she moaned, horrified and embarrassed. "What on earth has gotten into you?" she scolded the dog. "Please forgive him, Mr. Armstrong."

"It's Keenan, remember?"

"That depends, are you planning on suing me?"

He laughed. "No. I don't think so."

"Then Keenan it is." Seeing that he was genuinely amused, Jalila relaxed and laughed at the situation. "I'll go and put him outside."

"That won't be necessary," he said, pulling himself off the floor. "I'm sure that was just Cujo's way of saying hello. Beside, I own a Great Dane, too. I'm used to getting knocked down." He walked over to Cujo and, to complete this stunning phenomenon, her dog allowed him to scratch Keenan behind the ears. "My, my. Aren't you a handsome boy?"

Jalila shook her head. "Now I think I've seen everything. He usually doesn't like men. Up until now, my father is the only man Cujo doesn't bark his head off at. And even he can't make any sudden moves." Keenan's rich laughter deepened and something wickedly delicious stirred within Jalila.

"In that case, I'm going to take it as a good sign that he likes me."

"You should." She went and picked up the flowers, pleased that she'd lost only a couple of petals.

"Is there somewhere I can wash up?" She turned.

"Uhm, yeah. You'll have to go upstairs." Jalila

fought back the feeling of déjà vu. "The first-floor bathroom is still being renovated."

He handed over the bottle of champagne. "I'll be right back."

She nodded and gave him directions to the bathroom. When he took off up the stairs, she went into the kitchen to put the flowers in a vase. After that she forced herself to return to grilling her dinner. While waiting for Keenan to return she kept praying, "Please stay out of my closet. Please stay out of my closet."

Jalila exhaled a sigh of relief when she heard the back door slide open.

"Now what do you know about grilling?" he asked, his voice a light tease.

She flipped over her steak. A few flames licked but missed her hand before she glanced back over her shoulder at him. "Please. I know my way around a grill."

"Mmm-hmm," he said dubiously.

"Join me for dinner? I have another steak marinading."

He hesitated. "I don't want to put you to any trouble."

"No trouble at all. In fact, I took out some vegetables in the kitchen earlier. Maybe we can make some kabobs?"

"I'll do it," he offered.

She lifted an eyebrow at him.

"Just because I have a cook doesn't mean that I don't know my way around a kitchen. I'm a progressive kind of guy," he bragged. "You hold down the grill and I'll be in the kitchen."

"Well, all right then." She laughed.

It took Keenan no time at all to skewer the kabobs

and bring them out to the grill. A half hour later, the two sat at the patio table with a hearty meal in front of them. Since the champagne didn't exactly go with the meal, Jalila made some margaritas. Music was playing through the outdoor speakers.

"Now this is the good life," Keenan said, easing back from the table and his now-empty plate. "I have to say that I had my doubts about you manning the grill, but you knocked this out of the park."

"Well, thank you very much." They clicked their glasses and then she lifted her chin proudly into the air. She loved the way the evening breeze was blowing through her hair and the tequila gave her a nice buzz.

The sun was setting and the sky was a beautiful palette of indigo, lilac and dusty rose with flecks of gold.

"It looks like a painting," Jalila whispered, gazing up at the sky. "I love this time of day."

"Me, too," he said.

She glanced over and they shared a smile. "Usually I'm too busy to stop and just appreciate the setting sun, but the times that I do, I just feel this wonderful calm."

"I know what you mean."

For a long while, the two of them, Cujo at their feet, remained silent, watching as the sun disappeared and the night fell like a curtain, leaving only the patio light to shine on them.

"Mind if I ask you a question?" she asked.

"Sure."

"How did you get into the television business?"

He shrugged. "Well, I've always loved movies and television. Who didn't, living in this town, right?"

She nodded.

"But growing up, I first thought that I was going to become a car dealer like my father."

"Really?"

"Yeah." He nodded. "It's probably where I inherited my salesmanship skills. It comes in handy in this business. But then, somewhere in high school, I liked the idea of becoming a lawyer, then in college I got this chance to intern at NBC—even got to work on *The Late Show with Jay Leno* in the early nineties. Once you're around it, it's easy to get bitten by the bug."

"Do you still like what you do?"

"I love it," he admitted honestly. "Despite the long hours, the headaches, the ulcers and the prima donnas. There's a certain energy in this business, wheeling and dealing and whatnot. It can consume you."

"It doesn't sound like you have much time for a love life."

He frowned.

"I mean—personal life."

He cocked a grin at her. "No, you're right—on *both* counts. At least, that's what my ex-wife thought, too."

Jalila waited, not daring to speak for fear that he wouldn't continue. Something flickered across his handsome face. Had his marriage dissolved from more than them simply outgrowing each other as he'd previously claimed? Had he been hurt?

"Anyway, I don't want to bore you."

"Nooo," she said eagerly, and then realized that she needed to tone it down a bit. "I mean, you're not boring me at all."

Still he remained quiet.

"In fact," she added, "my friends say that I'm a pretty good listener."

He nodded. "I agree with them."

Jalila was flattered by the off-hand compliment, but knew that he wanted to move on. "We're out of margaritas."

Keenan glanced down at his empty glass. "So it appears."

Just then the Fugees's "Killing Me Softly," the extended instrumental version, began to play. The song triggered a memory and Jalila closed her eyes and smiled to herself.

"Ahh," Keenan said.

She opened her eyes to find him staring at her. "What?"

"That's what I want to know. What's that smile about?"

She shook her head, embarrassed to share.

"No, no. Give it up. When a woman smiles like that she is definitely remembering something good."

"Well…" Jalila's face warmed with embarrassment. "It's just that…my high-school sweetheart and I danced to this song at our prom."

"Was this the gay guy?"

She drew a deep breath. Of course, he'd know about that. "Unfortunately."

Keenan stood and then held out his hand.

Confused, she glanced up.

"C'mon. Let's dance. Who knows, maybe after tonight you'll think of *me* whenever you hear this song."

There was a look on his face that said he was just as surprised by his words as she was, but still she placed her hand in his and stood. He draped one arm around her waist, creating a sphere around them where the world had drifted away and an undeniable heat simmered. Their bodies brushed against each other while they rocked in time to the beat. Jalila felt like she had a high-school crush, especially the way she had trouble meeting his gaze.

Was he feeling what she felt right now or were her overcharged hormones and sex-starved body making a fool out of her once again?

"I bet you're dangerous on the dance floor," he mused with a crooked grin.

"I manage to stay on two feet." Just as the words left her mouth, Jalila stepped on Keenan's foot. "Oops. Make that three feet."

He laughed, his firm body quaking and rubbing against her. Now she couldn't decide whether she was experiencing pleasure or just going through pure torture. At long last she lifted her eyes and found his intense gaze drinking her in.

"I've been trying to figure it out," he said.

"What's that?"

"How a woman as beautiful, smart and kind as you are could have any trouble in the man department."

"It's not about *getting* a man—it's about finding the *right* one."

They stopped dancing, but didn't move away from each other. In fact, Jalila realized belatedly, Keenan was moving closer. He was so close that she was sure that at any moment he was going to kiss her. At the feel of his warm breath against her upturned face, she closed her eyes and waited with aching anticipation for the magic that she was sure to come.

And she was *not* disappointed.

His lips were soft. His tongue was gentle, and he tasted divine. She stretched her arms up his chest and pressed closer. Keenan's responsive growl caused the ache between her legs to intensify.

Keenan's hands left the small of her back only so they could roam freely through her thick hair. His strong fingers were incredibly erotic. Within minutes, desire seized her and left her trembling.

What are you doing? the voice in the back of Keenan's head said. He ignored his conscience by squeezing his eyes tight and deepening the kiss. He didn't want logic or reason to ruin this moment. His hands left her curtain of thick hair to roam between their bodies and settle on her soft lush breasts.

He swallowed her sigh as her body sagged against him. Instinctively, he swept her up into his arms and carried her inside the house.

Jalila broke the kiss and glanced around. "Where are you taking me?"

"To your bedroom," he answered simply. "Any objections?"

Their gazes locked and Jalila's entire body ignited. "No," she whispered.

"Good."

Chapter 9

Keenan carried Jalila into her bedroom like it was a scene straight out of an old black-and-white classic movie. But when he kicked the door closed in Cujo's face and they began to tear at their clothes, things got a little more X-rated.

Jalila knew that Keenan had broad quarterback shoulders. But to see them and his bare chest made her pulsing clit throb. Apparently, she wasn't getting out of her clothes fast enough because with one tug, Keenan ripped her delicate lace bra. Her full D-cup breasts bounced out, her toffee-tipped nipples stood erect and ready.

Keenan's eyes widened as a growl of hunger filled the room. In the next second he launched toward her.

They toppled onto the bed. Jalila in just her ripped bra and panties, Keenan in his black silk boxers.

"Oh, Gawd," he groaned, taking one breast into his mouth.

"Oooh." Jalila's head fell back as she arched upward. *It's been so long.*

Keenan moaned while his free hand cupped and squeezed her other breast.

Damn that feels sooo good. Jalila squirmed, her body covered in goose bumps. Keenan shifted his weight so he could sample the other breast. When he moved, his hard cock rubbed against her upper thigh. Her panties went from damp to soaking wet in point-two seconds.

"You taste so good," he murmured, skimming a hand down her body. "Look at these pretty titties." He pulled at her marble-size nipples and then released them so he could watch them bounce and jiggle before his eyes.

A lazy smile turned up Jalila's lips.

Keenan's hand slipped inside her panties. He ran his middle finger deep inside her slick honeypot. "Damn, baby. You're so wet." He eased in another finger and stirred them around.

Her body's juices made a smacking sound against his lubricated hand. Pleasure surged through her body as she rotated her hips counterclockwise to his hand.

"Mmm. You like that?"

"Y-yes," she panted. "Oooh." Air seeped from her lungs. The room spun while her body's temperature rose. She wanted to say "slow down" in order to make the moment last longer but her pussy screamed for him to go faster.

"C'mon, baby. Don't hold back," he whispered.

That was the *last* thing she was doing. Everything was short-circuiting, left, right and center.

Keenan inched down her body, leaving bright red passion marks in his wake.

Jalila started shaking.

"Are you comin', baby?"

She couldn't answer. A white light flashed behind her eyes as her body candy-coated his hand.

"Aww. That's my girl," he praised. "Let me get a good look at you." Keenan grabbed the waistband of her panties with his teeth and then dragged them down and off her body.

Still floating down from her orgasmic high, Jalila's eyes fluttered open to see Keenan planted in between her legs.

"Open up for me," he ordered.

She hesitated.

He leaned forward and kissed her brown lips. "C'mon. Let me see you."

Emboldened, Jalila reached down between her legs and spread herself open, exposing her pulsing and glistening pink clit to his greedy eyes.

"Let me see you play with it," he said.

The request took her by surprise, but she so wanted to please him that she complied. With two fingers keeping herself open, Jalila used her other hand to slip more fingers into her wetness.

Fascinated, Keenan watched her masturbate, then he leaned forward and blew a soft, steady stream of air around her clit.

Her eyes rolled up, her breasts tingled. Jalila felt wanton and free at the same time.

"Let me get a little of this." Keenan reached toward her, dipped his fingers in and stole some of her honey and then rubbed it up and down his thick cock.

Jalila smacked her lips, hit with the sudden craving for chocolate. Just thinking about how good he'd taste was enough to send her over the edge. "Aww."

"That's what I'm talking about," Keenan bragged. "Has anybody ever told you how beautiful you look when you're comin', baby?" He moved closer, his warm breath teasing. "Such a pretty pussy."

Jalila held her breath.

"You want me to help clean you up?"

She swallowed.

"Hmm?" He flicked his tongue across her clit.

Air rushed from Jalila's chest, her mind spun.

"Hmm?" Another flick.

"Oooh."

"Is that a yes?" Flick.

Jalila nodded.

"I can't hear you, baby." Flick.

"Y-yes."

"Good. Because I can go for some dessert." He hooked her legs over his shoulders and then sat up. This lifted Jalila's body up so that all that remained on the bed were her shoulders and head. There was no way to avoid watching him devour her.

Slowly and deliberately his tongue unfurled so deep within her it caused a series of orgasms to erupt in quick succession. Her toes curled and uncurled behind his head. All the while, he feasted and moaned as if she was the best home-cooked meal he'd had in a long time.

Everything he did caused tears of joy to flow like a river from her eyes. When she was finally limp as a wet noodle, he lowered her body and then hovered over it.

Jalila was suddenly overwhelmed with a case of shyness. *Never* had any man made her scream the way he had for the past half hour. Hell, she hadn't even done anything for him yet.

"Why are you blushing?"

Instead of confessing, she reached for his erection and was surprised at just how smooth and hard it felt. Had she been blind she doubted that she would have been able to tell it from a steel pole.

Keenan struggled to act as if Jalila's soft fingers weren't doing a number on him. So much blood had rushed to the tip of his cock, it had darkened to a shade of blue-black. However, he remained determined to play it cool and allow her time to get familiar with his body.

"How big is it?" she asked with wide-eyed wonder.

"Why? Are you afraid it won't fit?"

She blushed again, which he found strange. "You're not a virgin, are you?" Surely he hadn't missed that fact.

"No," she admitted to his great relief. "But it has been a while."

His brows climbed. "How long?"

"Two years."

Keenan's eyes widened. He couldn't possibly have

heard her right. Two years sounded like it should be a crime.

"You probably think that's a long time," she said.

"Just a little bit," he joked, but then he thought about it. Two years. Her body must be extremely tight right now. The ache in his cock intensified at the thought. Had he been a weaker man, he would have hopped right up and climbed between her thick thighs and gone to town.

Patience, he reminded himself. Patience was going to get them both where they needed to be. "I'm surprised you haven't jumped my bones by now." He chuckled.

"Believe me, I'm getting to that," she warned.

"I have condoms in my pants pocket and we can do whatever you like."

"Whatever I like?" she asked, brows lifted.

Keenan leaned back against the pillows and folded his arms behind his head. His cock sat straight up like a black pillar. "It's all about you, baby. Have your way."

"In that case…" Jalila crawled down in between his legs and then opened her mouth wide.

Keenan's eyes nearly rolled out of his head as he sucked in a long breath through his teeth. He held his breath as he watched Jalila's mouth sink farther and farther down his long cock. She took her time, letting her mouth adjust to his size. Soon, he could feel the head squeeze toward the back of her throat.

It was exquisite, amazing—just so goddamn good that it sent shivers down his spine and then shot out toward his toes. "Damn, baby." Keenan squirmed, feeling pre-cum drip down her throat. At this rate, he was going to explode before they even got started. He reached for her just as her head bobbed back up. Her lips smacked the tip of his mushroom-shaped head.

"Oh, Gaaawd," he groaned.

Down she went again.

Keenan started to sweat. Maybe he was out of his league. Baby girl had the potential of turning him out. Flippin' the script. Have him writing checks to pay her mortgage. Her throat squeezed and he actually felt his eyes water. "Damn, baby. You're going to make me cum."

Jalila released him and smiled. "That's sort of the point." She reached across the bed for her discarded panties. She wrapped the lacy material around the base of his dick, effectively cutting off circulation and guaranteeing that he would stay nice and hard for some time.

She went back to sucking him, concentrating on the plump head while rubbing her panties up and down his thick shaft.

Keenan ran his fingers through her hair, knowing he had, at best, thirty seconds before he shot off. When it was time, Jalila glanced up, her mouth still working its magic. It was her turn to watch him come.

"Oooh, Gaaawd!" His face twisted from the raw pleasure that seized him.

Jalila's mouth popped off as his hot creamy lava erupted and gushed down the sides of his still-hard cock. It was quite beautiful.

Panting hard, Keenan smiled wickedly. "That wasn't supposed to happen," he said.

"Says who?" She laughed.

He was pleased that she'd overcome her shyness. "Says me." He grabbed her and settled her under his arms so they could exchange a few light kisses. He dipped his hands between her legs to make sure she was still wet.

It was definitely time.

Seconds later, condom on, Keenan asked, "What position do you want to be in?"

Missionary? Doggy-style? Top side? Jalila had a hard time choosing.

"Tell you what," Keenan said, grinning. "Why don't we do a little of everything?"

"That works for me," she murmured, watching him above her. Trembling with anticipation, Jalila couldn't wait another minute to end her two-year drought.

"You ready," he asked.

Hell, yeah. "Yes."

Keenan eased the tip of his dick in first and then teased her by slowly sinking into her. Turns out he was right. Her body was as tight as a drum, and sliding into her slick narrow pathway caused an army of sweat beads to pop out along his hairline.

Jalila automatically wrapped her legs around his waist while her hands slid down and cupped his firm, muscled ass cheeks. When he was buried as far as he could go, she gyrated her hips, making it difficult to tell exactly who was screwing whom. In no time, their bodies were hot and covered with sweat.

The house was filled with sounds: Keenan and Jalila's bodies slapping together, the headboard banging against the wall and Cujo howling in the hallway.

"Give it to me, baby. Give it to me," Keenan panted, his chiseled chest heaving.

"Oooh, Keeenaaan."

"That's right, baby. Scream my name." He stopped, flipped her over and even took a second to kiss her pear-shaped booty before ramming back into her with one long stroke.

Words eluding her, Jalila settled on another orgasmic scream.

"Gawdayummm," Keenan panted. "So tight."

Jalila heard nothing. Behind her eyes were heaven and stars.

However, there was no rest for the weary. Keenan peeled off one condom and replaced it with another. "Hey, I got an idea." He proceeded to fold her body over like a taco and then entered in a way in which she watched him grind into her from the backside. She had a clear view of his mountainous cock sliding in and out of her. And, being so close, she flicked her tongue out to tease his balls.

"Jesus," Keenan moaned, his voice cracking. To prolong the moment he did a few strokes and then changed up to grind his hips in small, but intense circles. But when his cheeks tightened, Jalila knew he was about explode again.

"That's right," she panted at him. "C'mon for me."

"Aww." He released her.

Jalila quickly unfolded herself and removed his condom. "Here, let me clean you up."

He tried to pull away, claiming his dick was sensitive now. She didn't want to hear it. They were in a competition of endurance and she was determined to win.

She quickly lapped him clean and then watched as he returned the favor.

As the night rolled on, they lost count of how many orgasms they shared. But the last one, Jalila performing the backward helicopter, practically knocked her into a deep comalike sleep. Never had she been so relaxed or satisfied. Hell, she was even dreaming about fairy dust and unicorns, if you could believe it.

Hours later, she slowly woke up, stretching and smiling. Her body was sore and tingly, but in a good way. She peeked over at the clock and saw that it was well past noon. But she didn't care. Jalila closed her eyes, stretched again and rolled over to reach for that incredible lover who had made her feel like a woman again.

However, her hand hit nothing but empty space. One eye peeked open and then the other. "Keenan?" She sat up and blinked in surprise to see Cujo lying at the foot of the bed.

Woof!

Now why did it sound like he'd just called her a fool?

Chapter 10

Twenty-four hours after that amazing sex-fest, Jalila was still waiting for Keenan to call. This particular situation was a first for her. Not that she hadn't ever had a one-night stand. She had—complete with awkward breakfasts at the local IHOP where they would each pretend that they were actually going to continue seeing one another. But this was actually a guy sneaking out of her house while she was still asleep. That was foul. "Wait. You don't know whether he *snuck* out," she reasoned aloud. "He could have been called away on business."

It was a shaky excuse at best, but it was one that she was desperately clinging to at this point. She was on entirely new ground and she didn't know what to do. Her first inclination was to call him, but that didn't seem right. He'd left *her* bed. Therefore, he should call her. She was certain that was in the rule book somewhere.

After forty-eight hours, Jalila was concerned.

After seventy-two hours, she was pissed.

Needing to vent, Jalila grabbed her camcorder. "All right, YouTubers, this is your girl, Jalila," she said tightly. "I know it's been a while since I've done a video, but your girl has been running around lately. You know how it is. Anyway, let me cut to the chase. Right now, I'm pissed the eff off." Jalila recounted the entire evening. Cujo's birthday, Guy X dropping by, dinner, margaritas, music, dancing. "I'm telling you, I couldn't have dreamed a better evening," she said. "Next thing I know we're kissing, right? And then he's carrying me up to my room like I'm Scarlett O'Hara in damn *Gone with the Wind*.

"But none of that had jack to do with what came next," she admitted, staring into the camera lens. "Gi-iirrrlzzz, when I tell you that brother man put it down, I mean brother man *put it down*." She clucked her tongue and rolled her eyes. "I'm screaming, he was growling and the dog was barking. It sounded like animal kingdom up in here." She shook her head and held up her hand like she was in the middle of church service. "So, after we're going at it for a couple of *hours* and I pass the eff out, how come this brotha creeps out of here like the police showed up at the door?

"Gone. Ghost. I mean, am I that chick that gets played like that? Yeah, I've put up with my share of losers, shoe-sniffers and the like, but *damn*. Hell, the only thing that was missing was money on the nightstand. Look, I am a strong—and I do mean strong—black woman and you know what? My ass is still waiting for the phone to ring. How pathetic is that?

"I don't know. Maybe he's waiting for me to call him. But I ain't calling. Why should I call? He's Mr. Lightfoot." She shook her head. "And before you ask, his butt hasn't been in no accident. I've checked all the hospitals and called all the police stations. Bottom line, brotha man rolled up in here, hit it and then quit it. Now I'm stuck looking like Boo Boo the Fool."

Disgusted with herself, tears glossed her eyes. "You know what? I'm gonna have to holler at y'all later. I'm too emotional right now." She turned off the camera. She knew without looking that the recording was way too long and that she would never upload the video to her channel—especially since Keenan viewed her channel. Right now it just felt good to vent.

Her waiting game continued.

"You slept with your producer?" Fantasia shouted wide-eyed in the middle of Las Brisas restaurant.

Jalila wanted to crawl under the table.

"When the hell did this happen?" Martina snapped, whipping back her ice-blue hair.

Jalila forced a casual shrug. "Last week. And he's my *ex*-producer. No way am I going to do that show now."

Martina continued to look incredulous. "After all that time I put in vetting those men? Oh, you're doing the show."

"Not gonna happen."

"Why the hell not?"

"I just told you why not. Weren't you listening?" Jalila's irritation mounted.

Martina chuckled. "No. You just told us how you got laid—and surprise, surprise, you still ain't got a man."

"Ouch." Jalila flinched.

"Martina, behave," Fantasia chastised.

"What? I'm just telling it like it is. The whole point of this was for her to find herself a man, a soul mate, a husband. At least that's what y'all told me. Now if you're saying that you don't want that—cool. You know how I feel about a brotha puttin' a sista on lock anyway. Frankly, I'm tired of hearing the girl whining all over town and on the Internet about how she can't find nobody. *But* if this is something that you still want, why are you going to let some fancy Hollywood producer play you? You better get your head in the game."

Jalila shifted in her chair, listening.

"Do the show," Martina insisted. "Prove to Mr. Hollywood that one monkey don't stop no show."

Fantasia glanced over at Jalila. "I hate to admit it, but she has a point."

Jalila didn't want to, but she felt herself begin to sulk. "If I do the show then that means that I'll have to see him again."

"Not necessarily. Given how he hasn't called you back, he'll probably steer clear of you."

Despite trying to put on a brave face, Jalila's anger gave way enough for her to admit the awful and embarrassing truth. "You ladies just don't understand."

"Make us understand." Fantasia reached over and covered her hand.

"It's just that—that night…"

"Yeah?" Martina and Fantasia leaned in.

Jalila still fumbled for the right words.

"He was good, wasn't he?" Martina guessed with a wicked smile creeping across her lips. "Go ahead. Tell the truth and shame the devil. He knew his way around a bedroom, didn't he?"

"The bedroom? Hell, my body," Jalila finally confessed. "Girlz, that man had me doing things I had no business doing the first time with a man."

"Whoooooo!" Martina screamed and then clapped her hands and stomped her feet. "I *knew* it. I knew it just by looking at his fine ass that he could lay the pipe."

The other diners swirled their heads in their direction.

"Will you keep it down?" Jalila asked, her face burning with embarrassment.

"I knew it, I knew it, I knew it," Martina carried on.

Fantasia bobbed her head in shy agreement. "The thought *did* cross my mind."

"Well, at least one of us got his butt," Martina said. "I know I was sweating him myself."

Jealousy kicked Jalila in the gut. "You were?"

"You weren't?" Martina tossed back at her. "The man is gorgeous. Broad shoulders, big chest and an ass I betcha I can bounce a quarter off. How could a woman not look at him and think of sex? Shoot, I bet he could power drill—"

"Okay. Okay. I get it." Jalila paused. "And yes he can."

"Whoooooooo!" Martina screamed.

Jalila and Fantasia laughed.

"So you're going to do the show?"

Jalila was tempted. "Maybe I'm just embarrassed by how much of a ho I acted like."

"See. That's why you don't have your kitty-kat on lock that long. Can't let that pressure build like that. It ain't natural. Sheeeit. You sure he snuck out? Maybe the paramedics carried him out. You check the hospitals?"

Jalila cracked up.

"I can see him now, lying in a hospital bed with a broke dick."

The girls howled until there were tears running down their eyes. Jalila needed this, and after an hour of female bonding, her confidence was restored. Maybe Martina was right. Heck, maybe she was the one that was reading too much into what had happened the other night. There were no promises made, no vows broken. It was just…sex. Nothing more—nothing less.

"I'm so glad that I talked to you girls about this."

"That's what we're here for," Fantasia said. "Does this mean that you'll do the show now?"

"Well, since I still don't have a man—I don't see why not."

"Then let's make a toast." Martina held up her glass.

Jalila and Fantasia followed her lead.

"To Jalila, may she find her soul mate on *Queen of Hearts*."

"I'll drink to that," Jalila said and then tipped her glass against theirs. Who knew, maybe it just might happen.

Keenan felt like an asshole—and that was putting it mildly.

Every time he picked up the phone to call Jalila, he hung up. What exactly was he going to say? *Hey, thanks for that night of incredible sex but I'm just not looking for a relationship right now?*

The words were true, but complicated by the fact that he knew that she *was* looking for a relationship— a relationship that he was supposed to be helping her find.

For the past week, Keenan hadn't been able to concentrate on anything. His mind just kept playing that wonderful night over and over in his head. No one woman had the right to taste and feel that damn good. Not to mention the number of times he'd had tears in his eyes.

Tears!

Oh, no. He shook his head. The situation just wouldn't work. He'd vowed five years ago that he would never let a woman leave him strung out again. Besides, he knew what Jalila was all about. She wanted the whole enchilada: the ring, the house, the two-point-five children. Keenan had already tried that path before. It wasn't for him.

His interest in Jalila Goodwyn started and ended with a television series. Business. Nothing more.

Then why the hell were you so eager to take her to bed?

"Hell, she's beautiful," he argued with himself. "We'd been drinking and then the music and then…I kissed her." He swallowed the thick lump clogging his throat as he remembered. "And…damn the things she could do with her mouth." He expelled a long sigh and his body shuddered with a phantom orgasm.

The taping for *Queen of Hearts* was to start next week. So far, he hadn't heard a word about whether Jalila was pulling out. He was relieved *and* disappointed at the same time. If she elected to still do the show, then he had every intention of steering clear of the set. Nitara was more than capable of overseeing everything. He needed to focus on finding new material for the winter and summer seasons.

He spent most of the morning networking and combing through some potential material with the William Morris Agency before rushing back to his office for an afternoon conference call with NBC studios. However, when he walked into the office, Dee Dee was blasting the Fugees's "Killing Me Softly" from her iPod.

"Turn that off," he snapped.

When Dee Dee jumped, he softened his tone. "I mean, *please* turn that off."

She rushed over to her iPod and shut it off, still looking as if he'd slapped her or something. He marched into his office.

"Oh, you have a visitor," she called to him just as his hand landed on the doorknob.

He turned. "Who is it?"

"Tenetria."

Keenan's heart sank. He didn't need this right now. "Did she say what she wanted?"

"Why don't you come in here and ask me?" Tenetria shouted through the door.

Keenan rolled his eyes.

"Sorry," Dee Dee whispered, frowning.

Keenan drew a deep breath and then marched into his office like a soldier off to war. The minute he entered, his gaze zoned in on his ex-wife sitting behind his desk with her legs propped up.

"Comfortable?"

Tenetria smiled. "I figured that you wouldn't mind if I made myself at home."

"As a matter of fact—" he closed the door "—I do mind." He walked toward his chair and then waited for her to stand up.

"Aren't you at least going to say hello first, sweet-heart?"

His brows lifted. "Sweetheart?" He chuckled. "Endearments usually mean you want something."

Tenetria lowered her legs from his desk and slowly rose to her feet. The moment was undoubtedly meant for him to get a good long look down her pink shirt. "I just wanted to try the chair out for size," she taunted. With a catlike smile, she walked her fingers up his chest.

Keenan's face turned into stone as he swiped her hand away. "I'm not in the mood for any of your games." He moved around her and dropped into his chair.

"Now to what do I owe this wonderful honor?" he asked sarcastically.

"I need some money," she said.

"Ha! Don't tell me that you've already run through the ten and a half million you got in the divorce."

Tenetria shrugged. "I may have made a few bad investments."

"I've been there before." Keenan's gaze raked over her so that she didn't miss his meaning.

"Ha-ha. I'm serious." She lowered herself into the chair across from his desk.

"I'm serious, too. And in case you've forgotten, we're divorced. I'm no longer your personal ATM. If you made some bad investments maybe you should write Congress and apply for a bailout. I can't help you."

"You can't or you won't?"

"What difference does it make? The bottom line is that I'm no longer capitalizing your drug habits, shopping sprees and eighteen-year-old boyfriends."

"There's no need to get nasty."

"What can I say? You bring out the best in me." He glanced at his watch. "Now, if you don't mind, I have a phone conference to prepare for." He left the sentence hanging in the air between them.

Bitter disappointment twisted Tenetria's face. "Please don't make me beg." Her chin dropped a few notches. "I really do need some money. The house has been foreclosed on, the Mercedes has been repossessed and what money I did invest was tied up with some jackass in New York running a ponzi scheme. I have nowhere to go. I'm flat broke. I wouldn't be here if I wasn't."

Keenan's heart tugged and he dropped his harsh tone. "What about your parents?"

Tenetria rolled her eyes. "I can't go back there," she murmured.

What she meant was that she *wouldn't* go back there—not after she'd treated everyone like dirt when she had money. She wasn't humble like her sister Nitara. Money had changed Tenetria, and to go crawling back empty-handed would be a humiliating experience for her—which was exactly why Keenan was eager for her to do so.

"I was thinking that maybe I could stay with you for a while," she said, giving him a smile. "I can earn my keep." She stood up and made her way back to his desk. "I could pick up around the house, cook a few meals and even keep the bed warm for you at night."

"I have a maid, a cook and electric blanket that can do all of that quite well, thank you."

"C'mon, Keenan. You're not about to let me live out on the streets, are you?"

"How on earth can you make it sound like I'm doing this to you? You broke *my* heart, remember? And I still did right by you. I gave you the house, the cars and half of everything I owned. Now that it's all gone you want to come back and *play house?*"

Guilt flickered across her face.

"Naw. I don't roll like that," he said.

"I'm not saying it's a permanent situation."

"What about Nitara—can't you stay with her and Martin?"

Tenetria stomped her foot. "I'm not staying with my family. I won't be a laughingstock."

Keenan laughed in her face. "Sounds to me like you don't have a choice."

She switched tactics. "C'mon, baby." She sat on the

desk. "We've been through a lot together, and I know I put you through a lot of unnecessary changes. But I've changed."

As her mouth moved, Keenan envisioned a snake hissing.

"I'll do right by you. I swear."

He wasn't trying to hear any of this.

"You loved me once…and seeing how you're still not with anyone, maybe you still love me." She slowly crossed her legs so he was sure to see that she didn't have on any panties.

"Tenetria—"

"Shh." She pressed a finger against his lips. "Don't say anything." She placed her foot in his lap and then leaned back and started unbuttoning her top. "Just think about it, Keenan. You and me. We used to be good together."

The office door burst open and Nitara marched inside. "Keenan, do have those contracts for—" She stopped, her mouth falling open.

Tenetria hopped off the desk and turned, her silk bra falling out of her shirt. "Hello, sister dear."

However, Keenan didn't pay any attention to the drama unfolding between the two sisters. His eyes zeroed in on the woman who'd walked in with his business partner.

"Jalila."

Chapter 11

Jalila blinked—and then blinked again. Still she was having trouble processing what she was seeing. Keenan was closed up in his office with a half-dressed woman. Was he truly one of *those* producers who operated using the proverbial casting couch?

"Did we catch you at a bad time?" Nitara asked, crossing her arms.

The half-dressed woman, who looked eerily like Nitara, responded, "As a matter of fact—"

"No, no," Keenan insisted. "Tenetria was just leaving."

Tenetria? Jalila ran the name down in her memory database. *His ex-wife?* This information didn't have the same emotional effect as her ex-fiancé telling her that he was gay, but it was certainly up there. It took everything Jalila had not to tear across the office and whack him upside his head. Somehow she kept the presence of mind to realize that she had absolutely no claim on Keenan. None whatsoever.

So why did Keenan look so guilty?

"But we haven't finished talking," Tenetria said, turning her wounded expression toward Keenan.

"Yes, we have." He took the woman by the elbow and ushered her toward the door.

"Wait a minute." Tenetria snatched her purse up from the desk as he propelled by. "Keenan, what about my situation?"

"We'll talk about it later," he hissed.

"But...but..."

Keenan shoved her out and slammed the door in her face.

Typical, Jalila thought. *Once he's done with a woman, he certainly knows how to get rid of them.* She ground her teeth together and coached herself to stay cool.

"Sorry about that," Keenan said, walking back over to his desk.

Jalila wondered if that was a personal apology or a professional one. She licked her lips and lifted her head. *One monkey don't stop no show.*

Nitara cleared her throat. "I just came to see whether you had the final contracts for Ms. Goodwyn. I didn't know that you were, ah...busy."

Keenan ignored the barb and pulled out his desk drawer. "Here you go." He handed Nitara a manila folder.

She accepted the folder and then turned to escort Jalila out of the office.

"Glad to see that you're still on board," Keenan said.

There. That said it all, didn't it? He wanted her to move on. Jalila stopped and glanced at him from over her shoulder. "Why wouldn't I be?" After a beat of silence, Jalila made the mistake of looking him in the eye.

"No reason," he said softly.

She nodded and then walked out of the office. When she cleared the doorway, it felt like her Jell-O-filled legs were about to drop her like a stone. Suddenly, her eyes burned as if the tears she fought were made of acid. *Keep it together, girl.*

"Are you all right?" Nitara asked. "I apologize about that. Keenan and my sister…well, it's a long story. I'm so sorry you had to witness that."

"It's okay," Jalila said.

"Tell you what, let's just use the conference room to sign these papers."

"Fine." Jalila marched behind Nitara to a spacious conference room toward the back of the building.

"Can I get you anything to drink?"

"Water would be great," she said, wanting to steal a moment alone.

"One bottled water comin' up." Nitara set the manila folder down on the table and exited the conference room.

Once the door closed behind her, Jalila released a long, frustrated sigh. Not until then did she realize that her heart was pounding as if it was trying to escape her chest. "Goddamn it, Jalila. What did you expect?" she asked herself.

Nitara returned with a cold bottle of water for her

and something that smelled like rum for herself. For the next hour, Nitara went over everything from the basics of the contract to Jalila's health history, also peppered in were permission and waiver forms, and of course, a confidentiality agreement. "I know you broadcast on YouTube," she said, "but we need you to refrain from mentioning anything about the show for now."

Jalila shrugged. "I can just take a little break from uploading videos for a while."

"Great. Taping begins Saturday," Nitara said. "The first night we're throwing a party out in Beverly Hills. There will be music and drinks. You and your girl-friends will work the room, talk to the men one on one. The cameras will film everything. At the end of the night, you and the girls will confer and then you will select three men out of the twenty-five that you'd like to date.

"From there, the three men will plan their court-ships for the next four weeks. This is the part where we will follow you around your job and your friends, parents and, of course, your dates. This is to give the audience a thorough sense of who you are. The taping schedule will start from 9:00 a.m. to 11:00 p.m. That will give you ten hours a day to yourself—some private time.

"We'll also arrange a room in your house where you can do a video diary. You'll talk directly to the camera and just tell America what you're thinking from day to day or date to date."

America? She would be talking to all of America?

Exactly what kind of ratings were they expecting to get out of all of this?

"After the four weeks, we, of course, will edit everything and splice it to get our thirteen episodes. In the last episode you'll select who you'd like to be a 'queen' to. You can either choose to keep dating, or perhaps you can propose."

"Propose? Me?"

"Well, maybe we'll get all three men to propose and you select which proposal you'd like. Oooh. I like that idea. Let me write it down."

Jalila frowned. "Don't you think that's a bit staged?"

"It's a television show."

Jalila didn't have a response to that. Still, who would get engaged to someone after having known them for only four weeks?

"Don't worry. If you like the guy, you can have a really long engagement. If it doesn't work out maybe we'll bring you back for season two."

Season two?

After signing her name to an endless stack of paperwork, Jalila was tired and her writing hand was cramped.

"Looks like that does it," Nitara said, stretching out her hand. "I guess we'll see you on Saturday."

"I guess so." Jalila shook her hand and stood to leave. As she walked out of the conference room and walked the main office, she prayed she would avoid seeing Keenan again.

No such luck.

Keenan stood at Dee Dee's desk, talking about something. As she walked by he stopped.

"Goodbye, Ms. Goodwyn," Dee Dee said, smiling.

"Bye," Jalila said, rushing for the door. She could feel Keenan's eyes follow her. He allowed her to escape like the chicken she was. *Damn him.* When Jalila was safe in her car, she clutched the steering wheel, filled her lungs with air and let out a long-winded scream. "Aaaaaaaarrrrrgggggggghhhhh."

Did it feel good? Yes.

Did she feel better? No.

One thing for sure, she wasn't about to let Keenan get the best of her. She would do the show, she would find herself a man—a *good* man—and then Mr. Keenan Armstrong could kiss her naturally tanned ass.

"Do you want to tell me what the hell is going on with you?" Nitara asked, storming behind Keenan as they returned to their private office.

"Drop it, Nitara. I don't want to talk about it right now."

"You don't want to talk about it? Well, too damn bad," she shouted. "Does this office look like a hotel suite to you? Are we suddenly running a porno outfit around here and you forgot to tell me?"

"No, it doesn't look like a hotel. Nor does it look like my old childhood bedroom and you certainly don't look like my mother."

"Then maybe I should get your momma on the phone, smart ass."

Keenan drew a deep breath. "Calm down, Nitara. I already apologized."

"Calm down? Did you see the look on Ms. Goodwyn's

face? We're supposed to be professionals. I'm surprised that she didn't run out of here, telling us to take our show and shove it."

"There are other women out there who could take her place," he tossed out, dropping into his seat.

"What?" Nitara stepped back and held up her hands. "Did I just step into the *Twilight Zone* or something? *You* are the one who insisted that we build the show around her. Am I right or am I imagining things?"

Keenan swallowed. He realized that his glib comment stemmed from his disappointment that Jalila was continuing with the show—even though she had every right to do so. He didn't want a relationship, but he didn't want her to continue looking for a relationship. "That doesn't make sense," he reasoned aloud.

"What do you mean that doesn't make sense? Dee Dee and I were in here when you pitched the idea!" she said incredulously.

"What?" He frowned, and then realized that he hadn't been listening to her. "Oh, I wasn't talking to you."

"Well, excuuuuuse me if I thought my standing here and bumping my gums together actually meant that I was engaged in a conversation."

Keenan slammed his hand down on his desk. "Well, damn it, I said that I didn't want to talk about it right now!"

Nitara jumped. In all the years that she'd known Keenan, she had never seen him this angry. "What did Tenetria say?"

"Who?"

Nitara arched her brow at him. "Tenetria. My sister. The woman who was in here—"

"Oh, her." Keenan waved off her concern. "You know Tenetria. She just needs some money and thought that little strip show was going to get her what she wanted."

Nitara was confused by Keenan's casual attitude about what she thought was at the heart of his anger, but apparently she was on the wrong track. Her mind raced. If Keenan wasn't upset about Tenetria…then what *was* upsetting him? "How did the conference call with NBC go?" she probed.

"Fine. Fine." He turned toward his computer and pretended to be busy.

She wasn't buying it. Turning, Nitara walked over to her desk. All the while, she tried to fit the pieces of this puzzle together. No matter how hard she tried, she couldn't get the picture to come together. But one thing she knew for sure, something was definitely going on and she was going to get to the bottom of it.

Chapter 12

On the first day of shooting, Jalila, Martina and Fantasia were all picked up from Jalila's place in a black VIP stretch limousine. (What global warming?) In the back was every possible amenity to ensure a fun ride up to the famously posh Beverly Hills. For her own personal memories, Jalila broke out her handy camcorder and started filming herself and her friends acting like fools.

"Ooh, girl, *Cristal!*" Martina screamed, quickly working to pop the cork. "Ladies, we're about to *party!*"

Fantasia giggled like a thirteen-year-old with concert tickets to see the Jonas Brothers. "I'm so excited. I'm so excited." She turned toward Jalila. "Are you nervous? Are you nervous?"

Jalila laughed. "Why do you keep repeating your-self?"

"I don't know. I don't know. I've been doing it since I woke up this morning. Ahh. We're going to be on TV!"

"Damn straight," Martina chimed, pouring and passing the champagne glasses to them. "Y'all make sure that you get in a shout-out to my business, Horse Tail Weaves. I'm expecting business to go through the roof." She pumped up her hands and swung her demure chestnut-brown hair from side to side.

"Wait. Wait." Fantasia held up her glass to Jalila. "Don't forget Body by Jalila. This show is going to blow your business up as well."

"Provided that I don't make a big fool out of myself." Jalila laughed half-jokingly.

Martina downed her first glass of champagne in one long gulp and then said, "Oh, you're going to be fine. America is going to love you."

Jalila smiled, but she certainly had her doubts about that.

"I've got one question though," Martina said. "Are we all in agreement that whoever you *don't* choose I get a good crack at?"

"What?" Jalila laughed. "Now I'm really scared to see what kind of men you selected for me."

"Oh, don't pay Martina any mind. You know her libido is always stuck in overdrive."

Martina looked affronted. "I'm just saying, there's no reason to let a couple of good dicks go to waste."

The girls howled.

Jalila followed Martina and downed her first glass

of Cristal as Fantasia fumbled and found a button that blasted music from the speakers.

"Whooo!" Martina danced in her seat. "You know what I've always wanted to do?" she yelled above the music.

"What's that?" Jalila asked, laughing.

Without answering, Martina stood and popped her head out of the limo's rooftop and yelled, "Whh-hoooooo hoooooooo!"

Jalila and Fantasia followed suit. "Whhhhooooo hooooooo!"

The wind whipped through their hair as they bounced to the music. Jalila couldn't remember when they'd had more fun. In no time at all, she forgot her nervousness about having to speed-date her way through twenty-five men on national television, and she even forgot about the sleazy Hollywood producer who had pulled a fast one on her.

The limousine pulled into the lush drive of a sprawling Beverly Hills mansion. The women's eyes sprang wide as their mouths dropped open.

"Who in the hell lives here?" Martina finally asked. "And is his ass single?"

"What makes you think it's a he?" Fantasia said.

"Sheeit. For this house, I wouldn't mind considering switching teams," Martina admitted.

Jalila and Fantasia turned their stunned expressions to their friend.

"See. That's y'all's problem. You're too small-minded." She lowered herself back down into the cab, giving Jalila and Fantasia a brief moment to roll their eyes at their uninhibited girlfriend. When the limo parked under the portico, the chauffeur hustled to the back and opened their door.

One by one, the ladies placed their hands into the driver's and climbed out of the back. To the side there was a convoy of media vans from E! News, *Entertainment Tonight* and even the TV Guide Channel.

"Oh, my God! Oh, my God," Fantasia started repeating herself again. "This is really happening."

The front door to the mansion opened up and out stepped Nitara. "Ladies, welcome to the set of *Queen of Hearts*."

Jalila smiled as she spun around and then walked toward the door. "This place is beautiful," she praised.

Nitara gave a brief welcoming hug and then glanced around.

"It is, isn't it?"

"Who owns it?" Martina asked, cutting to the chase.

"Keenan, our executive producer."

Jalila's smile fell from her face as she froze in place.

The reaction didn't elude Nitara. "Is something wrong?"

Dizzy, Jalila tried to recoup, but it was her girls who came to her rescue.

"Oh, she's just nervous, that's all," Fantasia said, sliding an arm around Jalila's waist. "National television and all."

Nitara smiled reassuringly. "Well, don't be. Everything is going to be just fine. C'mon in and I'll show you around."

The girls shared a look, but then followed the co-executive producer into the house—Keenan's house. The outside of the house was nothing compared to the beauty that lay within. Stunning Italian marble floors, grand cathedral ceilings and expensive artwork made Jalila conscious about touching anything she couldn't afford to break.

Amidst the beauty, a full-scale crew was laying cable cords and hoisting large lighting panels.

"Don't worry. Everything will be in place by the time taping starts at eight o'clock," Nitara assured them. "Speaking of which—" she glanced at her watch "—we need to get you into hair and makeup. Follow me."

Jalila didn't know whether she should appreciate or be insulted that it took more than three hours to get her primped and camera-ready for the big night—especially since she was in the skin-care business herself. But after one glance at the end result, she completely understood that what Hollywood makeup artists created were works of *art*—not something the ordinary woman could achieve in thirty minutes or less.

Perfectly tweezed and arched eyebrows combined with even more length on her already long eyelashes had a stunning effect. Her cheeks were sultry, her lips plumped and glossy. Her long black hair, usually rippling with small body waves, was flatironed to within an inch of its life. She looked like herself, but not really.

"I'd say that we look like Barbie-doll versions of ourselves," Fantasia assessed. "Can't go wrong with that."

Nitara breezed in, her eyes once again on her watch. "Okay, ladies. It's over to wardrobe. Let's go. Let's go."

The women scrambled behind the fast-walking producer. As they headed to another room, Jalila noticed that the activity in the house had increased. It sounded as if a small country had gathered downstairs in anticipation of tonight's performance.

Jalila went from being nervous to cresting on a full-blown panic attack. This was really happening. She was really about to go on national television.

"Jalila, this is Jennifer. Jennifer, Jalila." Nitara made introductions. "Jennifer brought over some really nice dresses for you to try on for tonight."

Jennifer smiled broadly as she offered Jalila her hand. "Nice to meet you."

"Oooh, chile," Martina cooed. "Check this one out. I wonder if this one would fit me." She held up a short, shimmering black number that was clearly a few sizes too small.

"Uhm, maybe you should try something from the rack over in the back," Jennifer said, rushing to rescue the dress.

"Why? What's wrong with this one?" Martina challenged.

Jennifer blanched. "Well, uhm, see, our sizes run a lot smaller than normal. So, like, an eight is like a four."

"Mmm-hmm." Martina slammed the dress back onto the rack. "You skinny heifas better have brought something for real women who have curves."

"I know that's right," Fantasia agreed—not realizing that as they walked away, together they looked like the number 10.

Jennifer turned her relieved attention back to Jalila. "So, are you ready to transform into a television star?"

Jalila drew a deep breath. "As ready as I'll ever be."

"Quiet on the set," the director, Bill Wolfe, yelled, and the clamoring ceased immediately. "Places, everyone."

The show's host, Jon Krammer, a cute, almost nerdy African-American version of Ryan Seacrest, stood before camera number one with a stunningly white smile, ready to go.

"Aaannnddd *action!*"

"Good evening, America. Welcome to *Queen of Hearts.* I am your host, Jon Krammer, and tonight I'll be introducing you, America, to our twenty-five eligible bachelors and a very beautiful and special bachelorette."

Camera number two panned across the room to a line of gentlemen dressed in black and white tuxedos. They stood smiling as if they were contestants in a Mr. America pageant. "From this pool of bachelors, our bachelorette will select three men who will go on to date her and try to win the *Queen of Hearts.* In the end, only one man will win.

"Before all of that, let me tell you a little something about our queen. Her name is Jalila Goodwyn. She's a thirty-year-old entrepreneur who owns and operates the day spa Body by Jalila here in the Los Angeles area. Other than being gorgeous, Jalila is looking for a man who can balance and complete her life. According to

Jalila this man must have passion and enjoy the smaller things in life. He must be a sports fan as well as an animal lover. He must be open and honest, and according to her, handsome wouldn't hurt.

"Jalila is the only child of a retired high-school principal and English teacher who have been happily married for thirty-five years. She loves life, children and animals. So without further ado—" Krammer turned toward the line of men. "Gentlemen, are you ready to meet your queen?"

"Yes, sir," twenty-five strong baritones shouted.

The sound operator jumped.

"Then I present to you and America, Ms. Jalila Goodwyn."

The moment Jalila heard her name, the vat of butterflies that were fluttering in her belly ceased, and she strolled into the grand room with a bright smile. Judging by the looks on all the men's faces, she had made the right choice in selecting a bright red strapless cocktail dress that hugged her curves.

"Hello, gentlemen."

The men broke out in smiles, signaling their relief that the producers had hit a home run with their selection.

Krammer walked up to Jalila's side and greeted her with a smile. "Good evening, Ms. Goodwyn."

"Good evening," she said, remembering Nitara's instructions not to look directly into the cameras. She would only do that during the sidebar tapings and the video-diary portions of the show.

"Now, America," Krammer said, turning back toward the camera. "For your information, we're not about to throw this beautiful woman into this den of hungry wolves alone. We have a little more heart than that." He chuckled at the lame joke.

"Jalila will have a little help in selecting her potential king. Tonight we brought along Jalila's two best friends, Martina Hudson and Fantasia Silver."

On cue, Martina and Fantasia strolled into the room. Fantasia looked jittery—her smile visibly wobbled. However, it was the usually gregarious Martina who surprised Jalila. With the cameras rolling she now resembled a deer caught in headlights—eyes wide and mouth hanging slightly open.

"So, ladies," Krammer addressed the two best friends. "Do you think that you can help your best friend here select the man of her dreams?"

Fantasia cleared her throat. "W-we're certainly going to try."

Krammer shifted the microphone to Martina, but she was unable to say anything. Her eyes still bulging.

"Oookay. Looks like one of you is a bit camera-shy." He chuckled. "All right, ladies, let's go find Jalila's potential mate."

"Aaaaannnddd—*cut!*" the director shouted. "Mark it."

Jalila exhaled a long breath and turned toward her friends.

Krammer immediately asked, "How was that take? Did my hair look okay?"

Martina finally snapped out of her dazed expression and blinked for the first time. "Whoo, girl! How did I do?" she asked nervously.

"You're doing fine," Jalila assured her, laughing and wrapping an arm around her friend's shoulders.

While the camera crew rearranged themselves around the room, someone turned on some soft classical music and the craft service people started handing out flutes of champagne.

Nitara pushed her way through the crowd. "You ladies doing okay?" she asked, seeming a bit too bubbly.

Jalila bobbed her head. "I think so. I haven't passed out, so that's a good sign."

"Well, you look fabulous." Nitara addressed the other women. "Fantasia, try to breath and relax. Uh, Martina, well, you know—blink—if you can."

"Yeah, yeah. I was just…you know." She waved off the producer's concern. "I'll do better."

Jalila felt a little sorry for her friend.

"All right, Jalila, we're going to take you over here to camera number three so you can do a few sidebars. You know, your first impression of the men and that sort of thing. After that, you just come out and mingle. Just relax and be yourself. Try your best to ignore the cameras and everything will be fine."

Jalila nodded as she allowed Nitara to escort her across the room. She only caught about half of what the producer was saying because she was talking a mile a minute. When the camera rolled again, Jalila did feel much more relaxed.

The first brother to introduce himself walked and talked like a real-life wet fantasy.

"Hello, I'm Dontrell Smith."

Jalila slid her delicate hand into his. "Nice to meet you." She smiled.

"No. Believe me the pleasure is all mine."

He winked and Jalila's knees nearly knocked together. "So, Dontrell. What exactly do you do?"

"I'm a personal trainer. I own a chain of health clubs in L.A., Atlanta and New York."

Jalila's gaze raked over his impressive body. "Nice."

He smiled. "So if ever you're in the mood for a *really* good workout, I'm your man."

The line was a little cheesy, but he was fine enough to pull it off. "I'll definitely keep that in mind," she told him. Belatedly, she remembered the cameras and blushed when she realized that the whole world would see and hear their sexual innuendo. She'd need to pull back before she was branded a "ho" and her parents would be forced to find a new church.

She went back to mingling. There were a lot of charmers, though some were working too hard and some seemed to think that she needed to try to impress them.

Another brother who had potential was Tion Johnson—mainly because of his striking resemblance to her favorite actor and fantasy Idris Elba.

"Tion," she repeated, sipping on her third glass of champagne. "Now that's an interesting name."

"Why, thank you."

"And what is it that you do, Tion?"

"I work in the governor's office. I'm hoping to make a name for myself in politics."

"So you work for the Governator?"

He chuckled. "What can I say? It's a job."

For the next twenty minutes, Tion and Jalila were engaged in a deep conversation about the 2008 presidential election.

"I don't think we'll have another race that exciting in our lifetime," he concluded.

Jalila agreed. She liked the fact that this man was not only easy on the eyes but was intelligent. Both were incredible turn-ons.

Two hours later, the night drew to an end. It was going to be a hard decision. The crew taped Jalila and her girlfriends going off to a separate room to confer.

"Welcome back, ladies," Krammer said, after the men had lined up to hear Jalila's selection. "We have all been waiting on pins and needles. Have you made your selection, Jalila?"

"I have." She smiled warmly at the crowd.

"Okay, guys. When Ms. Jalila calls your name, you'll step forward and accept this silver bracelet. On it is a heart-shaped charm with Jalila's name on it."

Jalila cocked her head. The bracelets were a little cheesy, but whatever. She stepped forward. "First of all, it was a pleasure meeting all of you. I really had a great time tonight. Unfortunately, I can only choose three of you to move on to round two." Her smile turned apologetic. This was sort of brutal—dumping people on national television.

"With that being said, my first pick is…Dontrell Smith."

Dontrell stepped forward, his smile and confident stroll giving Jalila a thrill. "Dontrell, do you accept this bracelet to become my potential king?" Okay, that was cheesy, too.

"Yes, I do." He winked.

Jalila leaned forward and snapped the bracelet around his wrist. "My second choice is…Tion Johnson."

Tion stepped forward and they performed the same ritual.

"With the help of my girls, my last and final choice is…Evander Taylor."

Evander, a commercial real-estate developer, stepped forward. Handsome, smooth and a real lady-killer, if ever there was one. But most important, he knew how to make her laugh.

"Well, there you have it, America," Krammer said into camera number one. "Our bachelorette has made her choices. Tune in next time and watch as one of these men will go on to win the love of our *Queen of Hearts.*"

"Aaaannnnnnddddd *cut!*"

Chapter 13

Keenan vowed to stay away from the *Queen of Hearts* set. It was a promise that was not just necessary but essential to his mental well-being. However, it didn't stop him from wondering—no, obsessing—over how the taping was going at his place. How did the bachelors react upon seeing their potential prize? Keenan frowned. Of course he knew what their reaction would be, the same as that of any red-blooded man confronted with a beautiful woman.

The real question was how did Jalila react to seeing them? Did she find them attractive? Did she click with any of them? Was there a spark?

He shook the troubling thoughts from his head. What was he, a glutton for punishment? Of course she would be attracted to some of them. That was the whole point. Keenan gave himself a mental kick in the butt. The worst part of this was that he was responsible for all of it. He had decided to have this grand speed-dating party for *Queen of Hearts* at his house.

His house.

"Yes, I'm definitely a glutton for punishment." He drew a deep breath and glanced around the room where a fabulous birthday party was being thrown for one of the senior executives at HBO. He'd forgotten which one. Keenan had only accepted the invitation as a distraction, and it wasn't proving to be a good one at that. It had been two weeks since he'd slept with Jalila and instead of moving on, something was constantly pulling him back.

Maybe because it was the lousy way you ended things. Keenan let the thought echo in his head while he faced that awful truth. There was no excuse for what he'd done. Fear of falling for her or not, he owed Jalila if not an apology, an explanation.

Yet, he hadn't been able to do it. *Still* couldn't do it.

"Are you having a good time?"

Keenan turned and barely stopped the groan from falling from his lips. "Tenetria."

"Ah, so you do remember my name," she said, somehow both smiling and looking as if she'd spent the past hour sucking on a lemon at the same time.

"Trust me, it's seared into my memory for the rest of my life."

She cocked her head. "That's just about the sweetest thing you've ever said to me."

"Really? I thought that was when I told you that I wanted a divorce," he volleyed.

"Good point. How about the second sweetest thing?"

He smiled. "So what are you doing here?"

"I was invited."

"And you never miss an opportunity to party."

"I needed something to cheer me up. You know, me being homeless and all." She reached for a drink from a passing waiter.

Keenan shook his head. He did not want to be pulled back into any drama involving his ex-wife. "If you're truly homeless, then go back to your parents' place."

"I'd rather live on the streets," she quipped, tipping up her glass.

"That's your pride talking."

"And how much pride do you think I'm swallowing by asking to move back in with you?" she challenged. "Surely, you don't think I'm having a good time begging you to take me back?"

"I don't know. You looked like you were having one hell of a time turning my office into something like the champagne room at some strip club."

Amusement flashed in Tenetria's eyes. "All right. Maybe that part was fun." She inched closer to him. "You know, my situation still hasn't changed."

He stepped back. "And my answer hasn't changed. You're a grown woman and it's time that you start taking care of yourself."

He set his empty drink down on the bar and turned to leave. At the door of the posh Avalon Club, he handed his ticket to the valet. While he was waiting, his BlackBerry vibrated against his leg. "This is Keenan."

"The party is a wrap!" Nitara declared.

"Great. How did it go?" he asked, not really wanting to know.

"Fabulous! We managed to break only a few things in your house."

"Ha-ha."

"No. Everything went great. You were right. The cameras absolutely loved Jalila. And she was so relaxed and went along with everything. Her girlfriends were another story. But hey, I'm sure we can cut out a lot of their nervous twitches and wide-eyed looks in the editing room. Overall, the night was a big success. Jalila had the men eating out of the palm of her hand. Even some of the cameramen wanted to pass her their number." She laughed.

Keenan scowled. "Well, that's good. I'm pleased to hear everything went so well." He kicked at the concrete.

"Yeah, footage is headed over to Mack Media for editing. Guess I'll drop by after everyone clears out of here to see how it's going." She sighed.

"No need." Keenan chuckled. "I'll swing by and take a look at it."

"Really? You're sure you don't mind?"

Keenan smiled, holding the phone as he walked up to his car, slipped the valet a folded bill and then slid in behind the wheel. "Mind? Isn't that the real reason you called?"

"That transparent, huh?"

"A little, but don't worry about it. I guess I need to earn my paycheck every now and then. Consider it done. Go home and be a wife to your husband."

"Are you kidding me? As tired as I am, I'm hitting

the shower and then the bed. If Martin so much as touches me, he'll be pulling back a nub." She laughed.

"Hey. Stop all this black-on-black crime."

"Yeah, yeah. Whatever. I'll catch up with you tomorrow."

"Deal. Good night." He shut off the phone and then sped out of the restaurant's parking lot and traveled east.

Mack Media was an editing house contracted to handle most of A.M. Production's television projects. Editing, whether film or digital (which everything was nowadays), was a tedious job. It would take hours, days and weeks to sift through frames of footage and splice and cut them for just one forty-seven-minute cohesive segment to air to a viewing audience.

When Keenan entered the media house, he was greeted by two men who looked like college students, Jesse and Lamar.

"Hey, guys. What's up?"

"Nothing but the late hours," Jesse, a cocky blue-eyed grunge rocker, retorted. "I see you and Nitara finally took the plunge into reality TV."

"We're in the business of giving viewers what they want, right?"

"Whatever pays the bills," Lamar agreed.

The men exchanged brief handshakes and then immediately got down to business. Keenan peeled out of his jacket, pressed his weight into a cheap office chair and leaned over the controls. "All right. Let's see what we have here."

Jesse and Lamar uploaded a couple of digital disks

and numerous pictures came up on two different thirty-inch screens. "Right, we're first going to separate all the sidebar clips from the bachelors and the women. That'll help us streamline, but the rest of it is going to be much harder," said Lamar.

Keenan nodded and then felt a punch to the gut when Jalila's smiling face came on to the screen.

"Wow," Lamar said, eyes bugging. "Now, she's a knockout!"

"Is there any way I can pass her *my* phone number?" Jesse asked. "I know I'll treat her right."

"I can't believe *she* has any problems finding a man to tap *that*."

Keenan ground his teeth as his face heated. "Do you two mind? We've got a lot of work to do here tonight."

The editors looked at each other. "Oookay," Lamar said under his breath. "Someone is grumpy."

Keenan held his tongue and then continued to stare at the screen. Was Jalila wearing a dress or red body paint? One wouldn't have to have much imagination to know what she looked like naked.

The image of Jalila writhing beneath him flashed in Keenan's mind and his cock hardened instantly against his leg. He scooted his chair up so he could hide his erection underneath the control panel.

As the footage continued to run, Keenan's irritation quickly gave way to a fierce jealousy. He watched help-lessly as Jalila smiled, winked, flirted and even kissed the cheeks of those grinning a-holes vying for her hand.

Hell, did she have to look like she was having *that* much fun? "Hey, who's that guy?" Keenan inquired, pointing to the screen closest to him.

"Uhm, I'm not sure," Jesse said, and then scanned the clipboard. "A Dontrell Smith. One of the guys she chose at the end of the night. According to production notes we need to make sure we keep a lot of footage of him tonight."

Keenan's scowl returned. She chose him? He cocked his head to the side, thought that the man was just a'ight—nothing to write home about. He looked a little too bodybuilderish to him. Probably on steroids. Probably had a small dick.

On the other screen, Jalila was laughing. "Hey, roll sound on this one," Keenan ordered.

"All righty." Lamar cued the sound.

"So, Dontrell. What exactly do you do?"

"I'm a personal trainer. I own a chain of health clubs in L.A., Atlanta and New York."

Jalila's gaze rakes over his body. "Nice."

He smiles. "So if ever you're in the mood for a really good workout, I'm your man."

"I'll definitely keep that in mind."

"Humph." Lamar chuckled. "I can't believe that cheesy-ass line worked."

"Do you two mind?" Keenan snapped. "We're supposed to be professionals here."

Jesse and Lamar sank down in their chairs. "Yes, sir." From that moment on, they knew they were in for a long night.

Chapter 14

After an eventful day and night, Jalila had returned home late and collapsed on her bed, dress and all. Her only mistake was not putting Cujo outside for the night, because the sound of his barking early the next morning ensured her waking up with a head-splitting migraine. Someone somewhere was pounding on something.

"Go away," she moaned into her pillow.

A bell was added to the mix.

When the pounding, the barking and the ringing of the bell continued, she tried to bury herself under the pillows. The racket only intensified until she had no choice but to bolt out of bed with a major attitude. "I'm coming!" she shouted.

Jalila marched out of the bedroom in last night's dress and torn stockings to give whoever it was at her door a good piece of her mind. Reality didn't settle in until she threw open the door and Cujo leaped at a surprised cameraman.

"What the—" Bam! He and Cujo hit the tiled porch.

Jalila was instantly awake. "Cujo, no!"

Growling, with his canine teeth exposed, Cujo made it clear that he was in the mood to have the cameraman for breakfast.

"Cujo, stop! Oh, my God."

The rest of the crew, including Nitara, scattered.

"I'm so sorry. I'm so sorry." She grabbed Cujo's collar and tugged. "Are you all right? Give me a second. I'm going to just put him in the backyard. I totally forgot you guys were coming."

She dragged Cujo, barking and slobbering like a rabid animal, through the house. Getting the dog to the backyard was harder than usual because she still had on her stockings. She seemed to slip and slide more than anything else. Once Cujo was in the backyard, she felt as if she'd had a complete workout. The camera crew still looked hesitant to come inside the house.

"Please, c'mon in." She smiled reassuringly. "I swear it's safe."

Nitara crept in first, her eyes darting around as if she expected the bogeyman to leap out at her. "Girl, what are you doing with something that big in here?"

"A single girl needs protection," Jalila joked. "C'mon. Make yourself at home, I'm just going to run up for a quick shower and I'll be right back." She turned and raced up the stairs, her face still burning with humiliation.

After her shower and a quick change, the rest of the day went rather well. Cameras rolling, Jalila gave America a quick peek into her life. She led the cameras through her house, introduced her dog—through the sliding glass door since the cameraman didn't want any more up-close-and-personal encounters with Cujo for the rest of his life.

Next, she took the camera crew to Body by Jalila, where she introduced her employees and explained her business and her products.

Sidebar:

"So how is it that you got into this business?" asks the fresh-faced Jon Krammer.

Jalila takes a deep breath. "Well, like most teenagers, I went through an acne stage. My mother and I bought practically everything that we could find to help clear up the problem. Nothing worked. In college I started going to a dermatologist who loaded me up with prescription creams and they didn't work." She laughs. "So, finally my grandmother heard what was going on and simply suggested that I try some old homemade remedies. You know, products that didn't have all these chemicals in them. So we broke out the basics. Oatmeal, honey, the whole nine. Next thing I know my face started clearing up.

"Then my girlfriends started asking me what I was using and could I make some products for

them. So I did, and one thing led to another."
Jalila smiles brightly for the cameras.

The next stop was at her parents' place. When Jalila
had told her parents about the crew coming over, she'd
asked them to behave normally. However, when they
opened the door, her brain couldn't process this version
of her mother, dressed like Donna Reed, replete with
pearls and diamonds.

"Oh, hello, dear," Bettye Goodwyn cooed and gave
Jalila a dramatic kiss on the cheek.

Her father, God bless him, showed up at the dinner
table in a suit and tie that he must have dusted off from
his high-school-principal days. Too bad it was a little
too tight after his retirement diet—i.e., a whole lot of
all-you-can-eat buffets.

Jalila tried her best to hide her amusement, but when
their normal meatloaf or lasagna dinner was replaced
by some fancy French food her mother had never
cooked before, Jalila excused herself from the table in
order to have a good laugh in the bathroom.

Sidebar:

"So how do you feel about your daughter
going on national television to find her soul
mate?" Jon Krammer asks.

James and Bettye look at each other.

"Well," Bettye says. "It *is* a little different. I
have to admit I wasn't too thrilled when she first
told me."

"Why is that?"

"It's just not how we did things back in our day."

James reaches over and covers his wife's hand. "We just want Jalila to be happy," he says. "And if this little experiment helps her find what she's looking for then we're behind her one hundred percent."

Jalila smiled at her doting parents as the cameras rolled. Their happiness was so apparent it only deepened her desire to find the kind of love that they'd shared for thirty-five years. To her surprise an image of Keenan flashed before her eyes. She quickly shook it out of her head.

She wanted love…not lust.

The next day, Jalila was more prepared. She was up and dressed by 7:30 a.m., Cujo was in the backyard and she even had coffee made by the time the camera crew arrived. She was only dealing with half a crew because the other half was with Dontrell Smith, taping his preparations for today's date.

Jalila didn't know what was in store. Only that the date was going to last most of the day and well into the night. At noon, flowers were delivered and she had to do at least four different reaction takes before the director and Nitara were satisfied. Once that was done, she was finally allowed to open the note that came with the flowers.

"'Hope you like water. Dress light,'" she read. Now what on earth did that mean?

At two o'clock, she found out. In all of her thirty years of living in Los Angeles, Jalila could honestly say that it had never occurred to her to go surfing. Something about playing in a polluted ocean with sharks didn't quite tickle her fancy.

But today that was apparently about to change.

But Jalila wasn't a fool. She didn't have to be an Einstein to know that Dontrell chose to have their first date frolicking on the beach because he wanted to see her in a swimsuit.

When he picked her up, she was wearing an electric-blue bikini, a white sarong and heels.

"Oh, my…*damn!*" There was no need for a second take of Dontrell's reaction.

"I assume that you like it?" Jalila asked, turning to give him a 360-degree view.

"What's not to like?" He grinned and offered her his arm.

Sidebar:

> "Man, when Jalila opened that door, my mouth just hit the ground," a laughing Dontrell says into the camera. "I gotta hand it to her, she's got a banging body. I think we look good together. Those other brothers don't stand a chance next to me."

Jalila slipped her arm around Dontrell's bulging bicep and smiled openly at him. And though he was not at all hard on the eyes, in her mind she couldn't stop comparing him to Keenan. Both men exuded an extraordinary amount of confidence and strength. However, Dontrell was a little more flashy, with his bulging muscles and formfitting clothes.

To be fair, Dontrell couldn't have picked a more beautiful day to surf at Malibu. The sky was a blinding blue and the winds were a gentle caress. The camera crew took a few playful shots of Dontrell and Jalila walking on the beach, sometimes pretending that they were fascinated by something in the sky.

When it came time for her surfing lessons, Nitara produced a wet suit for Jalila to change into, and two new surfboards, made by some company who'd paid for advertising and product placement, were given to them.

"I don't know about this," Jalila said as she stood on the sandy beach with the water just high enough to cover her feet. "There are living things in there."

Dontrell chuckled behind her. "Don't worry, I'll protect you." Holding his surfboard in one hand, he draped the other around her waist.

Despite his words, Jalila was anything but comforted, and the farther she crept into the ocean the more the frown on her face twisted in fear. The water was astonishingly cold and she kept thinking that something was crawling across her toes. It was gross and she was squealing like a teenager in a horror movie.

Dontrell apparently thought that she was adorable and loved that she kept clinging to him and bumping up against him. Eventually, she calmed down long enough for Dontrell to try to explain the tides and how they affected surfing. For beginners, it was best to surf at the lowest possible tide, which generally happened later in the day. But since she was with him, he promised to pay extra attention to her so that nothing would harm her.

When he delivered those words, his face was mere inches from hers. His eyes made it clear that he wanted to sneak a kiss, but Jalila demurely turned her head.

"Aaaaannndddd…*cut!*" The director, whose name Jalila couldn't remember, waded out into the ocean in his own wet suit. "Let's go back and hold the pose where you were staring into each other's eyes. I think we can really work that with some music."

Dontrell and Jalila nodded, but they were both clearly uncomfortable replaying—or faking—an extended intimate moment. The rest of the surfing lesson went from bad to worse or from funny to funnier, depending upon one's point of view. Each time Jalila tried to follow Dontrell's instructions on how to go from sitting to standing on her surfboard, she ended up doing some interesting backflips. These always resulted in her swallowing a mouthful of water or getting some nasty seaweed tangled in her hair. When Dontrell finally ended the lesson, Jalila nearly wept with joy.

Sidebar, camera one:

"I don't know if she cared for the surfing too much," Dontrell admits. "But she was a trooper. I'll give her that." He laughs. "I like a woman who's willing to go outside her comfort zone. Take some risks. I'm really hoping that she'll like the next part of our date. I've planned something really nice."

Sidebar, camera two:

"I *never* want to see a surfboard again in my life," Jalila says, pulling seaweed from her hair. "It's not for me. It's too dangerous. It's gross. And there are living things crawling around your feet!" Jalila waves a finger straight at the camera. "Guys, just stick to walking on the beach. The women will love you for it. Do you see my hair? Now you know sistahs don't like getting their hair wet!"

After a quick beach shower, a change into a long white summer dress and an emergency hair and makeup rescue, Jalila joined Dontrell for the next phase of their date. Turns out it, too, would be on the beach—a beach picnic. On a huge blanket, Dontrell had sprinkled rose petals. Beside it, he had dug a deep hole in the sand and lit a couple of fire logs.

The whole setup was beautiful. In the picnic basket were sandwiches, strawberries and even some marshmallows to roast over the open fire. Jalila was almost willing to forgive Dontrell for her horrible surfing lesson. However, after such an intense workout, she'd hoped for something a little more filling than sandwiches.

They quickly fell into easy conversation, but when the sun began to set, Jalila's mind was transported to the sunset she'd watched with Keenan. She could almost taste those thick juicy steaks they'd shared, and instead of the light champagne she was drinking now, she craved the heavy tequila-laden margaritas she'd whipped up.

"Earth to Jalila," Dontrell said.

"What?" She blinked and jerked her head toward him. "I'm sorry, what did you say?"

"You zoned out on me," he responded.

"It's the sunset," she admitted. "It's my favorite time of day."

He looked toward the sky. "Don't be fooled by the colors. It's just smog," he said, killing the moment. "L.A. has the worst smog in America. If it wasn't for the surfing I would have left this city a long time ago."

Jalila loved L.A. "Where would you go?"

He shrugged. "Hmm. I don't know. Maybe Florida or somewhere east." He smiled at her. "Think you can see yourself in Florida?"

She shrugged, not wanting to hurt his feelings. "Florida is okay."

He bobbed his head. "I'm looking at Miami to open my next club. They have nice beaches. And Lord knows, with a body like yours, you could put most of those hard-body babes to shame."

She laughed at his exaggeration and decided to change the conversation. "So tell me something about you," she said. "How come a man like you is still single in L.A.?"

He shrugged and took a long sip of his champagne. "I just haven't found the right girl. You know, the one that's hot enough to show off to your friends, yet sweet and innocent enough to take home to the parents."

"Well, I don't know about innocent." She laughed.

"Don't tell me that you're one of those naughty girls."

Jalila shook her head. "I didn't say that either."

Still smiling, Dontrell's eyes narrowed on her. "Uh-huh. When was the last time you were with a man?"

"What?" She was suddenly acutely aware of the cameras.

"Ahh. Must have been recently," Dontrell said, his smile entirely too cocky.

"You're putting words into my mouth." She tried to ruin the shot by looking straight into one of the cameras, but the director didn't call "cut."

"It's all right. I understand that women have urges." He reached for her hand. "It's just that *if* we ever got serious, I would expect us to be in just a one-on-one thing."

Jalila felt as if she was subtly being cast as a loose woman or something. "For your information, it's been quite some time since I've with someone—intimately."

His brows shot up. "Really?" Both he and the cameraman eased closer. "How long has it been?"

Feeling the pressure, she lied, "Two years."

Keenan spent most of the day debating whether he would return to Mack Media and put himself through another night of editing with Jesse and Lamar. It wasn't as though the guys didn't know what they were doing and his jealousy was becoming too large to ignore— by him or by the guys at Mack Media.

However, his only other choice was to somehow

convince Nitara to oversee the editing process. That was hardly fair since she spent most of her days at the actual filming. So, either he watched the taping in person or he sat in a darkroom and supervised the editing.

He couldn't win.

He knew that tonight's clips were centered on Jalila's first date. He'd actually thought about having a few drinks or stabbing out his eyes before going in, but at the last minute he'd thought better of it.

When Keenan entered the studio, he didn't miss the silent glances that passed between Jesse and Lamar. No doubt they anticipated another night of Keenan snapping their heads off. He vowed to do better.

But, when the footage started rolling, all bets were off. First of all, how was it possible that Jalila grew more beautiful with each passing day? And why did his body keep responding like a prepubescent teenager's every time he saw her?

"Holy moly!" Jesse and Lamar exclaimed in unison when Jalila popped up in an electric-blue bikini that should have landed her the cover of *King* magazine. Lamar froze the footage and the three men sat there drooling like idiots.

Keenan couldn't speak, and his erection now threatened to bust the seam of his pants. After a lengthy silence, he finally reminded the men that they had a job to do and they were wasting time. But as the footage of the date wore on, Keenan increasingly felt like he was on the verge of having a stroke. Every chance this

Dontrell clown got, he was touching, hugging and trying to win a kiss from Jalila.

Whenever Jalila spurned muscle-head's advances, Keenan's chest would swell with pride while the little voice in his head cheered, *That's my girl.*

Most of the surfing material was funny, but the intimate beach picnic was not. "Turn up the sound from camera number one," he ordered.

Clip:

"So tell me something about you," Jalila says. "How come a man like you is still single in L.A.?"

He shrugs and takes a long sip of his champagne. "I just haven't found the right girl. You know, the one that's hot enough to show off to your friends, yet sweet and innocent enough to take home to the parents."

"Well, I don't know about innocent." She laughs.

"Don't tell me that you're one of those naughty girls."

Jalila shakes her head. "I didn't say that either."

Still smiling, Dontrell's eyes narrow on her. "Uh-huh. When was the last time you were with a man?"

"What?"

"Ahh. Must have been recently," Dontrell says, his smile entirely too cocky.

"You're putting words into my mouth."

"It's all right. I understand that women have

urges." He reaches for her hand. "It's just that *if* we ever got serious, I would expect us to be in just a one-on-one thing."

"For your information, it's been quite some time since I've with someone—intimately."

His brows shoot up. "Really?" Both he and the cameraman ease closer. "How long has it been?"

Jalila paused. "Two years."

Keenan growled as he jumped up out of his seat, grabbed his jacket and stormed out of the studio.

Jesse and Lamar watched him leave and then shared a suspicious look.

"Do you get the impression that there's more to this story than what's on the monitor?" Lamar asked.

"Yes, indeed."

Jalila was slowly falling asleep in the tub. She'd never known that a date could be so exhausting. Of course, if the camera crew hadn't been there, their nine-hour date would have been reduced to about three. The thought of all those people coming back in the morning was a little too overwhelming. It had been less than a week. She still had three more weeks to go.

She reflected on her day and had to admit that as far as dates went, it had been one of her better ones. But was there a love match? She wasn't too sure. Dontrell was nice, good-looking, but something was missing.

Bam! Bam! Bam!

Jalila jumped.

Cujo started barking.

"Who in the hell?"

Bam! Bam! Bam!

Woof! Woof! Woof!

"Oh, good Lord." Jalila got out of the tub and grabbed a short silk robe. As she raced to the front door, she realized the thin material was sticking to her wet body.

Bam! Bam! Bam!

Woof! Woof! Woof! Cujo circled in front of the door.

"Who is it?"

"Keenan! Open up!"

Chapter 15

Jalila blinked. *What in the hell is Keenan doing here?* She peeked through the peephole to make sure it wasn't one of her girls playing a game on her. "What do you want?" she shouted through the door.

"Open the door!"

"Why?"

"Open the goddamn door!" She jumped at the order. Maybe something was wrong. She quickly undid the locks and when she turned the knob, he shoved his way inside. "You got a lot of explaining to do."

"Hey!"

Woof! Woof!

"What's this bullshit that you haven't been with a man in two years?"

Woof!

"Cujo, go lie down," Keenan barked.

Cujo's happy face fell as he turned and did as he was told.

Jalila watched in astonishment as she shut the door. "How did—?"

"Why on earth are you trying to lie on national television like that?" he charged.

Jalila tried to process what the hell he was yelling about. "I don't see what the big deal is. You seem determined to act like that night never happened so why can't I?"

He stepped toward her. "I never said—"

"You never said anything," she shouted back. "You just crept out of here like a thief in the night and then started acting like I didn't exist. Well, screw you. I don't owe you an explanation why I didn't brag from the rooftops that we fucked!"

"I never said—"

"*Again,* you never said anything!" She tossed up her hands and her robe threatened to spill open. "How in the hell did you think that made me feel? Do you even care?"

"Of course I care."

"Yeah, I bet. Up until the time you had a half-naked woman draped across your desk."

"Tenetria is my ex-wife."

"That makes it all better." Jalila's face darkened as her chest heaved.

The latter catching Keenan's undivided attention.

"You know what?" She turned and opened the door. "Just get out. Go."

He didn't move. He was too taken by how her anger had transformed her into a raving goddess.

"Get out!" she shouted. "I don't care if I never see you again."

Keenan's gaze took in the length of her body. Did she know that there were soap bubbles racing down her legs? And did she have any idea what that was doing to him right now? His gaze finally slid back up to her face and his heart squeezed.

Jalila sucked in a small gasp because she recognized the raw desire written across his face. "No," she whispered, shaking her head. But her body was already responding. Her nipples were suddenly hard and aching. "It's not going to happen."

Keenan moved forward, his eyes locked with Jalila's.

She wasn't aware that she'd started holding her breath, but her lungs started to burn as hot as the rest of her when he stood mere inches away from her.

He reached up and caressed the side of her face. When she closed her eyes and shivered, Keenan smiled like the devil he was. Removing her hand from the doorknob, he pushed the door closed.

At the soft click, Jalila knew that she was doomed.

Keenan whispered a command, "Look at me."

Jalila's lashes fluttered open and she stared into eyes so black with desire that she nearly erupted with her first orgasm.

"If there's one thing I want you to know—" he hooked his finger onto her silk belt "—it's that I will *never* forget that night." With a gentle tug, the belt slid open, exposing Jalila's curvaceous body. Keenan's gaze drifted down her face while he licked his lips. "Look at you." He cupped one breast and ran the pad of his thumb against its hard nipple.

Jalila shivered again and tilted back against the door for support.

"You like it when I do that?"

She nodded and, as a reward, he took possession of her other breast. His thumbs circled and counter-circled, causing thick, hazy clouds to form in her head.

"Ooh, yeah. You really like that, don't you?" Keenan leaned forward and brushed a feathery-light kiss against her open mouth. "I betcha I can have this anytime I want to, can't I?" He lowered his head and wrapped his mouth around a wet, strawberry-scented nipple.

"Oh, God." Jalila's head fell back with a sigh. In the back of her head she knew this whole thing was crazy. How could she just let him come roaring back into her life like this? What right did he…?

Keenan's mouth abandoned her large breasts to travel south. Jalila lost the ability to think clearly. On his knees, Keenan was eye level with her pulsing cherry. She waited, dying with anticipation and fearful that he was about to make her beg for what she wanted—needed from him.

Sensing her impatience, Keenan glanced up and smiled. "Open your legs."

Without hesitation, she did as he commanded. With their eyes still locked, Keenan pressed a soft kiss against her lower lips.

Jalila groaned with disappointment. It wasn't enough, she wanted more.

"Did you kiss that brotha today?" he asked hoarsely.

"What?" She struggled through the lusty haze in her brain to make sense of his words. Who on earth was he talking about?

Keenan kissed her pussy again. "I saw you showing off your body to him today." Another kiss. "Strutting in your bikini, tryin' to get a brotha hard. Maybe you want him here tonight?"

"No, I—"

"No?" Another kiss. This time he slipped in his tongue and took his time letting it slide across her clit. He watched as her knees start to fold. "It sure looked to me like you wanted that steroid junkie. You're trying to tell me I'm wrong?"

"Y-yes," she confessed and then realized that it was the truth.

"Open it up for me," he panted, his desire cracking his voice.

Jalila reached down and exposed herself before his greedy eyes.

Keenan sucked in a ragged breath. "Look at this pretty pussy." He leaned forward, gliding his tongue in as far as it could go, his nose breathing in her feminine scent.

"Awww," Jalila sighed, her knees bending farther until they rested against his shoulders.

He curled and uncurled his tongue against her G-spot, sapping her liquid candy. She was so sweet and hot, he couldn't stand it. His cock pounded against its confinements and throbbed for release. While still lapping up her juices, Keenan reached down and freed his erection.

Tears swelled in Jalila's eyes as she ground against Keenan's loving mouth. A tidal wave of pleasure rushed through her as she seemed to climb higher and higher on the clouds in her mind. She could feel the crescendo building, her soul being swept away by forces unseen.

While stroking himself, Keenan worked his mouth and tongue as if it was qualifying for his own Olympics. At the feel of her clit pounding double-time, he knew his baby was on the verge of her first orgasm. To make sure that he would receive every drop, Keenan reached for her legs and helped her hook them around his shoulders so he could support her full weight.

Then he went to town.

"Oooh, Gaaawwwdd, Keeeeenaaaan!" Jalila's muscles quivered, once, twice and then a rush of honey poured from her body and into Keenan's mouth. But it wasn't over. His thorough cleanup had her right back where she started from: on the brink of insanity. This time her hand was buried in his short hair and she kept his face smashed against her honeypot. After her second orgasm hit, Keenan climbed back onto his feet.

Thinking that it was her cue to return the oral favor, Jalila started to sink to her knees, but Keenan grabbed her elbow. "Touch me."

She blinked, confused.

He took her hand and glided it to his steely erection. The moment her soft hand wrapped around him,

Keenan felt a few drops of cum slide from the tip of his thick mushroom head. "See what you do to me, baby?"

Slowly, Jalila's fingers stroked his long shaft. Their eyes remained locked until he dipped his head and slanted his hot mouth against hers. What was it about this woman that intoxicated him so? Why hadn't he been able to walk away as he had so many times before?

The temperature in the house climbed. The lovers were headed into sensory overload. Someone moaned, or maybe both of them did, they weren't sure. They only knew that this night was just beginning.

Keenan broke the kiss so he could bury his face in her hair and nibble on her earlobe. "God, I've missed you," he gasped. "I miss how you tremble when you come. I miss how you scream out my name."

Jalila smiled, loving the knowledge that she had touched him. Why else would he sound so jealous?

"I ought to make you call that Popeye-wannabe right now and tell him who fucked you good the other night."

He wouldn't!

"I sure the hell would," he said, as if hearing her thoughts. "Look at you, shaking. You want it right now, don't you?"

"Y-y-es."

"That's what I thought." He grabbed her by the arm and spun her around to face the door. "Humph. Telling *him* that you ain't had any in two years." He stripped the silk robe from her shoulders. "Ooh." He cupped her firm ass and gave it a good, hard squeeze. "Girl, you just don't know what I'm about to do to you."

Jalila stood still with her breasts press firmly against the cold front door while she listened to Keenan strip out of his clothes. Then there was the rip of a condom packet. It seemed like forever before he touched her again, but when he did, it wasn't with his hands or mouth, but with the tip of his dick.

"Spread your legs." Instantly, her legs sprang apart, wrangling a soft chuckle from him. "Aren't you the eager beaver?"

She smiled at the double meaning, but then her eyes closed when he started teasing her pulsing clit with his dick instead of just entering her and ending the torture.

"Work up that booty for me," he said, kissing her shoulder. He grinned when she hesitated. "Oh, you must want me go home then?"

"No."

"Then let me see you pop it."

Jalila snapped up her hips and let her butt jiggle against him. She felt ridiculous and started to giggle.

"See. I knew you had it in you," he praised and popped her on an ass cheek. That just caused it to jiggle some more.

"Please, Keenan," she said, not wanting to play anymore. She wanted him. Now.

"Please, Keenan, what?" he asked, rubbing his dick against her wetness, then all on and around her clit. "What can I do for you?"

"Please, I need you inside of me."

"Need me *inside* of you? What's with all this proper

stuff? It's just me and you here, baby. Tell me what you really want." On her shoulders his kisses turned to little nibbles and then finally he was planting huge passion marks across her back.

She hesitated.

"I can't give you what you want until you tell me what it is," he reasoned.

"I want," she panted. "I want…"

Again, he laughed at her trying to be all proper. "You want me to fuck you, Jalila?"

"Y-yes."

"Then tell me you want to be fucked."

She wiggled, trying to tempt him into entering her, but he was having none of that.

"Say it," he ordered, teasing her with just an inch of his dick at the edge of her sex. "Tell me you want to be fucked."

She closed her eyes. "I want you to fuck me."

"What?" He pressed forward, giving her another inch.

"Fuck me, Keenan. Please, fuck me."

"As you wish." With a smile, Keenan slid gently into her slick, but tight body. Once he was buried up to the hilt, he rotated his hips in a deep grind. "I ought to call that steroid brotha you were with tonight and let him hear how I got you wide open right now."

"Awww."

"Mmm-hmm. You hear how this pussy is talking back to me?"

Their bodies slapped, while fresh honey poured down Jalila's legs. She cried out in ecstasy. Within a few strokes, she was struggling to catch her breath. "That feels so good," she moaned. "What are you trying to do to me?"

"The same thing you're doing to me," he said, breathing heavily. "When you wake up in the mornings, I want you to think of me. When you're at work I want you to think about me. And when you lie down at night, I want you to reach down like this—" His slid his arm down between her legs and zeroed in on her hot spot. "I want you to play with this pussy and remember how I tear this up, each and every time."

Keenan was grinding as deeply as he could, hitting her back G-spot like the home-run king.

"Oh, my…awww…I'm cooomming," she moaned.

"Well, come on then, baby." His flat abs bounced hard against her firm booty, causing it to wiggle and jiggle like Jell-O.

Jalila started coming, screaming and crying at the same time.

Keenan was next. He grabbed a fistful of her hair and stroked so hard and deep that it sounded as if the front door was about to bounce off its hinges. "Ooohh…Jaaalilaaa," he growled. What poured out of him felt like rocket fuel blasting him into the stratosphere. When he finally drifted back to earth, he discovered himself panting against the back of Jalila's shoulder.

Pulling out of her, Keenan turned and headed toward the stairs.

Jalila knelt on shaking legs and retrieved her robe. "Where are you going?"

"To your bedroom," he said simply and then glanced over his shoulder. "Are you coming?"

She smiled. "Yes."

"Good." He winked. "Now get your fine ass upstairs."

Chapter 16

Jalila was positive that she was paralyzed from the neck down. When the morning sun peeked through her bedroom's high windows and warmed her naked body, she couldn't find the strength to so much as lift her toes she was so exhausted. The same thing couldn't be said for her Energizer lover. Clearly he had awakened with a morning hard-on and was looking for a hole to bury it in.

"I know you're awake," he whispered.

Jalila moaned.

Keenan chuckled. "What happened to all that bragging you were doing last night?" He pulled her closer so that she could curl up against his hard frame. "I guess that means I won and you owe me breakfast in bed," he said, kissing her mussed hair and then her shoulders.

Breakfast? "Uuuh," she groaned. No way was she going to be able to climb out of bed and actually do some work.

"You know breakfast is the most important meal of the day. Should I tell you what I'd like to eat?" Keenan eased a hand down in between her thighs. "Something sweet," he murmured. "Something that I can really sink my mouth into." He brushed aside her hair and then nibbled on the base of her neck. "I want something that smells like strawberries but tastes like honey."

Finally understanding his meaning, Jalila smiled. "Oh, is that right?"

"That's right."

She turned her head and her long lashes fluttered open.

Keenan smiled. "Good morning, beautiful."

"Morning." She noticed the droplets of water in his hair, sparkling like diamonds in the morning sun. "You already took your shower?"

"Just got out." He brushed a kiss against her nose.

"No fair. I wanted us to take one together."

Keenan's eyebrows hiked. "Well, a man can never be too clean."

She laughed and then scattered kisses against his scruffy chin. "You need a shave."

"I thought you'd like the rugged look." He leaned down and rubbed his cheek against hers.

Jalila squealed at the irritating friction. When she tried to roll over so she could face him, every muscle in her body screamed. All those positions last night had come back to haunt her.

"My poor baby." Keenan helped her roll over. "I told you not to try that spinning helicopter move again."

"You did no such thing."

He shrugged. "Well, I meant to, but I was too busy rolling my eyes to the back of my head."

Jalila laughed.

"Now what are we going to do about my breakfast?" he inquired.

She smiled wickedly into his twinkling brown eyes and couldn't decide whether what she felt for him was the beginning of love or just lust. "I don't know. What did you have in mind?"

"How about I show you?" Keenan slowly inched down the bed, raining kisses down her body as he went.

"Has anyone ever told you that you're insatiable?" she asked.

"No. Because this only happens when I'm with you," he admitted, cupping his large hand beneath her butt.

When his tongue dipped inside to taste her body's morning honey, Jalila released a long dreamy sigh and stretched her head back against the pillows. This was one hell of a way to wake up in the morning. In the distance she heard a door slam close. A second later, Cujo was barking up a storm.

Keenan's head popped up. "What in the hell?"

"Oh, hell, it's that dog again," someone's voice drifted up from outside her window.

"Omigod! It's nine o'clock." Suddenly it hit with a backup generator of strength, and Jalila scrambled out of bed, wrapped the top sheet around her body and raced to her window.

"Okay," Keenan said.

"The camera crew!"

"Awww hell." He finally bolted out of bed, but then tripped over the sheet that she had stretched from the bed to her body over at the window. He hit the floor with a thud and then bounced up as if he was made out of rubber. "Where're my clothes? What did I do with my clothes?" He scrambled around in a circle, frantic.

Ding-dong!

Woof! Woof!

"Oh, God. What are we going to do?" She glanced around, raking a hand through her hair.

"I need my clothes. Where're my clothes?" He sounded like a broken record.

Woof! Woof!

"Did you bring them up here?"

"What?"

"You undressed downstairs, remember?"

Keenan slapped his hand against his forehead.

"I'll go get them," she volunteered. "They're scared of Cujo so they're not going to come in. Just stay here and I'll be right back." She raced to the bedroom door.

"Jalila."

"What?" She turned around.

"You can't go down there like that."

She glanced down. "Oh, right." She found her robe near the foot of the bed and then raced to the door.

"Hurry," he hissed.

"I'm hurrying. I'm hurrying."

Once again, Jalila was racing toward the front door.

Keenan's clothes were right where he'd left them—discarded on the floor.

Woof! Woof!

"Cujo, stop!" She unlocked the front door and poked her head out.

The cameramen were already standing ten feet back.

"Can you guys give me a few more minutes while I put my dog away?"

"Sure. Sure. Take your time," one of the guys said. "We'll wait."

Woof! Woof!

"Thanks." She closed the door and then rolled her eyes. "C'mon, Cujo. Let's go in the backyard."

Cujo, of course, put up his usual struggle. When she finally got him into the backyard, she tossed him a doggy biscuit and then raced toward the stairs. "I'll be back down in a second," she yelled toward the front door and bolted up the stairs.

Rushing into the bedroom, she handed Keenan his clothes and then doubled over to try to catch her breath. "I'd better jump in the shower," she mumbled.

"No. No. No."

"No?" She glanced up and then blinked at the shredded mess Keenan held up. "What the hell?"

"Look at my clothes," he said, alarmed.

Her bewilderment only lasted a few seconds. "Cujo," she whispered. "I am so sorry. Cujo must have gotten bored and just…"

"Sorry? Now what am I supposed to wear?" He held up his pants—little more than thin strips dangling from a waistband.

"Well, maybe you could wear something of mine," she suggested.

"You have men's clothes here?"

Jalila shook her head. "Well, no. Not exactly."

He frowned. "Then what on earth could you possibly have that could fit me?"

"I don't know." She shrugged and then looked him over. "Maybe a…skirt or something."

"I'm going to pretend that you didn't say that. Do I look Scottish to you?"

"Hey, don't snap at me. I'm trying to help." She folded her arms. "Nobody told you to leave clothes downstairs for a Great Dane to play with."

"I was a little preoccupied…and I don't remember you complaining about me taking my clothes off last night."

Jalila snapped her mouth shut because she wasn't quite sure if he was hurling an insult or a compliment at her.

"Ms. Goodwyn?" a male voice filled the house.

She gasped. "They came into the house."

"Great." Keenan huffed.

Jalila once again rushed toward the door.

"Wait," he called after her. "What are you about to tell them?"

"I'm going to tell them that I'm about to jump in the shower. They won't come up here for that. That should give us some more time."

Keenan had another thought. "Nitara."

"What?"

"Is Nitara here?"

"I don't know. I didn't see her."

"She's going to recognize my car." He started panicking again. "I've got to get out of here before she shows up." Keenan darted toward the window. "Is this ledge sturdy out here?"

"I don't know. I've never had the compulsion to go out there and try it out."

"Okay. Uhm. Give me your robe."

"What?"

"Your robe. I'll wear the robe."

Following his irrational thinking, Jalila stripped out of her robe. At the sight of her naked body, Keenan experienced another erection.

Jalila's eyes bulged. "Stop that."

"What do you want me to do?" He gestured toward his hard-on. "Sometimes it has a mind of its own."

"Well, hurry up and put the robe on and cover up," she ordered.

Keenan slid an arm through the sleeve, but there was no way the short robe was going to fit. "Oh, just forget it." He tossed the robe down and then hurried into the bathroom.

"What are you doing?" she hissed.

Keenan quickly returned, wrapping a towel around his hips. "This is just going to have to work," he said.

"You know, we could just go downstairs and tell them."

"Yeah, that should go over well with the network." He went to the window and pulled it open. "It'll look like I'm running some kind of scam."

"Are you sure that you want to do this? What if you break your neck?"

"It'll make one hell of a story on the six-o'clock news," he joked. "I'll call you later." He gave her a kiss and then swung one leg through the window.

"Keenan, I don't know about this," Jalila said worried.

"I gotta think." He paused. "Look, just go on with the taping today and then we'll think of something later."

"Ms. Goodwyn?" the cameraman called out.

"Yeah. I'll be right down," she yelled and then returned her attention to Keenan. "I still don't like you going out on that ledge."

"I'll be fine." He kissed her again. "But thanks for worrying about me."

"But what about my date tonight?"

"Go. But I forbid you to have a good time." His eyes held a stern warning.

"Forbid?"

"No kissing—and no bikinis." He swung his other leg out the window. For a second, if anyone was looking, they would've had a great peek at Keenan's big package. "I'll come see you after taping. Eleven o'clock."

Jalila smiled. "Eleven o'clock," she repeated. However, she felt guilty about seeing Tion tonight. She hadn't gone into this expecting to lead men on.

Keenan slid out of the window and down onto the ledge.

Jalila watched him for a few seconds and then shut the window.

Nitara was running late.

She'd experienced some car trouble after her husband left for work and had to call around for a ride out to Jalila's place. She'd tried to locate her M.I.A. business partner to no avail. *He's probably sleeping in late with a booty call.* In the end, she had to settle on convincing Dee Dee to pick her up. With the crew settling in to their shooting schedule, it wasn't really necessary for her to be on set every day, but she'd always liked to stay on top of things whenever she and Keenan had a production in the works.

"I really appreciate this," Nitara said. "I owe you one."

"It's not a problem," Dee Dee said with her usual sunny disposition.

"You don't have to stay out on the set all day. I can get a rental car delivered out here later."

"Don't worry about it. I'm actually curious to see how everything is going."

"It's going pretty well. The first date went well, but I gotta tell you, it feels like the show is missing something. I dunno. We need a 'wow' factor or something." She shrugged. "Jalila is a fascinating girl and all, but what distinguishes our show from any other reality show?" Nitara stroked her chin in contemplation. "We need to kick it up a notch—a plot twist or something."

Dee Dee slowed the car down. "What's that?"

"What?" Nitara followed Dee Dee's line of vision and tried to assess exactly what the young assistant was looking at. Before she could ask, her gaze finally zeroed on something moving on Jalila's roof.

"Is that a man?" Dee Dee asked.

Nitara squinted, hating that she didn't have her

contacts in. She reached for her purse and then pulled out her rarely used eyeglasses.

"It *is* a man." She leaned forward. "And if I'm not mistaken, he's just wearing a towel."

"Oooh," Dee Dee said. "I thought you told me she said she hadn't had sex in two years?"

"I guess the streak is over," Nitara said. "Hold up."

Dee Dee pulled over.

"Is that who I think it is?"

"Who?"

"It can't be."

"It can't be who?" Dee Dee asked, impatient.

"Your boss."

Dee Dee did a double-take. "Keenan?"

Nitara reached back into her purse and pulled out her camera phone. "The camera crew is probably inside the house and Keenan is on the roof naked. Suddenly things are starting to make some sense."

"What are you doing?"

"Getting some footage."

"For what?"

"For the show. I think we just found our plot twist."

Chapter 17

"It's hard out here for a single girl," Martina announced into the camera. "A lot of that has to do with the fact that times have changed since our parents and grandparents hooked up. Women are more empowered and able to do things for themselves. Technology has made the world a lot smaller. Men—and women—have a lot more options." She shrugged. "Frankly there just isn't the same need to get married."

"I don't know about that," Jalila interjected. She and her two best friends were settled around a table at their favorite restaurant, Las Brisas, dishing with the cameras—and therefore America—about the perils of dating in the new age.

"I do," Martina continued. "The whole point and need for marriage is no longer valid. Women have

changed—for the better We once leaned on the opposite sex for protection, stability and security. Men
needed someone to feed them, clothe them and force
them to ask for directions." She chuckled.

"Oh, don't listen to her," Fantasia chimed in. "You
can probably tell that she's never been a real fan of
marriage."

"And why should I be?" Martina challenged. "The
only true reason that men and women need each other
is for sex."

"See what I mean?"

Jalila laughed and shook her head at her friends.
"See what I have to put up with?"

"Well, what are your thoughts on love and marriage?" Jon Krammer asked, sitting behind the frame
of the camera.

"Well." Jalila hesitated. "I don't agree with my
friend Martina." She glanced over at her. "Sorry."

"Don't be sorry. You'll learn sooner or later."

Jalila waved off the comment. "I think that marriage
is more than the sum of what one individual can get out
of it." A soft smile touched Jalila's lips. "Don't get me
wrong. I do agree that sex is important—and with the
right person even…magical. The right man can help
free you from all your inhibitions. It's wonderful to feel
free to do and share your innermost fantasies."

"What she means is, a woman needs to get her freak
on every once in a while," Martina clarified. "I'm sure
a lot of women out there know what we're talking
about. You're a lady in the streets and a freak in the
sheets."

Krammer laughed.

Martina's words hit closer to home than Jalila wanted to let on, but that was exactly what she was experiencing with Keenan. Their feverish and wild lovemaking left her feeling like a lady and a sex freak all at the same time.

"Oooh." Martina elbowed Jalila. "What's that smile all about?"

"Huh?" Jalila suddenly realized that she'd spaced out in the middle of her interview. "Uh, nothing. I was just thinking."

A knowing twinkle flashed in Martina's and Fantasia's eyes, and to Jalila's great relief, her two best friends didn't drop dime on her on national television. Of course, she hadn't had a chance to tell the girls the latest development between her and Keenan—which was probably a good thing.

Her thoughts roamed. *What exactly is my relationship with the philandering television producer?* During all that heavy panting and caressing there hadn't been any words of love or even a serious case of like. Hell, they hardly even knew each other, come to think of it.

Jalila's smile slowly evaporated as she contemplated the situation. Here she was participating in a reality TV show in which her lover-slash-TV producer was fixing her up with other men to help her find her soul mate. She was dating different men during the day and then screwing Keenan's brains out at night. Why did her life suddenly sound like one of those twisty romantic novels by Adrianne Byrd?

"Is sex an important factor for you?" Krammer asked.

The cameras zoomed in for a close-up.

"It's uh…sure. I mean, everyone wants to have that great chemistry—and forever is a long time."

"How important—say on a scale from one to ten?"

Martina jumped back in. ":Shoot. It's a twenty."

The girls giggled.

"What about you?" Krammer asked Fantasia.

"Oh, I don't know." She blushed. "Maybe a five."

"Five!" Jalila and Martina echoed in disbelief.

"Yeah," Fantasia defended. "If you love the guy then sex doesn't matter."

"Then your man ain't hittin' it right," Martina accused.

"Martina!"

"What? If her husband is watching then I'm just helpin' her out."

Jalila squirmed, wanting to get off the topic.

"And what about you, Jalila?" Krammer asked, returning his attention to her. "Given that you haven't had sex in two years."

Jalila's face heated, remembering the lie she told yesterday.

"Two years?" Martina echoed. Her eyes bulged. "I thought…" She suddenly remembered the cameras. "Oh, yeah. I forgot," she said unconvincingly.

Fantasia suddenly got busy pushing the ice cubes around her glass with her straw. She clearly didn't want any part of confirming or denouncing Jalila's lie.

Jalila continued to squirm. "Well, sex is still important to me," she said. "I'm not saying that I don't believe in sex before marriage or anything. It's just hard finding that right person to connect with."

"It's not *that* hard," Martina mumbled under her breath.

Finally Krammer showed Jalila some mercy and changed the subject.

Of course, Jalila couldn't stop thinking about what Keenan would say once he watched that bit of footage in the editing room. But what was she supposed to do—admit that she'd lied to Dontrell *and* America yesterday or confess that she got her freak on last night?

What a tangled web we weave.

Nitara and Dee Dee scrambled around the office, setting up a few personal cameras. There was no way that they could use any of the professional equipment for what Nitara had in mind, but this was better than nothing.

"Are you sure that this is a good idea?" Dee Dee whispered.

"Of course not," Nitara said, rushing around the room. "I'm making this up as I go along. It's not like we can just confront him and think he's going to confess. Keenan keeps things too close to the chest for that. Do you think that he'll be able to see this camera over here on the shelf?"

Dee Dee cocked her head. "You're probably going to need to put something up there to cover up the red light when you hit Record."

"Oh, good point." No sooner had Nitara rearranged the leaves of a potted plant beside the camera than Keenan waltzed into their private office.

"Afternoon, ladies."

Nitara and Dee Dee gasped, jumped and spun around.

Keenan frowned. "What's going on? Did I interrupt something?"

"You know," Dee Dee said, her voice cracking. "I think I better get going. I have a lot of filing that needs to be...uh, filed."

"Oookay," Keenan said, his gaze bouncing between the women.

"Bye." Dee Dee waved, inching toward the door. "If you need anything I'll, uh, be right out here...uh..."

"Filing?" Keenan filled in for her.

"Yeah. Yeah." Dee Dee rushed out the door.

Keenan turned toward Nitara. "Maybe we should go back to drug-testing our employees."

Nitara laughed—a little loudly as she hit the record button on the remote in her hands behind her back.

Keenan's frown deepened as he settled in behind his desk.

Nitara stood in the center of the office, trying to think of a way to get Keenan to open up about his love life. It was something he rarely did. "So, uhm, how's everything going with editing?" To Nitara's amazement, Keenan's face flushed.

"Oh, about that. I had to head out of there early last night." He shrugged. "It's no big deal. The guys there are doing a great job. I just, uh, had something come up."

Nitara hid her smile. "Oh? I hope nothing serious."

"Oh, no. No. Everything's fine. I, uh, just had to go and see someone about something."

"Sounds…mysterious." She eased into the chair in front of his desk. "So everything's fine?"

"Oh, yeah. Everything is great," he said, avoiding eye contact.

"Well, you know, you don't have to keep checking up on the guys down there. I've seen some of what they've been able to put together. They're doing good."

"Are you sure?"

"Reality television is turning out to be a lot easier than the scripted stuff."

Keenan bobbed his head. "Is that why you're not on the set today?"

"Yeah. Wolfe pretty much has everything under control. We should've jumped into this reality stuff a lot sooner. Low-maintenance." A thought suddenly occurred to her. "Unless you want to go. You haven't been on the set yet…and Jalila is scheduled to go on her first date with bachelor number two—Tion Johnson, I think."

Keenan's face darkened. "I think I'll pass." He tried to smile, an action made difficult by the fact that his back molars were grinding together.

Nitara found his reaction amusing. "You know, if I was a betting person, I'd say that Tion will win this thing hands-down."

Keenan's head snapped up. "Why do you say that?"

"Oh. Little things." She sighed. "The night of the party I saw a little spark there between the two of them. I guess I could be wrong."

He cleared his throat. "Did Jalila *say* she liked this, uh, Leon guy?"

"Tion," she corrected. "She had to like him. She chose him, didn't she?"

A twitch now etched along Keenan's jawline. "I guess."

"Plus, I believe that he works at the governor's office. They say that he's a rising star in the world of politics."

"A politician? Ha."

"What's so bad about dating a politician?"

"Let's just say that there's one time to trust them."

"When is that?"

"When they're not breathing."

They shared a laugh before Keenan turned his attention to his computer.

"Soooo." Nitara searched for an opening.

"Soooo?" Keenan stared at her.

"So you've been busy lately," she said, and then wanted to kick herself.

"No busier than usual." He shrugged. "I had a talk with Sam over at Creative Artist Agency. He's sending over a few potentials for the winter lineup. Comedies. One of them was passed over by Will and Jada's production company. Rumor has it that they're getting out of television and sticking with the big money in movies."

"Then you want to go back to scripted material?" she asked with mild surprise. "I figured that if this reality thing was a hit…?"

There was a visible shift in Keenan's expression.

"You know," Nitara hedged. "Maybe next season we'll get a bachelor on the show—call it *King of Hearts?*"

"Humph. We'll see," Keenan said noncommittally.

Nitara nodded, frustrated that she wasn't getting anywhere. "Maybe you're right. It's more difficult for these types of shows to produce a match when it's the guy who's choosing."

"That sounds like a sexist thing to say."

"It's true. From *The Bachelor* to that God-forsaken *Flava of Love* crap, the men are just looking for a little arm candy. None of them have gone on to have any successful relationships. Once the cameras are gone so is the love."

"Don't be glib. Men aren't as hard to figure out as women think."

"Really?" She folded her arms. "You're not such an easy nut to crack. Here you are, divorced for five years and I don't see you diving back into the cesspool or as some call it, the dating scene. I mean, sure you have a few one-nighters, but nothing serious. I don't get the sense that you even think about it."

"That's different."

"How is it different?"

He shrugged. "It just is."

"I think that you just blew your own theory out of the water," she said. "Maybe *you* should go on the show."

Keenan laughed and tossed his head back. "Never gonna happen. I'm happily single. Thank you very much."

Nitara frowned. Maybe she'd misunderstood this whole thing. There was a real good chance that Jalila was nothing more than a fling for him. However, that hardly explained his chaotic moods the past couple of weeks. And more important, why would he risk ruining their show for a one-night stand?

She stared at him.

He looked up. "What?"

"Oh, nothing." She felt disheartened.

Keenan turned his attention back to the computer while Nitara thought for a moment. "Keenan, you know, just because things didn't work out with Tenetria, it's not a reason to just throw in the hat."

He didn't respond.

"Does that mean that you don't want to talk about it?" she asked.

"I've avoided talking about it for five years. I don't see any reason to start talking about it now."

"Maybe that's *exactly* the reason why you need to talk about it now. You can't just give up. Everyone deserves love. Everyone deserves to be with that special someone."

Keenan pushed back in his chair. "Why do all women believe that stuff?"

She looked at him in stunned surprise.

"Women have been sold this fairy-tale crap that men simply can't live up to. There are plenty of people who live their whole lives without finding *the one*. Love is just a…lucky shot in the dark. I should know. I tried." He drew a deep breath. "I was a good husband. I provided for my wife. No, I couldn't always be there. I worked long hours and maybe I traveled too much. But all the things I was brought up to believe that a good husband does for his wife and family, I did. And what did I get for my troubles? A wife who cheated and lied…" He shook his head.

"Tenetria and I had been changing since college—but no matter. I was good…and faithful. I didn't deserve what she did to me." He grinded his teeth and got lost in his painful memories. After a long silence, he said, "She should have come to me. It would have been better just to ask me for the divorce.

"When I discovered them…something broke in me. That kind of betrayal…I don't think it's something that I can ever get over. I don't ever want to be in that position again—to be that vulnerable." Their eyes met again. "You know, when you get married you hand over this power that you pray your partner will never use against you. You hand over your heart. You promise to love, cherish, and…I dunno."

Nitara lowered her gaze. She knew that Keenan had been holding back these past few years, but she didn't know just how deeply her sister had hurt him.

"I'm sorry," he said. "I got all sentimental on you."

"No. It's okay. I'm glad you shared this with me." Nitara wiped a tear from the corner of her eye. No way was she going to use this recording for their show. "I'm sorry my sister hurt you."

"There's nothing for you to be sorry for," he assured her. "I'm a big boy. I can take care of myself."

Nitara nodded, but she was still curious about one thing. "So you don't think that you'll ever fall in love again?"

Keenan fell silent for so long that Nitara thought that he wasn't going to answer the question. Finally he said, "Not if I can help it."

Chapter 18

As much as Jalila had hated surfing, she discovered that she hated golf even more. Somehow Tion got in his mind that taking a woman out to an eighteen-hole golf course was a romantic thing to do. When he showed up saying they were going to sink a few holes, Jalila thought that he meant miniature golf—a cute game with funny, goofy sets. But standing in the middle of a boring green gold course, chasing a little white ball around was not her idea of a fun date.

Tion, bless his heart, clearly thought that he'd hit a dating home run. His love of all things political was at first a turn-on or at least rather intriguing. But the man could go on for hours, arguing in circles about any subject having to do with politics. Two hours into her date, Jalila wanted to beg the cameraman or the director for a pair of toothpicks to help prop open her eyelids. It was a shame because Tion really was good-looking.

They showed up at the golf club, where plenty of members stared at them, wondering who these people with a whole camera crew following them around were. Before going out to the green, Tion suggested that they stop at the bar and order some drinks.

Jalila smiled and figured why not. At the bar, she ordered a wine cooler while Tion ordered a double shot of brandy, a surprising choice since it was just past noon. When their drinks arrived, Tion turned on his stool toward her and smiled.

"I sure hope that you have a good time today."

"Well, I've already warned you that I've never played golf before so I hope you're patient."

"Aw. Don't worry about it. It's just a game. You're going to be just fine." A sly smile slid across his face as he stared at her—first at her lips and then slowly his eyes lifted to meet her gaze.

She smiled back, wanting to be polite. The truth of the matter was that after her second night with Keenan, she couldn't conjure up so much as an ember of the spark that she'd felt for Tion the night of the party. In fact, she felt guilty for even being out on this date.

Tion smiled and leaned forward. He was so close that when he spoke, his warm breath drifted across her cheek. "You look so hot in that outfit."

She glanced down at her mid-thigh pink shorts and white cotton T-shirt. Pretty basic.

"You probably didn't know, but I'm a leg man."

Jalila had a horrible sense of déjà vu. "That's a leg man and not a foot man, right?"

He shrugged. "Feet are all right, but the legs are where it's at."

Jalila tried not to laugh at his weak game.

For twenty minutes, while they nursed their drinks, Tion rambled on about all the celebrities and politicians he'd played golf with over the years. If the name-dropping was meant to impress her, it didn't.

After drinks and renting a set of clubs for Jalila, the two of them finally headed out to the green. Tion grabbed her hand and held it. The director insisted that they take some B-roll footage of them walking and pointing at innocuous things like squirrels or trees. It was meant to help set the mood.

Jalila wondered if after the show she would feel strange not having a full camera crew following her around. At the first tee, Tion instructed her to take a few swings to see what her natural "stroke" was like—a cheesy joke that fell flat.

Jalila had no idea what she was doing and her first couple of swings looked more like she was trying to take a whack at a T-ball instead of a golf ball.

"Oh, no, no, no," Tion said. "It's all in your hips. Let me show you." He moved up behind her, pressed his body close and then wrapped his arms around her. "What you want to do is place your hand on the *shaft,* like this."

Jalila was suddenly hip to the game. This political nerd apparently had a few playa moves. Still, she felt… nothing.

No spark.

No chemistry.

Nothing.

Sidebar, camera one:

Tion grins brightly into the camera. "A golf course is the perfect place to bring a woman on a first date. Why? It's a sport that both men and women can enjoy together. It's an instant ice-breaker." He glances off into the green. "Whenever I come out here, it relaxes me. It's a nice outdoor activity that provides excellent opportunities be-tween shots. Plus, by the end of a good game, if two people aren't compatible, it's the end of the date." He chuckles at his loopy conclusion.

Sidebar, camera two:

Jalila stares straight into the camera. "Is it time to go home yet?"

Sidebar, camera one:

Tion says, "Yeah. I think she's digging it. She seems to be having a good time. Of course, I don't think I made a good impression on her when I missed sinking my ball in that last hole and I got angry and threw my clubs around." He nods. "And I probably shouldn't have made her retrieve that ball out of the pond, but it's impor-tant that a new golfer understand the price of these golf balls." He cocks his head. "Look, golf is a pretty intense sport." He laughs. "Yeah, I would love to bring her back out here. You know, if it all works out. Which I'm sure it will. She's seems to be digging me."

Sidebar, camera two:

Jalila stares into the camera. "Is it time to go home yet?"

At least the second part of their date was better. Tion escorted Jalila to her favorite Italian restaurant, Cicada,in downtown Los Angeles. The conversation over dinner of course involved more politics—which by this point was short-circuiting her brain. Still, there was an adorable sweetness about Tion. He was clearly not for her, though she suspected that he thought otherwise.

Whenever Jalila tried to bring the conversation back to her or anything that had to do with her life, it always ended up right back to the fascinating drama between the Democrats and the Republicans. She *loved* President Obama, but if this man said his name one more time, she was going to scream.

After dinner, Tion suggested that they go to his place where they could take a little dip in his Jacuzzi. It was a tempting offer until she remembered the hickies Keenan had planted all over her back.

The director and the camera crew liked the idea, mainly, Jalila suspected, because they wanted to get her back into a bathing suit. "I think I'm going to have to take a rain check," she said, smiling at Tion and a team of disappointed faces. "That golfing...really wore me out."

"Okay." He bobbed his head, clearly disappointed. "Not a problem."

When they returned to her place, there was a big deal with lighting. She and Tion had to say their good-nights an astonishing fifteen times before the director was satisfied with the take. The perils of reality dating.

Exhausted, Jalila stomped her way to the backyard to feed Cujo and let him into house. However, Cujo wasn't alone. There were two Great Danes in her backyard. She would have been alarmed if Cujo didn't look so happy with the arrangement. She was confused, but then something tickled her memory.

Turning, she raced up the stairs and into her bedroom. When she burst into the room she found Keenan, fully dressed and stretched out on the bed with his hands folded behind his head.

"What are you doing here?"

"Waiting for you. I told you I'd be here at eleven o'clock." He stood up from the bed and walked toward her. He took her hand in his and kissed them. "How was your date?"

"It was, uhm…boring."

"Glad to hear it."

She smiled and shook her head. "How did you get in here?"

"The same way I left—through the window." He laughed and then kissed the tip of her nose. "So I was thinking."

"About?" She laced her arms around his neck.

"About how we have yet to go out on a date."

Jalila arched a brow at him.

"So why don't you change out of those clothes and I take you out on the town?"

"Two dates in one day?"

"Yeah, but the first one don't count since you were supposed be having a lousy time. And—" he wrapped an arm around her waist so that she could feel just how excited he was to see her "—it wasn't with me." This time he leaned in for a long and deep kiss.

Jalila moaned.

"Of course we can always stay in, too," he amended.

"No. I think I'm going to take you up on this." She kissed *his* nose. "Give me five minutes." She peeled herself out of his arms.

"Five minutes." Keenan glanced down at his watch. "I'll be waiting."

One thing Jalila loved to do was dance. She had casually mentioned this to Keenan on Cujo's birthday and she was happy that he'd remembered. As a child and teenager, she had spent years in everything from ballet to jazz and even hip-hop lessons. But tonight, it was salsa.

The Rumba Room was perhaps the hottest salsa club in Los Angeles. Salsa was like lust set to music. There was something about the rhythm that really got into Jalila's soul. Suddenly her arms and hips had minds of their own and would get her to move in ways that were equally erotic and hypnotic.

Soon she was kicking and spinning like a top. All the while Keenan was there to hold and guide her.

"You're a good dancer," she panted.

"You're not so bad yourself," he said, taking her and spinning her around again.

Jalila's own salsa instructor had always said that salsa is performed to reveal one's steaming passion and desire. Jalila and Keenan's performance mirrored the way they made love: spicy, hot, sweat pouring down their bodies.

All in all, they were having the time of their lives.

After a couple of hours, the couple couldn't wait to make it back to Jalila's place. Since the club was closer to Keenan's, that's where they went. Once his palatial home had had the power to awe Jalila, but tonight all she cared about was making it to his bed.

Outside, someone in another car sat watching as Jalila and Keenan arrived at the Beverly Hills mansion. Nitara held her personal camcorder capturing the image of her business partner as he carried Jalila from his car into the house. After watching them go from Jalila's house to the Rumba Room and now here, Nitara felt confident that this *was* more than a fling for Keenan. He just didn't know it.

"Aaaannnddd *cut,*" she whispered, lowering the camera.

Chapter 19

It was different this time.

There was no dirty talk, no pretzel-like position and no test of competitive endurance. Their lovemaking was mind-blowingly tender and sensuous. Maybe there was something about being in Keenan's home—his domain—that caused Jalila to feel that she was somehow becoming more a part of him. It had gotten so that when he wasn't kissing her she was craving his taste. When he wasn't caressing her, she was aching for his touch.

When had her feelings for him changed? When had she changed? When had *they* changed?

Now pressed into the center of his king-size bed, Jalila watched Keenan through the mesh of her lowered eyelashes. The expression on his face reflected sweet ecstasy, and as he moved inside her, he kept whispering the Lord's name. Jalila reached up and ran her fingers down the sleek corded muscles in his back and then glided her hand onto his firm and flexing butt cheeks.

"Yes, yes. Oh, Gawd," she panted. Nothing she had ever experienced had felt this exquisite. She lifted her head and flicked her tongue against his taut nipple, moaning at the taste of him. How had she lived the past thirty years without this man being in her life?

Even though they were so deeply connected at this moment, she sensed that he was holding a part of himself back. There was a wall erected around his heart. "Let me in," she whispered, pulling his head down for a fierce kiss. The moment his tongue slipped into her mouth, she climaxed.

Keenan greedily swallowed her sighs and moans.

Still dizzy with desire, she languished between heaven and earth while he continued to grind inside of her.

Keenan's low growl was a sign of his struggle for control. It was a hard thing to do while Jalila sucked and nibbled at his bottom lip. Equally hard for him was to separate his heart from the physical sexual act. It seemed like he was fighting an impossible battle. This woman, whom he'd only known for a short period of time, had touched him so deeply and so completely that he felt once again in danger of doing something foolish.

Like falling in love. *It's just sex. It's just sex,* he tried to convince himself, but his heart just laughed at him.

"Let me in," she whispered again.

No. He didn't want to let her in. He didn't want to let anyone in. *Never again,* he repeated in his head, but the voice was so faint.

"Let me in," she insisted, quieting the voice inside his head. A fire began to build, low and hot. But soon the flames rose and intensified, scorching him inside and out. Then it seemed it was all too much to bear. His toes curled while his lungs threatened to collapse.

"Let me in."

"I…can't…"

Keenan grazed his mouth back across her full, lush lips. He didn't want any more talking. He surged deeper. She was hot and slick and tight, a velvet fist gripping him. He cried out, his voice hoarse, as pleasure engulfed him and left him quaking with after-shocks.

He lay still, panting like a man who'd just escaped with his life. Jalila peppered soft kisses across his dewy brow to cool him down. But her efforts only succeeded in causing his body to tighten in response. Still joined to her, he truly had a hard time discerning where he began and she ended. And at this moment in time, it didn't matter.

Keenan didn't know when he'd fallen asleep but when he opened his eyes, Jalila was gone.

The camera crew was waiting for Jalila when she arrived home via taxicab. She tried her best to smooth things over with smiles and apologies since they had been standing at her front door for at least two hours.

"Where have you been?" Nitara asked, glancing at her watch. "You know, time costs money. This is costing the production and the networks."

"I'm so sorry. I really am. Please forgive me," Jalila said, shoving a key into the front door.

"Did you go out after your date last night?" Nitara asked, as she and the TV crew followed Jalila into the house.

"Huh, what?"

"Your dress," Nitara pointed out. "You look pretty jazzed up."

"Oh." Jalila glanced down. "Uhm…" She fumbled for a lie, but couldn't come up with anything. "Yeah, I just went out with, uhm, some friends."

"Really? With Martina and Fantasia?"

"Huh—yeah! We, uhm, just decided to go out for a little while. The time must have just gotten away from me and I just crashed over at Martina's place."

"I see." Nitara nodded along. "That probably would have been some good footage for the show. You know—girls' night out. Add a little realism about how it is out there in the clubs for single women in this day and age."

Jalila continued to dig a bigger hole for herself. "Well, you know it was sort of last-minute. Just—'hey, let's go out.'" She chuckled. "Plus, it was nice to get away from the cameras for a little while."

"Ms. Goodwyn." The sound tech approached her. "Do you want to get miked up so we can get started?"

"Oh, just give me a few minutes, I need to jump in the shower for a quick minute and I'll be right down."

The announcement of a longer delay didn't go over too well.

"You guys just make yourselves at home." Jalila was heading for the staircase when she heard Cujo barking in the backyard. "Damn. I have to feed the dog."

"Don't worry. I'll do it," Nitara suggested. "You go ahead and take your shower and I'll take care of the dog."

"Are you sure? Cujo can be a little…rambunctious."

Nitara waved off her concern. "Yeah, don't worry about it. My business partner has a Great Dane, too. Maybe I can pull this off." She chuckled.

"All right then. I'll be right back." She started up the stairs again when she remembered something. "Oh, wait."

"Hey, there's *two* dogs back here." Nitara turned toward Jalila as she rushed toward the back door. "Did you get a second dog?"

"No, uhm." *Think, Jalila. Think.* "I'm dog-sitting." That sounded good. "For a friend of mine."

Nitara squinted at the two dogs. "You know, this one actually looks like Chips." She leaned toward the back glass door. "He even has the same collar."

The dogs went wild, barking.

"How uncanny," Nitara whispered. "If I didn't know any better I'd say it *was* Keenan's dog."

"What? Nooo." Jalila laughed. "What would his dog be doing here?"

Nitara stood erect, her gaze leveled at Jalila. "Yeah. What indeed?"

While Nitara took care of the dogs, Jalila rushed through her shower, got dressed and then took the TV crew out to Body by Jalila, where they videotaped her as she ran her business. Of course they also captured a lot of celebrity and local gossip, mainly because that was what women talked about in this spa, just as they did in hair salons and nail shops everywhere.

When Fantasia finally came in to work her half a day, Jalila managed to escape the cameras long enough to steer her into the women's bathroom.

"What the—!"

"I need to talk to you," Jalila hissed against her ear.

Fantasia's high-heeled sandals slapped against the floor as Jalila practically dragged her through the women's bathroom door.

"We'll be right back," Jalila said, apologizing to the cameraman.

Once inside, Fantasia tried to wiggle free. "Can I *please* have my arm back?"

Jalila released her. "I need your help. I have a problem."

Fantasia's face scrunched. "What is it? What kind of problem?"

Jalila hesitated, wondering for a few more seconds whether she should confess this or not. What if she was wrong? What if she was just reacting to the moment, and as soon as someone snapped their fingers these wild and chaotic feelings that she'd been experiencing would disappear?

"Well? Are you going to keep me on pins and needles?"

Jalila took a deep breath. "I think…I'm in love." The moment she finally said the words, her heart started racing. "No. I know I am," she amended. "I've fallen for this really wonderful guy and…I don't know what to do."

A smile exploded across Fantasia's face. "Omigod, I can't believe it! Really?" She started bouncing up and down. "I'm so happy for you." Fantasia threw her arms around Jalila's neck and then held on for a fierce hug. "I knew doing this show was the right thing for you."

"Fantasia," Jalila croaked. "I can't breath."

"Sorry." Her friend released her. "Which one is it? Dontrell or Tion? I bet you it's Dontrell, isn't it? Oooh, that brother is fine. I bet you guys will make some beautiful babies."

Jalila frowned and shook her head. "No. No. You don't understand. It's not one of the guys from the show."

Fantasia's smile flipped upside down. "I don't understand. You haven't been seeing anyone else. Have you?"

"Well…yes…and no."

"Which is it?"

Jalila hedged. "I think it qualifies as a 'kinda sorta.'"

"That sounds…weird."

"We've been out on *one* date."

"One date?"

"Yeah."

"And you're in love?" Fantasia asked.

Jalila exhaled a long breath. "I know that it sounds ridiculous and a little hard to believe."

"More than a little hard."

"Well, you were willing to think I was in love with someone from the show a minute ago."

"That's different."

"How?"

Fantasia shrugged. "I don't know. Maybe I thought you were you using the term *love* loosely."

"Well, I'm not. And I know what I'm feeling." She took Fantasia's hand and held it tightly. "This feels more real to me than anything I've ever known."

"Now you sound overly dramatic," Fantasia said sarcastically.

"You know, if I'd wanted someone to dump on me, I would have called Martina."

Chastised, Fantasia apologized. "All right. How about we do this? Tell me why you think you're in love."

"There's just this connection—this incredible spiritual and sexual connection that I just can't explain." She shook her head. "You know, my mother always said that when the right man comes along, you'll just know it. And she was right. I just *know*. He's the one for me."

Fantasia jumped on one phrase. "*Spiritual* and *sexual?* You've only had sex once in the past two years. I mean unless it's…" Her eyes widened. "Nooo!"

Jalila bobbed her head. "Yes."

Outside the ladies' room, the sound tech removed his headset and looked over at Nitara. "Did you just hear that?"

Nitara smiled. "I heard every word."

Chapter 20

"I'm engaged!"

Keenan stopped in the middle of his business conversation and lowered his BlackBerry. "You're what?" he asked his sister, sitting across from him at the lunch table at The Ivy.

"You heard me," Keisha said, bouncing in her chair. She thrust her hand toward him and wiggled her fingers. "I'm getting married."

Keenan's gaze fell to the glittering diamond on her left hand. He couldn't suppress his surprise or shock. "Yeah, Tony," he said into his phone. "Let me call you back." He disconnected the call and then took his sister's hand. There was no doubt about the quality and expense of the beautiful diamond.

"Well, I…uh…"

"Aren't you going to congratulate me?" his sister said. She continued to bounce in her seat and beam at him.

"Congratulations," he finally spat out. He lifted a smile. "Who's the lucky guy? And why haven't *I* met him?"

"You have." She lowered her hand. "You remember Jaheim? We broke up last year."

Keenan frowned. "Not the brother whose tires you slashed that one time?"

"Okay. So it wasn't exactly a pretty breakup."

"And busted out his headlights?"

"Water under the bridge." Keisha waved off Keenan's questions. "The point is that he finally came to his senses, said that he made a mistake thinking he needed some space and came back to me."

"Did he make a mistake before or after you went psycho?"

"I wasn't psycho. I was just…a little disappointed that he didn't think the relationship was going in the direction that *I* thought it needed to be going. Now he's back, I got my ring and I'm happy." She started bouncing in her chair again. "Please, please, please say that you approve."

Keenan stood up from his chair and went around the table and hugged his sister. "I approve of anything that makes you this happy," he said, kissing her on the cheek and then mussing her hair the way she always hated.

"Hey! Cut it out." Keisha pushed him away. She smiled down at her diamond. "He did good, didn't he?"

"Yes, he did." He returned to his chair and continued to smile. "Married."

"What? You didn't think that I'd ever get married?"

Keenan recognized a trap when he heard one. "Of course I did. It's just going to be an adjustment thinking of you as someone's wife when up until now you've just been my kid sister. A pain in my backside."

"Very funny. But if you think that's hard, wait until you start thinking of me as someone's mother."

"Mother?" His eyes narrowed. "You don't mean…?"

Keisha bobbed her head. "Four weeks pregnant!"

"Four weeks?" Keenan tried to stare down at her belly, but the table blocked his view.

"I'm so happy!" Keisha squealed.

Other diners glanced in their direction.

Keenan blinked. This was a lot of information to take in at one time. In his head, he kept replaying all the childish games that he and his sister had engaged in over the years. All the practical jokes and potshots they'd taken in the spirit of sibling rivalry. His little sister was all grown up. That knowledge made him proud.

"Now all we have to do is get you hitched again," Keisha said casually.

Just like that, Keenan's joyous mood evaporated.

His sister cocked a smile at him. "C'mon. You can't just continue to mope around this town because of what that crazy bitch did to you. Please." She rolled her eyes. "I wouldn't give her the satisfaction."

Keenan picked up his fork and returned to his lunch. "Let's just drop the subject."

"No. I'm happy and I want my big brother to be happy. What's wrong with that?"

Keenan chomped on his salmon.

"I know that it would totally jack your *cool* image if it got out that you're this really sensitive ball of goo."

"I'm not goo."

"Trust me. You're goo." Keisha took a sip of her tea and then launched back onto her soapbox. "You need a woman in your life—and not just one to warm your bed and then skip out before the sun rises."

"You've been engaged all of…"

"Twelve hours."

"And now you're a relationship expert?"

"There you go again—lashing out at me. I'm not the one you're mad at."

Keenan drew in an impatient breath. "I'm not mad at anyone."

"Liar." She stabbed her salad.

"I'm not…" He glanced around the restaurant. "You know what? Just drop it." He shook his head. "I don't know why all of a sudden everyone is so concerned about my love life. Between you and Nitara, I feel like I'm just talking in circles."

"I'm going to set you up with a nice, good girl," she said and then ignored all his protests. "I don't care what you say." Keisha pointed her fork at him. "There's a woman out there who's perfect for you. I just know it. Don't ask me how. I just do—and I'm not going to let you give up until you find her."

Keenan's heart squeezed as a voice inside his head whispered, *I already found her.*

* * *

Bachelor number three, Evander Taylor, turned out to be a very sweet guy. Their first date consisted of a nice quiet evening at his place. His home was a quaint ranch-style home that looked small on the outside but was very spacious on the inside. The moment she (and the TV crew) entered the house there was a wonderful assault of aromas drifting from the kitchen.

"What smells good?"

"Dinner," he said, in a smooth husky baritone.

"You cook?"

"I dibble and dabble a bit. On tonight's menu is one of my all-time favorites, veal marsala. I hope you enjoy it."

"Hmm," she said, impressed. "If it tastes as good as it smells then you've just hit a home run."

He smiled. "Let me take your sweater."

She turned and offered him her back.

Evander leaned in close. "You smell good yourself." Jalila blushed, mainly because the flirtatious moment was done before a squad of twenty people.

He pulled her sweater off to reveal a sexy, form-fitting black dress.

"Wow." Evander grinned, but then he said, "What happened to your back?"

"What?"

"It looks like you have a rash or something."

Jalila's eyes bulged. She turned and grabbed the sweater and put it back on. "I, uh, tried this new lotion and…uh, I had a bad reaction," she lied. How on earth had she forgotten about the hickies?

Evander eyebrows ticked higher and an awkward silence blanketed the couple and crew.

Sidebar, camera one:

> Evander stares into the camera. "Sure didn't look like a rash to me."

Sidebar, camera two:

> Jalila smiles nervously. "I really do have very sensitive skin."

In the kitchen, Evander had clearly spent most of his day prepping and preparing dinner. Jalila drew a deep breath and her stomach growled in anticipation. Embarrassed, Jalila shot a look over to the sound tech. "I guess I'm hungrier than I thought."

Evander chuckled. "Glad to hear it. I love a woman with a healthy appetite." He retrieved two wineglasses. "How about we start this evening off right?"

"Sounds good," she said.

Twenty minutes later, she and Evander sat in the middle of his couch in a candlelit living room, sharing stories about their lives and past loves.

Turns out, Evander was an ex-NFL player (go '49ers!) who'd only played two seasons in the league. After being sidelined by a nasty knee injury, he'd fallen into his career in real estate, and, he insisted, "There're a lot of great deals in this current market."

Jalila nodded.

"I'm telling you. This kind of economic opportunity comes only once in a lifetime."

"Thank God," Jalila joked and returned to sipping her wine.

When dinner was finally ready, Evander escorted her to the dining room, where he pulled out her chair.

Evander wasn't a good cook—he was an *amazing* cook. The moment Jalila sank her teeth into the veal marsala, her mouth exploded with exquisite flavors.

"I take it you like it," Evander asked.

It wasn't until that moment that she realized her orgasmic moans were filling the room and a lot of the TV crew were smirking over her reaction. "Sorry. Yes, this is wonderful. Where on earth did you learn to cook like this?"

"My mother. She was a master in the kitchen."

"Well, this is excellent. Consider this a home run."

Sidebar, camera one:

Evander pumps his fist in the air. "Yeah, baby! You hear that? Home run! Dontrell and Tion need to hang it up—get outta the game. Trust me, I'm winning this queen's heart," he boasts. His face splits into a wide smile. "People out there, listen up. The way to *anyone's* heart is through their stomach. Ya feel me?"

Sidebar, camera two:

Jalila smiles into the camera. "I have to admit, he put his foot in this. I'm very impressed."

Back in the living room, Evander put on some smooth jazz. "I hope you like Najee."

"I love him. He always put me in the mood for…" She smiled and decided that it was better for her not to finish that thought.

"I know what you mean." Evander swayed his hips as he moved from the stereo back over to the couch. "How about a dance?" He held out his hand.

Jalila hesitated, but given the number of eyes watching her, she slid her hand into his and allowed him to pull her up against his body—a rather nice body—and lead her into a gentle rocking in front of the fireplace.

Evander turned out to be a pretty good dancer, even though she had to engage in the game of him constantly trying to press their bodies closer while she tried to pull back. All the while, guilt built up in the back of her mind. He was a wonderful guy: sweet, caring, funny, the kind of man she probably would have fallen for had she never crossed paths with Keenan.

The only reason that she was still participating in this show was because she was legally obligated to do so and, well, the network and Keenan's production company had sunk so much money into it. Her only option as she saw it was, at the show's finale, not to pick any of the bachelors.

Jalila sighed at the thought of how that was going to go over with everyone. That would certainly be a twist. Her decision might have the potential to make this show last just one season.

"You seem troubled," Evander said.

"What? Oh, no. I was just thinking…about how nice this evening has been."

He smiled and she leaned her head against his and continued to sway to the music.

Side bar, camera one:

Evander smiles. "Do I have the magic touch or what? I know how to wine and dine the ladies. Nah, let me stop playing. Jalila is a really nice lady. She's smart, beautiful and, quite frankly, if I didn't have all these cameras up in here I'd have been trying to make my move." He laughs. "Let me quit. I'm really feeling this girl. I didn't think that I would find someone of her caliber on this show. I'm glad I decided to take this chance."

Side bar, camera two:

Jalila shrugs. "He's sweet. I like him a lot. Any woman would be happy to be with him."

After three takes of their goodnight kiss, the *Queen of Hearts* limo took Jalila back to her house. All the while, her mind was spinning about the complicated situation she'd gotten herself into. Her heart told her that Keenan Armstrong was the man for her, but she was determined to fulfill her contractual obligations. She just hoped that in the end she would win the man she really wanted.

She climbed out of the limo at half past eleven grateful that the camera was leaving her a little privacy. After she entered her front door, she hoped against hope that she was about to embark on her *second* date for the evening. Heck, it was getting to the point that she couldn't remember the last time she had had a full eight hours of sleep.

She took her time going upstairs, not wanting to appear too eager. Slowly, she opened her bedroom door, a smile blooming across her face. But Keenan was not there. She crept farther into the room and then checked the bathroom. As a precaution, mainly because she was experiencing flashbacks, she also peeked into her closet.

He wasn't there either.

Curious, she went back downstairs and opened the back door. Cujo was alone.

"Humph." She glanced around. "Have you eaten, boy?"

Woof!

"You wouldn't tell me even if you had." She ruffled his ears and then led him to the kitchen, where she filled his dinner bowl. Afterward, she glanced around, pouting. When her eyes landed on the cordless phone, she picked it up, but then thought better of it. Maybe, since she'd been the one to leave his bed without waking him up, she needed to go to him.

Her smile returned as she glanced down at Cujo. "Looks like Mommy is about to take a little road trip."

Rushing back upstairs, she showered, oiled down and got dressed—in only a bright red coat and high-heeled pumps. "This oughta rock his world."

Woof!

Jalila laughed and then rushed out of the house. She felt wicked as she slid behind the wheel of her car and drove out to Beverly Hills. The whole time, she pictured his surprised face when he answered the door and she jerked open her coat. As she turned onto Keenan's vast estate, those familiar butterflies returned and fluttered wildly against her belly. She was so excited and nervous at the same time.

At the door, she collected herself, pasted on a smile and rang the bell. While waiting, Jalila quickly undid her belt and unbuttoned her coat. She wanted to be ready when he opened the door.

It took a few minutes, but she finally heard footsteps approach. She smiled in case he was taking a peek through the peephole. The locks disengaged and when the door swept open, Jalila yelled, "Surprise!"

However, it was Jalila that got the real surprise when the person at the door wasn't Keenan, but instead his ex-wife, Tenetria.

Chapter 21

An unmistakably evil smile slithered across Tenetria's lips. "I take it that you were expecting someone else?"

Jalila gaped, struggling to process the situation.

Tenetria's gaze slid down Jalila's body. "Those are nice. Are they real?"

Remembering that she was exposing her naked body, Jalila jerked her coat close, but she was still unable to find her tongue.

"I'm sorry, but Keenan is a little busy right now," Tenetria said. "Seems like he can only handle one woman at time. But I will tell him—*after* we're through—that you stopped by."

Jalila understood her meaning perfectly. She had just been played. She had blindly let Keenan use and humiliate her.

...if he's part of that crazy Hollywood crowd, I wouldn't trust him any further than you can physically throw him.

With a sob, Jalila turned and raced back to the car.

"Was it something I said?" Tenetria yelled.

As Jalila jumped behind the wheel, the woman's deep-throated laughter filled her ears. She started the car and slammed her foot down on the accelerator. Her tires squealed and a cloud of smoke jetted from her tailpipe as she took off down the long, curvy driveway.

Stupid. Stupid. Stupid. She banged her open hand against the steering wheel. How on earth had she allowed this to happen? She knew how the men in this town operated. She knew the rules of the heart-breaking game.

Jalila backhanded an overflowing river of tears, temporarily taking her hands off the wheel and swerving into a flower bed and then scraping against a line of sculpted hedges. She jerked the car back on the driveway and spun out on the main road, the back end of her SUV fishtailing for a few seconds. Finally, she sped off into the night.

Tears continued to pour and blur her vision. What was she thinking? Had she been thinking at all? In the time since she had first caught Keenan in his office with his ex-wife, Jalila had never once asked him about their relationship. She had never sought clarification about whether he was still playing the field or seeking to reconcile with his ex-wife. She hadn't done anything. Therefore, it was perfectly logical that Keenan had taken her silence as acceptance of his free-loving lifestyle.

This is what happens when you get caught up.

She shook her head. "Why does this always happen to me?" she moaned. "Why is it so hard to find a decent man in this *damn* town?" Not paying attention, Jalila sped past a police car. Blue lights flashed in her rearview mirror. "Oh, c'mon. Give me a break," she groaned, easing off the accelerator. Taking a deep breath, she pulled over. She wiped at her tears and reached over to the passenger side for her purse, but then realized that she didn't have it.

Jalila banged her head back against the headrest. "Just great."

Keenan had spent the evening wining and dining two of NBC's top executives at an exclusive club in downtown L.A. It was a good night. It looked like A.M. Production could possibly have three new shows in the winter lineup. They were all scripted—leaving them enough flexibility to get out of reality television. It had been an all-around good day—first the news from his sister and now this.

Keenan smiled and loosened up his tie. He was in such a great mood that he wanted to continue the celebration—and he knew just whom he wanted to celebrate with. The mere thought of spending time with Jalila caused his smile to widen and his dick to harden.

You need a woman in your life—and not just one to warm your bed.

Keenan swallowed as his sister's words came back at him. Now that he was alone, he allowed himself to really think about the direction his private life was taking. He would never admit this to Nitara or Keisha, but he had felt bouts of loneliness. It was no big deal. He was human. But since this…what—affair?—that loneliness had disappeared. In fact, every morning Jalila Goodwyn was the first thing on his mind. She danced in and out of his thoughts throughout the day and at night…

His smile widened. Now, thinking about it, he realized his feelings for Jalila, in the short time that he'd known her, were stronger than he'd felt for any woman. Was it possible that Tenetria had broken his pride and not his heart? Because right now, it felt as if his heart was soaring just thinking about Jalila. At that moment, he knew that there was a real chance that he was falling in love.

He laughed, probably looking like a crazy man.

When he arrived at Jalila's place, he was surprised to see that it looked locked down for the night. When he hopped out the car and rang the doorbell, Cujo went wild, barking and scrambling around.

Keenan waited. Rang the bell a few more times and then banged on the door. Was she asleep? He stepped back from the front door, glanced around and then up at the roof. "This is getting ridiculous," he muttered. Despite that, he climbed onto the roof and was thankful to find the bedroom window still unlocked.

Once Keenan was inside the house, Cujo leaped up and knocked him down onto the floor, where he proceeded to slobber all over him. "Down, boy. Down." Keenan chuckled. With a bit of a struggle he peeled himself from the floor. "I bet you missed Chips, huh?"

He scratched behind the dog's ear. Earlier, he'd stopped by and retrieved Chips when he knew Jalila and the TV crew were at her job.

He glanced around the room and then went through the house. "Where's your mom at, boy?"

Woof!

Keenan looked at his watch. It was well past midnight. Shouldn't she be home? Surely, she and whatever bachelor number she was on weren't still out on their date? Or were they?

Suspicion crawled up his neck while an unsettling anxiousness fluttered in his gut. He glanced down at Cujo, wishing he could interrogate the dog for some answers. Then he laughed at himself. Maybe they were just running late. He'd just wait around a little while longer.

An hour later, Keenan's tune had changed. He scooped his BlackBerry out of his pocket and started to call Nitara. After punching in her number, he thought about how his call would look to his business partner. Nitara would undoubtedly needle him about his interest in Jalila's whereabouts. He shoved his phone back into his pocket and stormed out the house.

Minutes later, he arrived at Mack Media. Jesse was off for the night, and Lamar seemed to welcome some company.

"I just came by to see how things are going," Keenan said. "Did you get the day's package for *Queen of Hearts?*"

"It was dropped off an hour ago. But I'm working

on some other dailies for Dreamworks. Got to get those in the can and ready for pick up by six."

Keenan's heart dropped, even though he nodded his understanding. "Mind if I use one of the stations to take a look?"

Lamar lifted a shoulder in a casual shrug. "It's your show, man."

Keenan sat in Jesse's usual workstation and, with a little help from Lamar, inserted the digital disc from camera number two. He tried to prepare himself mentally for seeing another man schmoozing and canoodling with his…what—his girlfriend? Lover? Woman?

Yes, your *woman,* Keenan's heart screamed. He pushed in the disc and watched. From the moment the footage started, Keenan experienced mild palpitations. Jalila's date, Evander, was a handsome and physically fit guy whom Keenan hated immediately. The way he smiled at Jalila was both primitive and sensual at the same time. What was worse, Jalila seemed to respond in kind.

Keenan leaned closer to the screen, convinced that he was witnessing some type of spark between the two and he didn't like it one bit. When Evander took off Jalila's sweater, Keenan's good humor returned. Evander and the cameraman zoomed in on the rash of hickies across Jalila's back.

When Keenan chuckled, Lamar glanced up. "What's so funny?"

"Aww, it's nothing." Keenan waved him off and then returned his attention to the screen. Jalila was adorable trying to lie her way through a reasonable explanation, but judging by Mr. Smooth's face, he wasn't buying it.

However, Keenan's amusement soon disappeared as the date continued. It was torturous watching Evander and Jalila laugh and talk over a glass of wine before a crackling fire. This Evander jerk was clearly a pro in subtle seduction. Keenan lost count of the times Jalila either blushed or laughed at the man's cheesy jokes. Her long winding moans at the dinner table shocked and then angered him. But that was nothing compared to the romantic cheek-to-cheek dancing to some incredibly slow jazz that followed.

Keenan stopped the footage and stared at the frozen image on the screen. His mind wasn't playing tricks on him. There *was* a spark of something between Evander and Jalila. It was undeniable.

His heart squeezed. It was time to end this. At this point, killing the show would cost him a fortune. Well, not only him, but Nitara and the network. But wasn't he undermining the show from the start?

"Are you all right, man?" Lamar asked, cutting into his thoughts.

Keenan blinked. "Uh, yeah." He ejected the digital disc and returned it to the production package. "You know what? I'm just going to head on out. I forgot I'm going to have an early morning myself. I'll catch up with you later." He and Lamar quickly exchanged fist bumps before he rushed out the door—heartbroken.

It was bad enough that Jalila didn't have her purse or her driver's license, but it was completely humiliating to be arrested for reckless driving—seventy in a thirty-five—zone and to have to try to explain to the female cop why she was naked under her coat.

She had never been arrested before, and her first trip into a holding cell wasn't too bad. Of course this *was* Beverly Hills—it was like being locked up in a nice hotel. Still, the officers were in no hurry to let her have her one phone call. It didn't matter because two hours later she still didn't know who she should call—her parents or one of her best friends. Any of them would come and get her. It was just the whole explaining the how and why of her arrest that complicated things.

Her parents would lecture, plus she didn't know whether she could get the whole naked thing past her mother.

Her friends would sympathize and might possibly throw her a pity party, which she needed, but there was no telling whether their money was funny or not so that they might not be able to bail her out. In the end, the decision was taken from her when Martina and Fantasia surprisingly just popped up and saved her from her nightmare.

"How did you guys know I was here?" she asked, after exchanging a brief hug with them.

Martina shrugged. "We got a call that said you were in trouble so we came."

Jalila frowned. "Who from?"

"Does it matter?" Fantasia said. "C'mon, let's get out of here."

Too tired to argue, Jalila climbed into the backseat of Martina's red convertible. During the ride back to her place, her girls tried to wheedle what had happened out of her, but Jalila was clearly so close to tears that they dropped the subject. Once they made it back to her place, Jalila raced up to her bedroom and quickly pulled on a pair of cotton pajamas and then crawled into bed. She just wanted to put this whole night behind her.

But she knew that she would have no such luck. When Jalila tried closing her eyes, Tenetria's evil smile stared back at her and her cackle filled her ears. It was time to give up and face facts, she told herself as fat tears dripped onto her pillow. There was no such thing as a Prince Charming for her—and she would never have her happily ever after.

Never.

Chapter 22

It wasn't too late, Keenan decided. What he'd witnessed tonight between Jalila and Evander wasn't necessarily the nail in the coffin of their relationship. Just because Jalila wasn't home didn't mean that she was off somewhere with Mr. I-Can-Cook. The best way to handle this whole situation was to pull the plug on the show. Of course that would mean pissing off a lot of people at the network, not to mention Nitara, but he could stand the heat if it meant that he would be able to keep the woman he loved.

Loved. He chuckled. It was the truth. He *did* love her. That information alone would—or should—get Nitara off his back. He just hoped that Jalila felt the same way.

Again, the image of her dancing in Evander's arms

flashed in his mind, but he quickly dismissed it. Jalila was just putting on a show for the cameras, he told himself—or rather, he tried to convince himself. With his mind set, Keenan drove home. Even as he put the key in the front-door lock, his mind ran through different scenarios on how he would deliver the news to Nitara, and—more important—how Jalila would take the news. Would she think that he was being presumptuous or would she be as thrilled as he hoped?

Memories of their previous night together soon flooded his mind. The way she'd felt, quaked, tasted and even the way she'd called out his name. He smiled with renewed confidence. *Yeah, she'll be thrilled.*

Woof! Woof! Chips shot toward him and then jumped up on his hind legs to plant his forepaws on the center of his chest.

"Hello, boy! Sorry I'm late." He rubbed Chips behind his ears.

Woof! Woof!

Keenan laughed. "How would you like to have a brother soon?" he asked good-naturedly.

Woof! Woof!

"It's nothing definite yet, but keep your paws crossed." He winked and then released an exhausted yawn as he headed up to bed. It was going to be a big day tomorrow, and if could hit the sack within the next twenty minutes, maybe he could squeeze out four solid hours of sleep. As he hit the top landing and started to peel out of his jacket, the faint scent of vanilla wafted under his nose.

He frowned. He hated the smell of vanilla. It was Tenetria's signature scent.

Still frowning, Keenan strolled cautiously down the long hallway. The scent grew stronger. When he reached his closed bedroom door, he stopped. Light was flicking beneath it. "Who's here, boy?" he asked Chips in a low voice.

Woof! Woof!

Whoever it was had to be familiar to Chips or the door would have been busted down and he would have come home to a crime scene. He turned the doorknob and slowly entered the room.

"Welcome home," Tenetria said, lying back in his huge bed. She wore a cotton-candy-colored bra-and-panties set that lifted and accentuated her every curve.

Keenan's jaw hardened. "What the hell are you doing here?"

Unperturbed, Tenetria kept her sensual smile in place. "Now is that anyway to greet a half-naked woman lying in your bed?"

"It's exactly the way to greet an unwelcome guest," Keenan said, tossing his jacket on a nearby chair. He leaned against the doorjamb. "Get dressed and then get out."

"Aww, come on," she said, purring like Eartha Kitt. "You don't really mean that."

"The hell I don't. Get dressed."

Tenetria's smile slipped. "Don't be rude."

Keenan flipped on the light switch, ruining her romantic mood. "You can either get dressed or I can throw you out dressed the way you are."

"You wouldn't dare."

He arched one brow. "You wanna bet?"

Tenetria's stony expression now matched his own. Finally reading the seriousness in his eyes, she bounced out of bed. "You're such an asshole. I don't even know why I bother."

He shrugged. "That makes two of us."

She glared.

"Since I didn't see a car out front, I take it I need to call you a cab?"

Tenetria snatched up a see-through robe. "You can't do that," she snapped. "I don't have anywhere to go."

"Oh. We're back to that again, are we?"

"Yes. We're back to that. My situation hasn't changed. You'd know that if you'd bothered to call me like you promised. I'm broke."

"Then call your family."

"I told you I can't go back to them with my tail tucked between my legs."

"You can, you just don't want to."

"*Fine!* I don't want to."

"And *I* don't want you here. So guess who's going to win that argument."

"Keenan, stop being an asshole and just help me out. I'll pay you back."

"It's not about the money," he growled. "You need to get it through your head that I'm not responsible for you. I'm not your safety net. You need to move on with your life. Lord knows that it's time for me to do the same thing."

"Oh. Let me guess. Just because you have a new toy, you feel free to kick me to the curb?" she accused. "Give me a break. What did you do, pick her up off

Hollywood Boulevard?" Tenetria shrugged. "Sure she has a good body and everything, but what kind of skank just shows up at a man's front door naked?"

Keenan frowned. "What the hell are you talking about?"

Suddenly, Tenetria's eyes gleamed and she tried to act casual. "Nothing." She marched over to the corner of the room where her bags were stacked neatly.

Keenan wasn't buying it. He knew Tenetria too well, and he knew that something was up. "That wasn't *nothing*." He marched over to her and took her by the arm. "What did you mean by that?"

"Please let go of my arm," she said, sounding almost bored. "You made it clear that you don't want me here so I'm leaving."

"Tenetria," he warned.

"What?" She arched her brows. "Are you going to beat it out of me or something?"

If only... He released her arm.

She smiled. "I didn't think so." Tenetria pulled out some clothes and started shimmying into a pair of tight jeans. "Of course if you wanted to *pay* me for some information then…"

"My God," he roared. "You never quit, do you?"

"Fine." She shrugged again. "It's no skin off my nose. I'm sure that you'll find out sooner or later."

He didn't like the sound of that. Keenan's mind scrambled. What on earth could she possibly know that was worth anything? When dealing with Tenetria, it could be anything…or nothing. He stared at her, wavering. Her smile was too cocky, he decided. "All right. How much?"

Her smile broadened. "Don't you know never to come to the negotiating table without a checkbook?"

"You're kidding, right?"

"Does it look like I'm kidding?"

Stomping back his irritation, Keenan warred with himself on whether to continue this game. "Fine." He turned and marched over to the dresser and removed his checkbook from his jacket. "Tell me what it is and I'll write you a check."

"Now I look stupid, is that it?"

"Is that a real question?"

"You write the check first and then I'll give you the information."

He glared.

She smiled.

"How much?"

"How about three hundred thousand?"

He laughed. "How about one thousand?"

"How about you kiss my ass?"

Keenan's eyes narrowed. "You better not be messing around with me."

"Now would *I* do that?"

Their hardened stares battled one another.

"Two hundred and fifty thousand," she amended.

"Ten thousand," he countered.

"I'm leaving," she said.

"All right. All right." He huffed. "One hundred thousand."

"Two."

"One-fifty. Take it or leave it."

She stared him down and then smiled. "Fine. A hundred and fifty thousand. You drive a hard bargain."

Keenan flipped open his checkbook and wrote out the check. When he tore it out and handed it over, Tenetria greedily snatched at it, but he held on to it. A small tug of war ensued, but she finally managed to take it from his fingers.

"Thank you very much." She smiled, folded the check and then stuffed it into her pink bra.

"Now tell me what was worth that kind of money," he said evenly.

Another shrug. "Well, I don't know if it's worth that much." She turned back to her bags and pulled out a blouse.

"Tenetria…"

"I'm getting to it. I'm getting to it."

Keenan folded his arms as he watched her take her time buttoning her blouse. "I'm waiting."

"All right. All right." She slid her feet into a pair of pumps. "It just that earlier tonight someone stopped by. I think I've seen her in your office before."

Keenan's heart stopped as his brain leaped to a conclusion. *No. No. No.*

"Some lady came by," she continued. "Well, I don't know if I should call her a *lady*. I mean you gotta be some kind of ho or chickenhead to pop up at someone's house butt-assed naked in just some heels…don't ya think?"

Keenan groaned. "Jalila."

"Oh, was that her name?" Tenetria smiled wickedly. "She ran away so fast that I didn't quite catch it."

With his worst nightmare confirmed, Keenan closed his eyes and fought back a murderous rage.

At exactly six o'clock the next morning, Nitara hit Martina up on her cell phone. "I'm sorry, but she's not going to continue the show," Martina announced.

"Oh, God, no," Nitara moaned. "No, no. No. Are you sure? Let me talk to her."

"We've tried, but right now, she doesn't want to talk to anybody. She just wanted me to tell you that she doesn't want to continue the show. Period."

Nitara felt sick just thinking about the amount of money at risk. They had sold the show off on spec and now they wouldn't be able to deliver. It would be the first time they'd ever failed to do so and it could severely damage their reputation. Of course this mess wasn't exactly *her* fault, but she felt responsible all the same.

"Did you tell her that I was the one that called you last night?"

"No. She didn't really harp on that, thank God. We hadn't come up with a good lie to explain how we knew that she was in jail. Then again, I'm still a little hazy on why you were following her around myself."

"Let's just say that I suspected that there was going to be a twist at the end of the show."

"Does this have anything to do with that asshole of a business partner of yours?"

"Did she tell you about their relationship?"

"I know bits and pieces," Martina admitted. "I just know this whole thing has turned into one big mess and I'm not happy about it. Jalila is my best friend and I don't like seeing her hurt—no matter how much I've warned her about it."

"Look, I had nothing to do with what was going on. In fact, Keenan hasn't told me anything. Let's just say that I sort of stumbled onto the story."

"So you figured it was okay for you to just go snooping around in her private life like some Peeping Tom?"

"Hey! Don't jump on me. Jalila signed up for a reality show, which by definition is giving the production company permission to snoop around in her private life. No one forced her to do this so why are you attacking me?"

"I don't know. My girl is hurt and I gotta take it out on somebody. Better yet, send that damn Keenan over here and let me really go off."

Nitara expelled a frustrated sigh. "Please. Just let me talk to Jalila."

"No. It's over. You two can go and find someone else's life to ruin." Martina slammed the phone down, ending the discussion.

Chapter 23

Keenan didn't sleep a wink. Instead, he sat up all night after his evil ex-wife left and just stared at the clock. He didn't bother trying to call Jalila's house. He knew that there was no way in hell that she would take his call. This was going to require him groveling in person. Right now he needed to figure out his best way to approach the situation. Unfortunately after five hours, he was still drawing a blank.

At one point his ego tried to tell him that it wasn't like he'd violated any vows. They had made no promises to each other. After all, she had caught him once before in a compromising position and she had let it go. So maybe this wasn't as big a deal as he feared. When he finished that line of bullshit, Keenan gave serious thought to just showing up at her place on bended knee and trying to explain how crazy his ex-wife was and that nothing was going to come between them.

But why would she believe that? *Because it's the truth.* He laughed. Hell, if he was her he wouldn't believe him. That's how seriously effed-up this whole thing was.

After considering all of his options thoroughly, he realized that there was only one thing to do: beg.

Chips lifted his head from Keenan's lap and shared a mournful gaze as if he was experiencing the same pain as his owner. He reached up and licked one side of Keenan's face.

"Thanks, but cut it out." Keenan went to the bathroom to wash his face. It was seven o'clock in the morning. Now was as good a time as any to drive over and plead his case.

The front doorbell rang, surprising him and then filling his heart with hope. He rushed to the door in record time. But once again, his hopes crashed onto the shore of reality when he jerked open the door only to see Nitara standing there.

"What are you doing here?"

"Well, good morning to you, too," she said, pushing her way into the house.

"Look, Nitara, this really isn't a good time."

"We have a problem," she said, interrupting him.

"I was just on my way out," he continued.

"Jalila is backing out of the show," she countered.

"What?"

"You heard me. Your up-and-coming superstar of

reality series television just pulled out of the show. She won't even take my phone calls."

Keenan's shoulders deflated. Even though he had had every intention of canceling the show on his own, this latest development told him that Jalila wasn't just dumping the show, she was dumping him. "I'd better get over there and talk to her," he said, rushing out of the door.

"What do you plan to say to her?" Nitara yelled after him.

"I don't know yet," he shouted back. But before he could open his car door, Nitara had caught up with him and pressed her hand against the door. "Where's Tenetria?"

"What?" He blinked.

"My sister. Surely you remember her? She was here last night, wasn't she?"

Keenan's face twisted in confusion. "Yes—but how did you know that?"

"It doesn't matter how I know. The better question is when were you planning on telling me that you've been sleeping around with the bachelorette of our show?"

Keenan drew a deep breath and rolled his eyes, then expelled it in a long sigh. "Believe it or not, I was going to tell you today." As she stared at him, he could see that she was warring with whether she should believe him or not. "Nitara, I know that this looks bad but—"

"*Looks* bad? What exactly were you planning to tell the network? You know how much money they've put into this? They'll have to scramble for a replacement at the last minute, and we may never get them to work with us again. This could ruin our reputation. Yours *and* mine. I mean, really, of all the women to have an affair with."

"It's not just an affair."

"No? Then what is it?"

Silence.

"Were you screwing her when you came up with this show?"

"No."

"So the affair happened, what—during? After the cameras left for the night? And since you made it clear to me the other day that you weren't interested in a relationship, that leaves me to conclude that you were undermining the show on purpose."

"No. No." He huffed. "It's a long story. It's complicated. Just—just let me go over there and talk to her."

"Again—and say what?" Disappointed, Nitara shook her head. "You know, we've been friends for a long time. And it just surprises the hell out of me that you would deliberately risk both our reputations for a cheap fling—a meaningless affair."

"It's not meaningless! *I love her.*"

Nitara jerked back at his bark, but then a soft smile curved her lips. "I thought so. Now we're getting somewhere."

Keenan frowned. "What do you mean 'you thought so'?"

Nitara smiled. "I just needed to hear you say it."

More confused than ever he cocked his head at her. "You knew? How?"

"Well, it's not every day I see you climbing out of a woman's windows wearing only a towel around your hips."

Keenan's brows stretched in surprise. "If you knew, then—"

"Then I've been waiting for you to come to your senses. Now get on over there and tell her what you just told me." She leaned forward and kissed his cheek. When she pulled back there were tears in her eyes. She loved this man who had once been her childhood crush and more than anything she wanted him to be happy— wanted him to be loved the way he deserved to be loved. She had known for some time that it would never be with her. "You better get going," she said. "Good luck."

"What about the show?" he asked, opening his car door.

Nitara drew a deep breath. "I expect you to absorb all the losses, of course," she said, shrugging. "What else?"

He nodded. "What else." Keenan slid behind the wheel and started the car. "Thanks, Nitara."

"For what?"

"For understanding…and for being the best friend a guy could have."

She winked. "Don't mention it."

He returned her wink and then sped off, hoping to win the queen.

Jalila had no plans to get out of bed, despite only sleeping in twenty-minute intervals. In the spirit of commiseration, Cujo had climbed onto the empty side of her bed and lay there watching her. Under normal circumstances, Jalila wouldn't have allowed him to be sprawled all over her good sheets, but this morning she took comfort wherever she could find it.

The bedroom door crept open and Jalila quickly slammed her eyes shut. She listened to the soft padding of Martina's and Fantasia's footsteps as they walked over to the bed where she and Cujo were curled up.

"Now I'm sure that this is against the law even in California."

"Just leave her alone, Martina." Fantasia sat on a small corner of the bed and then gently brushed Jalila's hair from her face. "Jalila, are you awake, honey?"

Jalila hesitated. She couldn't decide if she wanted her friends' sympathy or their silence.

"If you like," Fantasia said, as if knowing that she was awake, "I can go down and fix you a big breakfast. How'd you like that?"

"Forget that," Martina said. "If you want we can go over and cut that bastard's dick off."

"Martina!"

"What? He's got it coming."

Something about her friend's indignation made Jalila smile.

"Aww. See there? She is awake," Martina said.

"Jalila," Fantasia inquired.

Jalila finally rolled onto her back and cracked open her eyes. "As much as I think…you-know-who…deserves dismemberment, I don't think that it's worth any of us going to jail."

"You sure? You gotta get caught in order to go to jail."

Jalila chuckled. "I'm positive. I just want to put these past few weeks behind me."

Fantasia looked as though she wanted to cry for her friend. "You still haven't told us what happened. It might make you feel better."

Jalila doubted that, but as her two best friends waited with bated breath, she decided to come clean. Especially since she'd just told Fantasia the other day about how much she thought she was in love. Love. What the hell did she know about love? Other than that it was painful and elusive as hell?

Jalila pushed herself up and then leaned back against the headboard. For added comfort Fantasia took her hand and gave it an encouraging squeeze. Finally, Jalila gave her friends the 411 on what had transpired between her and Keenan during the hours after her reality show. Of course, Fantasia knew more of the story than Martina, but the women shared looks of indignation when she got to the part where she showed up at Keenan's place and ended up flashing his ex-wife in just heels and a smile.

"You had no clothes on underneath that coat last night?" Martina said, her eyes as big as saucers. "Wow. You really have turned into a bona fide freak."

"Martina!" Fantasia snapped.

"What? I'm just making an observation."

Fantasia rolled her eyes and returned to the discussion at hand. "You mean that he still lives with his ex-wife?"

"What kind of sick bullshit is that?" Martina asked.

"Who knows?" Jalila moaned. "My father was right. I shouldn't have trusted a Hollywood producer any further than I could throw him."

"There is that," Martina agreed.

Fantasia continued to look mournful.

"Well, I don't know which was worse, flashing his ex-wife or being frisked by a cop and trying to explain I'm not a flasher—well, not a professional one, anyway."

Ding-dong.

Cujo jumped at the sound of the doorbell.

Woof! Woof! He tried to scramble out of the bed but got caught up in the sheets and took a tumble over the side. He hit the floor with a hard thump, but sprang back onto his feet and took off running for the door.

Martina and Fantasia nearly leaped out of their skins. "Good Lord."

"Really! Can't you get a Chihuahua or something?" Martina complained. "That dog is entirely too big."

Ding-dong!

Woof! Woof!

"If it's the camera crew, tell them to go away!"

"It better not be them," Martina said, heading for the door. "I already told that Nitara chick that you weren't going to continue doing the show."

Ding-dong!

"Wait. I'll come with you," Fantasia said. "You stay in bed. After we get rid of whoever it is, I'll fix you something to eat. Would you like that?"

Jalila was all for a pampered pity party. "I don't know if I feel like eating."

"You gotta eat something."

Ding-dong!

Woof! Woof!

"We're coming. We're coming," Martina shouted.

When her girls left, Jalila inched back down into the bed and pulled the sheets over her head. Maybe if she was lucky she could get another twenty minutes of sleep.

Martina and Fantasia marched down to the front door, both prepared to do battle with the *Queen of Hearts* production crew if necessary. But when they snatched open the door they both blinked in surprise at seeing Keenan on the other side.

Cujo bounded out of the house, barking in an excited circle to see him.

"Hey, boy." He reached out and rubbed Cujo's sweet spot behind his ears. Keenan then returned his attention to Jalila's two wide-eyed, staring best friends. "Is Jalila here?"

"I like your nerve," Martina said, snapping out of her trance. "You gotta lot of balls coming around here."

Fantasia cut in. "Yes she is in. But she's not interested in seeing *you*."

Keenan's congenial smile dropped into a stony frown. "Excuse me?"

"You're excused," Martina said. "Now just turn your ass around and get ghost." She snatched the door from Fantasia's hand and sent it sailing.

With sharp reflexes, Keenan shoved his foot between the door and the frame and stopped it from slamming in his face.

Both women grabbed the door and tried to shove it closed, but Keenan had no problem pushing it back open with only one arm while they slipped and slid all over the hardwood floor. "If you two ladies don't mind, I'd like to speak with Jalila please."

"Cujo! Attack," Martina barked.

Cujo just cocked his head in confusion at the command.

"See?" she complained. "What's the point of having a dog this big if it don't do shit?" She stared at the dog and stomped her foot. "Cujo, I said attack! He hurt your momma, now *attack!*"

Apparently those were the magic words because suddenly the dog started a low growl in his throat. *Woof! Woof! Grrr!* His lips rolled up and revealed his long, pearly-white canine teeth.

Keenan blinked in surprise and then backed out of the house. "All right. All right." He reached for the door and slammed it closed. So much for being on the dog's good side.

"Now *that's* what I'm talking about," Martina praised and then held up her hand.

Fantasia smacked her a high five. "That most definitely deserves a doggy biscuit," she told Cujo and they all headed toward the kitchen.

Outside the door, a frustrated Keenan paced outside and then glanced up. He knew what he had to do.

Jalila hadn't dozed for more than a few minutes when something caught her ear. She peeled back the top sheet expecting to see Martina and Fantasia returning with a breakfast tray. Instead what she saw was Keenan climbing through her bedroom window.

"What the hell do you think you're doing?" she said, bolting upright in bed.

"At the moment, I'm risking my neck trying to see you." He stood up and shut the window.

"I gotta start locking that damn thing," she hissed.

Keenan rushed over to the bedroom door.

"Now what—"

"I don't want us to be disturbed and those damn Gestapo guards and aptly named dog you have downstairs would like nothing more than to have my hide if they see me up here."

"Good—because I don't want to talk to you, so you can just climb right back out of here."

"Shh. Shh." He locked the door.

"Get out!"

"Not until you hear me out."

"I don't want to hear anything you have to say."

"Will you please calm down and listen?"

"I'm going to call the cops if you don't get out of my house."

"Please, Jalila. You have to listen to me. I found out what happened last night and there's a huge misunderstanding." He rushed toward the bed.

She scrambled backward and jumped out the opposite side of the bed. "You get away from me. I'm not interested. Just get out of here and go back to your wife."

"I'm not married."

"Then your ex-wife!"

"There's nothing happening between me and Tenetria."

"Ri-i-ight. That's why every time I see her she's either spilling out of her clothes at your office or answering your door in Victoria's Secret." She shook her head. "I was sooo stupid. I didn't even ask you about your relationship with her after the last time. You had me so damn sex-crazy I couldn't think straight."

"Look, that's just Tenetria's way of starting trouble. She's manipulative and borderline crazy."

"I don't want to hear it."

"C'mon, Jalila. I wasn't even there last night. I had a meeting that lasted well past midnight and then I came here, but you weren't here."

"That's not what she said. She said that you two were *busy. Busy!* And that she would tell you I stopped by just as soon as you two were finished doing whatever it is you two do." Tears swelled in her eyes. "Get out."

"I'm telling you the truth, Jalila."

"Get! Out!"

Martina's voice drifted from outside the bedroom door. "Jalila, what's going on in there?" The doorknob rattled. "Why is the door locked? Jalila, what's going on? Is there someone in there with you?"

Keenan and Jalila ignored her friends trying to break into the bedroom. Instead, Jalila glared at Keenan while his gaze implored her.

"I mean it, Keenan. It's over. I don't ever want to see you again. Now please—leave."

"Jalila—"

"Martina," she shouted. "Call the police."

"I'm on it."

Keenan blinked in surprise. "All right. Have it your way," he said, finally giving up. "Goodbye." Instead of going back out the window, Keenan walked out of her bedroom door, with his head held high and his back straight.

Jalila watched with tear-brimming eyes and a broken heart.

Chapter 24

"He's in love?" Keisha said, astonished. "He actually said that?"

Nitara drew a deep breath and nodded. "The only problem is that Jalila doesn't want to have anything to do with him—or us—or the show."

Keisha lowered herself into the empty chair in front of Nitara's desk. She still couldn't believe it. "So that's why he's been so moody lately." She smiled. "It all makes perfect sense."

"Yeah, well, it doesn't do him any good if he can't be with the one he loves."

"Well, did he tell her that he loved her?"

Nitara shrugged. "I don't know. He refuses to talk about what happened when he went over there."

"When was this?"

"Three days ago. He hasn't been in the office since. I'm still stalling on what to tell the network."

Keisha frowned and chewed on her bottom lip. "We gotta fix this."

"We?" Nitara said. "How in the hell are *we* supposed to do that?"

Keisha mulled this situation over. "I know there has to be some way. Sounds to me like we've just got to convince Jalila that nothing is going on between Keenan and your evil sister."

"Hey," Nitara whined.

"What? It's true," Keisha said.

"I know, but—" Nitara shrugged. "She's still blood."

Keisha rolled her eyes. "So were Cain and Abel. What's your point?"

"All right. All right." The women fell silent.

"Well, I give up." Keisha tossed up her hands. "I don't know how to get them together. This is all just one big mess."

Just then, Dee Dee knocked and entered the office. "Ms. Murphy, I have ABC on line one. They're insisting they speak with either you or Keenan."

Nitara expelled a long frustrated sigh. "Tell them that we're both out at the moment."

"Yes, ma'am."

Nitara's gaze zoomed back to Keisha. "This whole thing could ruin us."

"You know if I wasn't already engaged I could have replaced her." Keisha beamed and then flashed Nitara her sparkling diamond.

"I heard about that. Congratulations! When's the big day?"

"We haven't decided yet. Probably in about six months. I know you're coming to my engagement party, right?"

"I wouldn't miss it for the world. I hope by then I've figured out something to prevent this company from going bankrupt."

"Is it that bad?"

"It's that bad. At this point, Jalila is the only one who can save Keenan both professionally and personally."

For three days Jalila stayed in bed, nursing her broken heart. However, her woe-is-me phase was stretching her friends' patience thin. Martina insisted with more frequency that it was time for her to pull herself out of bed, dust herself off and get back into the game. Those things were always easier said than done, and usually by people who had no idea what they were talking about.

Wanting to share this vast void with her YouTube subscribers, Jalila pulled out her camcorder. But when she hit Record all she could do was to stare into the camera lens and allow tears to roll down her face. No words. Just the naked reality of what a broken heart looked like.

This level of devastation for someone she hardly knew really didn't make that much sense. She knew that—she got that. Still, there was something more that bonded her to Keenan that defied logic. Their story wasn't a love-at-first-sight scenario. Heck, she'd been turned off when he'd approached her at Las Brisas.

Their story—her love for him—had started the night of that first kiss. That dance on the back porch while listening to the Fugees.

"Aaarrrggghhh!" Jalila buried her head under the pillows and tried to will herself into an animated state.

Cujo was tired of her just lying around. Wanting to get out and play, he'd brought everything from Frisbees to tennis balls to her room and dropped them by the bed, but Jalila had just rolled over and ignored him. Now he was nudging her with his cold nose and pulling the sheets off her.

"Will you cut it out?" Jalila snapped, snatching the covers back.

He whined as if she'd hurt his feelings, but Jalila had long known that Cujo had been a dramatic actor in a former life, so she didn't take the bait. When he raided her closet and dropped a pair of Nike running shoes on her head, she gave up.

"All right. All right. I'm getting up!" Jalila bolted out of bed. After she'd had a quick shower and thrown on some clean clothes, she grudgingly admitted that she did feel a *little* better. She still wasn't entirely ready to return to work, but she drove Cujo to a park and played with him for a while.

An hour of tossing a Frisbee around had a positive effect on Jalila's spirits. "Okay. So you were right about getting me out of the house," she said to Cujo, rewarding him with a few treats before heading back to her car. Feeling as though she was back among the living, she returned home and called her best friends to see if they were up for a late lunch at Las Brisas.

Once at their favorite table, Martina announced, "I said it once and I'll say it again. You can't keep your kitty-kat locked up too long. This whole thing could have been avoided if you were walking the cat on a regular basis. Now you're sprung, you think you're in love and we got to try to talk you off a ledge."

Fantasia dropped her fork. "You just open your mouth and any damn thing falls out. What the hell is with this kitty-kat stuff?"

Unfazed, Martina brushed her Barney purple-colored hair back from her shoulders. "Again. Don't get mad at me because I drop knowledge on the regular. Okay?" She returned her attention to Jalila. "What you're going through right now is just withdrawal. When…little sister—" She glanced at Fantasia and asked, "Is that p.c. enough for you?" Her purple head whipped back around. "Anyway. When *little sister* comes out of hiber-nation and then gets hook on some real potent *black steel* then you're like a crackhead looking for a hit. You're thrown off your game. You can't get your mind right. Classic symptoms of dick withdrawal."

"Martina!" Fantasia stomped her foot.

"What? Why are you always trying to shut me down? Let's face facts. Jalila and Keenan went on *one* date and the rest of the time they were screwing like jackrabbits. Now I ain't saying I blame you. Mr. Hol-lywood had it going on, but he straight played you—not once but twice. Do you listen to me? Nah, you gonna let the brotha creep back into your house—through the window. Now ain't that some mess? I still can't believe his ass did some Spiderman shit like that."

Jalila snickered as she nibbled on her Cobb salad. As she listened to her girl, it hurt her to admit that she brought up some very valid points.

"Let me ask you something," Martina said. "Do you still think you're in love with him?"

Defensive, Jalila folded her arms and struggled for an answer.

Frustrated, Fantasia waved a finger in Martina's face. "One of these days you're going to see how it feels. You're always just spouting all this nonsense."

"Who, me, get played?" Martina's purple hair bounced around her swiveling neck. "Naw, partna. It ain't happening. I make sure I stay two steps ahead of the catch-and-release game."

"What the hell is the catch-and-release game?" Fantasia and Martina asked in unison.

"You're kidding, right?"

Jalila and Fantasia glanced at each other.

"Very simple, ladies. Listen up." Martina waited until she had their full attention. "It's just what it says. You *catch* the dick and, when you're finished with it, you *release* the dick. If you want, you can write it down."

Jalila and Fantasia cracked up.

"I'm serious," Martina said. "Repeat after me, catch the dick…"

Jalila and Fantasia laughed and shook their heads.

"C'mon, class. Repeat after me," Martina insisted. "Catch the dick."

"Catch the…dick." They giggled.

"And release the dick," Martina finished with the flurry of an orchestra conductor.

When Jalila finished laughing, she wiped tears from her face and was genuinely happy that she had met her friends for lunch. "Okay. Since you're teaching us today, what do you propose I do?"

Martina picked up her wineglass and leaned back in her chair. "Do you *really* want to know?"

"You might want to think about this," Fantasia mumbled.

Jalila shrugged. "Sure. Why not? Lay it on me."

Martina's smile turned wicked. "All right. I think it's time for a little retribution."

Jalila frowned. "What do you mean?"

"I mean it's time that you learn how to fuck like a man. Dish out the same BS they do."

"What? She's supposed to go out and screw every man she sees—and that's supposed to prove something?"

"Not *every* man, but one in particular."

Jalila's and Martina's eyes locked.

Fantasia intervened. "No! No way. She just got rid of that jerk. Are you crazy?"

Martina shook her head. "No. What she did was let him get away with it. The only way you're going to get over this guy *quickly* is to take back the power you gave him. Once you do that then you can get on with your life."

"Don't listen to her," Fantasia said to Jalila. "You're doing good. You're out of bed and out and about. You'll go back to work soon and you can put this whole thing behind you."

Jalila ignored Fantasia while her gaze remained leveled with Martina's. "What would I have to do?"

Martina's smile returned as she gingerly sipped from her wineglass. "If I was you, I'd bust out that coat and high heels again. But remember—the whole point is to do this and then walk away. Keep your heart *out* of it."

Keenan was a wreck. He tried to deny it—to himself and then to everyone else, but they, like him, weren't buying it. Chips picked up his master's agitated state and started to stage his own form of retribution by giving him the cold shoulder. When Keenan came home, Chips refused to greet him with his usual vigor, electing instead to remain perched on his velveteen dog pillow in the dining room and ignoring him.

After three days, Keenan finally noticed that when he set Chips's dinner out, he didn't jump up and attack the bowl as was his habit. Figuring that he needed to entice the dog, Keenan retrieved some of his favorite treats from the cabinets and tried to coax him to the bowl.

Chips just hung his head low and covered his eyes with his front paws.

"What's the matter, boy? Are you sick?" Keenan asked with genuine concern. The last thing Keenan felt like doing was dragging his two-hundred-pound dog to the vet.

Ding-dong!

Keenan groaned and stood up from Chips's doggy bed. "All right. If you don't eat, I'll have to take you to the doctor and you know how much you hate needles and getting things shoved up your butt."

Chips whined.

Ding-dong!

"I'm coming. I'm coming." Keenan rushed to the front door only to have his day go from bad to worse.

Tenetria stood on the other side glaring at him. "You think your ass is slick, don't you?"

Keenan folded his arms and leaned against the door frame. "I take it that you're having a little problem with your check?"

"You stopped payment. I could sue you," she hissed. "It's against the law to write bad checks."

"And I could have you arrested for breaking and entering and then blackmailing me."

"I didn't blackmail you. I sold information. *Big* difference."

"Goodbye, Tenetria." Keenan stepped back and started to close the door.

Tenetria thrust out her hand in an attempt to block it from slamming in her face. "Keenan—"

"Tenetria," Keenan growled, his temper at long last exploding. "You have no idea how hard it is for me not to just snap you in half. It's not good enough that you had to ruin my life once, but you had to drop in five years later to do it again."

Tenetria jabbed her hands on her hips. "And people say that *I'm* always overly dramatic."

Keenan took a threatening step forward. "You have no idea what you've done to me—what you've cost me. And I'm not talking about money—though that's all you operate on."

Tenetria's gaze narrowed suspiciously. "What—is your little girlfriend mad at you? Is that what you're so upset about?"

"Why?" He tossed his hands. "Why do you hate me so much? What have I ever done to you to deserve this? Did I mistreat you or abuse you? What happened to that nice girl I dated back in college? Where did she go?"

Slowly, Tenetria's hardened face softened.

"Money changed you," he accused. "I gave you half of everything and it was never enough. We had to live in a certain area. We had to live in a certain house. You had to have this and you had to have that. And I made sure you got it. So what did you do?"

"Keenan—"

"What did you do?" he roared.

Tenetria jumped. This was the first time that they'd ever addressed her infidelity. When it had happened, Keenan had just turned away and given her everything in the divorce. What surprised her was that this was the first real show of emotion from him in years, and apparently it had a lot to do with that Jalila chick. Jealousy kicked her hard in the gut. "I'll tell you what *you* did," she said evenly. "You stopped loving me— so I started filling my life with things—cars, furs—"

"Drugs and men?" he finished for her. "That's a cop-out and you know it."

Tears sprang into Tenetria's eyes. "All right. So I made a mistake."

He sucked his teeth and rolled his eyes.

"I made several mistakes," she amended. "But that was a long time ago. I didn't appreciate what I had."

"Is this where you tell me how much you've changed again?"

"I have," she whined.

"You tried to fleece me of one hundred and fifty grand and then chased away the woman I love!" Keenan closed his eyes and shook his head. "For the first time in a long while I started to *feel* again. I found someone who was independent, smart, funny and valued me as a man. She wasn't some spoiled, petty and conniving woman who refused to think about anyone but herself and who refused to grow up."

Tears skipped down Tenetria's face. "But…I—" She sniffed. "What if I told you that I still love you?"

He shook his head. "If that's true…then you'd let me go."

Chapter 25

The next day, Jalila was a nervous wreck. The easiest thing to do was to back out of this and chalk it up as just one of Martina's wild ideas. But there was something to what Martina had said about taking back her power, proving to Keenan and to herself that she could celebrate her sexuality without engaging her heart.

For the second time in a week, Jalila left her house wearing baby oil and high heels underneath her bright red dress coat. However, this time she wasn't going to risk popping up at his house unannounced. Lord knew she wasn't bold enough to risk repeating that nightmare. The only other option was to chance catching him at his office. It was risky, since he shared an office with Nitara. But if she was there, she'd ask to speak with him in the conference room.

But what if he's not in or not expected in? She shook that scenario out of her head since she was making this thing up as she went along. It was close to five o'clock when she arrived at A.M. Production and found a clearly startled Dee Dee at the front desk.

"Ms. Goodwyn!" Dee Dee jumped up from her chair and beamed a smile at her. "Oh, thank God."

Jalila arched a lone brow up at her.

"I mean, uhm… Welcome back," Dee Dee amended, and then asked shakily. "Please say you're coming back to finish the show."

Actually, Jalila hadn't given the show a second thought. "Is Mr. Armstrong in?" she asked, electing not to answer the question.

"Actually, no."

Jalila's heart dropped.

"But he should be here in a few. He had a meeting with an agent and he usually works late on Tuesday nights. Ms. Murphy is gone for the evening."

Jalila perked up. "Great. Can I wait for him in his office?"

Dee Dee hesitated and glanced at her watch. "Uhm, well, I usually head out at five o'clock and I don't think I should just leave—"

"I do want to discuss the possibility of returning to the show, so I'm sure that he wouldn't mind my waiting in his office."

Dee Dee sighed in relief. "You have no idea how much you'd be saving our butts if you do." Then she realized what she said and tried to clean it up. "I mean, Mr. Armstrong and Ms. Murphy will be thrilled to have you back."

"So I can just go ahead and wait for him then?" Jalila asked, walking toward the office.

"Well, uhm—"

"Thanks. You're a sweetheart." Jalila continued her stroll toward the producer's private office. Once inside, she shut the door and placed a hand over her pounding heart. *You can do this. You can do this.*

Outside the office, Dee Dee picked up the phone and dialed. "Hello, Nitara? You'll never guess who's here."

Keenan debated whether to return to the office or cut his losses and just go home and let Chips continue to give him the cold shoulder. Tomorrow was a big day. He'd told Nitara that he would personally go down to the ABC studios and tell them that his company would be unable to deliver the thirteen episodes of *Queen of Hearts*. No doubt that news would jeopardize the three shows they were hoping to land for the fall and winter schedules, not to mention how the breach of contract could potentially drain his bank account.

In the end, Keenan decided to head back to the office. It was better to wheel and deal than to go home and mope with a dog who acted like he was disappointed in him. As he pulled into his office's parking lot, the Fugees's "Killing Me Softly" started to play over the radio.

Keenan parked the car and closed his eyes. Instantly, he was transported back to that the night....

"C'mon. Let's dance. Who knows, maybe after tonight you'll think of *me* whenever you hear this song."

When she stood, he draped one arm around her waist, creating a sphere around them as the world had drifted away. An undeniable heat simmered between them. Their bodies brushed against each other while they rocked.

"I bet you're dangerous on the dance floor," he mused with a crooked grin.

"I manage to stay on two feet." Just as the words left her mouth, Jalila stepped on Keenan's foot. "Oops. Make that three feet."

He laughed, his body quaking and rubbing against her. "I've been trying to figure it out," he said.

"What's that?"

"How a woman as beautiful, smart and kind as you are could have any trouble in the man department."

"It's not about *getting* a man—it's about finding the *right* one."

They stopped dancing, but didn't move away from each other. In fact, he moved closer. She closed her eyes and lifted her chin.

Her lips were soft, her mouth sweet. She stretched her arms up his chest and pressed closer. Keenan's hands left the small of her back only so they could roam freely through her thick hair. He felt her tremble.

What are you doing? the voice in the back of Keenan's mind had asked. He ignored his conscience by squeezing his eyes tight and deepening the kiss. He didn't want logic or reason to penetrate and ruin this moment. His hands left her curtain of thick hair to roam between their bodies and settle on her soft lush breasts.

He swallowed her sigh as her body sagged against him. Instinctively, he swept her up into his arms and carried her inside the house.

Jalila broke the kiss and glanced around. "Where are you taking me?"

"To your bedroom," he answered simply. "Any objections?"

Their gazes locked and Jalila's entire body ignited. "No," she whispered.

"Good."

Keenan opened his eyes, not wanting to go any further with the memory. It was just too painful. He turned off the radio and climbed out of the car.

As he walked into the office, Dee Dee hung up the phone and gasped. "Keenan, thank God you're here."

"Is there a problem?" he asked, noting her flustered face.

"Ms. Goodwyn is here," she said, lowering her voice.

Keenan froze, his heart squeezed.

"She asked to speak with you." She glanced at her watch. "I didn't want to leave her here alone, but I have to go pick my daughter up from day care. I called Nitara—"

"It's all right." He croaked and then coughed to clear his throat. "Uhm…you can go now. I'll go talk to her."

"This is good news, right? If she comes back and finishes the show?"

"Uhm…yeah." He didn't have the heart to tell Dee Dee that Jalila's return was as likely as a snowball in hell.

Dee Dee grabbed her jacket and purse and headed to the door. "Good luck," she said, holding up her crossed fingers.

I've got a feeling I'm going to need all the luck I can get. Once Dee Dee was gone, Keenan turned toward his closed office door and drew a deep breath. As he walked, his heartbeat sped up and his mouth dried out. *What will she say? What should I say?*

The short walk to his office felt as long as a country mile, but the moment he pushed open the door, the scent of Chanel No. 5 greeted him. A second later his eyes landed on her standing by the window in a bright red coat. She turned toward him and unbelievably a smile touched her lips. Maybe this wasn't going to be so bad after all.

"Jalila," he whispered—almost as though if he spoke too loudly it would scare her off.

"Hello, Keenan."

He liked the way her voice hugged his name. His gaze skimmed over her, drinking her in. "I've missed you."

"And I've missed you." She slowly untied her belt. "I was afraid that you weren't working today." She started unbuttoning her coat.

"Look, I know you were upset the last time, and—" He closed the door.

"Lock it," she said.

His brow arched in curiosity and he wondered if he'd heard her correctly. "I'm sorry."

She undid the second button. "I said, lock it."

Keenan's hand flew backward and fumbled with the lock.

Jalila's smile widened. "Good boy."

Silent, Keenan's eyes tracked the procession of her hands—one button at a time.

"I think you were saying something?" she prodded.

"Uhm, yeah, I, uhm…" He licked his lips as anticipation of what awaited him made the blood rush from one head to the other.

Suddenly, that last button sliding through its hole was the most erotic thing he'd ever witnessed in his life.

"What's that matter?" Jalila teased. "Cat got your tongue?" She peeled open the coat and revealed her beautiful, naked, honey-brown body.

Ever so slowly, Keenan's gaze dragged over every inch of her. His heart sped up so fast that he couldn't tell whether he was just extremely excited or truly on the verge of a heart attack. By the time his eyes reached her firm calves and sexy high-heeled shoes, he was convinced that his hard cock was about to do an Incredible Hulk and burst out of his pants.

Her eyes lowered to his erection and she flicked her pretty pink tongue over her candy-apple-red lips.

Keenan groaned, believing he was either going to drop from the palpitations of his heart or the painful throb in his cock.

Jalila's coat hit the floor as she sauntered toward him. "You know, a woman might think you don't like what you see when you don't compliment her on her outfit." She stopped before him and boldly cupped his erection. "Don't you think I look nice?"

He nodded, licked his lips and then added dehydration to his list of medical concerns.

Her smile slid wider as she stared into his eyes. "Boy, you just don't know what I'm about to do to you."

She's up to something.

"Jalila, about the other night—"

"Shh." She leaned forward, her firm breasts pressing into his chest. "I don't want to talk about that right now. "Right now I want to know whether Little Kenny can come out and play."

Little Kenny?

She squeezed his dick through his pants. "Or maybe I should call him *Big* Kenny?"

Now that's more like it.

She gave him another hard squeeze. "Take off your clothes."

Hell. She didn't have to ask twice. Keenan pulled his shirt open so fast and so hard that the buttons on his shirt were shooting across the room like bullets. He jerked down his pants and boxers at the same time, and then cursed when he had difficulty getting them off over his shoes. Despite that, he was still naked in record time, with his cock saluting its commander-in-chief.

"There's my friend." Jalila slowly and very dramatically bent over, her ass lifting high as she puckered her lips and placed a feathery kiss against the head of his straining cock.

"Ahh," he groaned and then reached for her.

Jalila stepped back, evading his hands. "Maybe we should talk first," she said, slinking away toward his desk.

"What?" *Did she say that she wanted to talk first? Please, God, don't say she wants to talk now!*

She sat down on the front of his desk. "I mean, you looked like you had a lot on your mind when you came in here. So maybe we should talk?"

"N-no. No." He licked his lips. "I—I was just so surprised to see you."

"Oh?" She leaned back, parting her legs in opposite directions. "Was it a good surprise or a bad surprise?" She walked her fingers through the soft, springy curls of her pussy and spread herself open.

Licking his lips had now become like a nervous tick. He couldn't stop himself.

"Keenan?"

"Hmm? What?"

Jalila cocked her head. "You seem distracted." She slid one finger deep into her wetness, stirred it around. "Mmm. I can't tell you how good this feels. I mean, after a long day, a woman needs to relax, you know?"

He bobbed his head. His eager eyes told her that he was ready to jump into the game at any time. Her sweet juices started smacking around her hand. But his eyes feasted on the sight of her honey polishing her clit. That damn nervous tick increased in frequency.

"Is there something you want to ask me?" she said.

Keenan stepped forward.

"Uh-uh." She shook her head. "You gotta tell me what you want first."

Keenan didn't know what he wanted to do first. So

many images raced through his mind that he was damn near stupefied.

"Oooh," she moaned, signaling that she had hit a good spot. "Awww." Her head fell back as she now moved her hips in a hypnotic rhythm. "Oooh, baby. I think I'm coming."

Keenan gripped his dick and started stroking as he watched her. *Damn, she's so beautiful.* "Come on, baby. Come on," he mumbled under his breath.

And come she did. Her mouth sagged open, her chest heaved and her breasts jiggled in the air. When her body calmed after the aftershock, her long lashes lifted and her gaze locked on his. "You look hungry."

Maybe it was a coincidence, but he was suddenly hit with a hard hunger pang.

"Are you hungry, baby?" she asked.

"Starving."

"I got some juicy fruit for you. Want some?"

"Hell, yeah."

She smiled. "Then come on over. I have all you can eat."

Keenan finally moved forward and knelt down. He looked up at her. Their eyes locked as his tongue slid into her, long and deep.

Air rushed out of Jalila's lungs, her hips jumped up. How had she forgotten how good he was at this? She tried not to come unglued as his tongue slipped and slid, dipped and glided. There was no slow building toward her second orgasm. It just hit her like a freight train. She screamed out, but still he continued to lap her up. It was too much, too intense. She tried to shove him away, her clit now hypersensitive, but he didn't move—wouldn't move.

Orgasms number three and four had her inching up the desk, knocking over paper, in-boxes and God knew whatever else. *Don't let him take over. Get it together, girl.*

That was easier said than done. Mercifully, Keenan stood up and looked for his pants. Jalila took the time to regroup. By the time he returned to the desk, condom on, she had stood up and walked away. "Now why do I get the impression that you want to fuck me?"

"Maybe because I'm naked and have a condom on," he smirked.

She smiled. "But what if I don't think you deserve it?"

His brows inched up. "What kind of game are you playing?"

"You don't like games?"

"I just like to know what the game is."

"All right," she said, walking around the desk, deliberately adding extra *oomph!* to her switching hips. "How about we play Jalila, May I?"

He frowned, his hand still leisurely stroking himself.

"Jalila, May I? is sort of like Momma, May I? You have to do whatever I say after you ask, 'Jalila, May I?'"

Keenan laughed. "All right. Let's play."

She winked. "Sit in this chair."

He started to move, but caught himself. "Jalila, may I?"

Her smile exploded. "Yes, you may."

It was a relatively short game, since they were both hot and bothered. To Keenan, this whole thing felt like a dream. He had his woman back and she seemed more than willing to let bygones be bygones. In his head he was planning how they could have a whole new beginning, starting with a real courtship: taking her to fine restaurants, hanging out at the park with their dogs or even just serving her breakfast in bed. He wanted to do anything and everything for her.

Most of all, he just wanted to love her.

Sitting in his leather office chair, Keenan watched as Jalila straddled the chair and then slowly lowered herself onto his painfully hard erection. He was grinding his back teeth to damn near powder at the snug, tight fit.

"Fuck me, Keenan," she whispered.

"Jalila, may I?"

"Yes, you may."

It was on. Keenan locked an arm around her waist while his hips turned into a supercharged power drill. Jalila couldn't catch her breath. When the chair sounded as though it was seconds from breaking, Keenan stood up and Jalila locked her legs around his hips. She held on for dear life, their bodies slapping hard.

Curling the top half of his body, Keenan sucked in one of her fat nipples and went to town. The next thing she knew they were on the desk, against the wall, on the floor. Neither one of them could get enough.

When Jalila neared exhaustion and was on what she knew would be her last orgasm, she bit her lower lip and purred as she came. Smiling, she collapsed against

Keenan's sweaty chest and waited for the room to stop spinning.

"Just think," he said. "It could always be like this."

A tidal wave of emotion flooded Jalila as she closed her eyes. Still a lone tear managed to escape and rolled down her face. She pushed up off the floor on wobbly legs and then looked for her coat.

Keenan frowned. "What are you doing?"

She picked up her coat.

"Where are you going?" he asked.

"I gotta get home. Feed the dog." She started buttoning her coat. "But hey, thanks. I really needed that." Jalila tied her belt.

"Wait a minute. Hold up." Keenan jumped to his feet and started to follow her to the door. "What the hell was this about?"

She frowned. "What do you mean?"

"Wh-what do you think I mean? You just came over here to fuck me and leave?"

Jalila folded her arms. "Well, yeah," she said, as though the answer was obvious. "Isn't that what we do?" She glanced at her watch. "I'd better go. Thanks again." She blew an air kiss at him and then rushed out.

When she slammed the door, Keenan just stood there, dumbfounded.

Jalila stood on the other side of the door, wondering if she'd truly seen hurt flicker across Keenan's face a second ago or whether it was wishful thinking. She waited a couple of seconds, wanting him to come after her. He would if he cared, right? But when the door remained closed, Jalila put one foot in front of the other and marched out of the main office.

She'd just slipped her key into the door of her SUV when Nitara whipped into the parking lot and drove over to her.

"Jalila, hey," Nitara called. "I'm so glad I caught up with you. I was in a meeting when Dee Dee called and told me you were here. I rushed over as soon as I could." She glanced around the lot. "Is she still here?"

Jalila hoped not—especially after all the racket she and Keenan had kept up. She opened her door and hopped in.

"Oh, Keenan's car is here." Nitara looked at her, her gaze suspicious. "Did you talk to Keenan?"

"I gotta go," Jalila said.

"So, about the show," Nitara said, ignoring the fact that Jalila was hell-bent on leaving. "I'm sure I don't have to tell you that you left us in a pretty tight pinch when you left the show."

Jalila slid the key into the ignition, but stopped short of starting the car.

"You know, we can script the ending if you no longer want to really date any of the guys. It's just that we've already put in so much money and time. I don't want to be crude but you *did* sign a contract."

The wheels in Jalila's head started spinning.

"It would really help us out if—"

"Actually," Jalila said, folding her arms, "If you still want me, I'll be more than happy to finish the show."

Nitara's mouth dropped open. "You would?"

"Why not?" Jalila shrugged. "I'm still single."

Chapter 26

For the next two weeks, Jalila resumed her role as the bachelorette of the reality television series *Queen of Hearts*. Martina and Fantasia thought that this was a sign that her high-heels-and-dress-coat routine had worked—she had reclaimed her independence and sexual power.

Jalila knew otherwise. As much she wanted to claim that she'd successfully kept her heart and emotions separate from the physical, it simply wasn't true. Sex with Keenan wasn't *just* sex. Somehow Keenan got into her blood, tangoed with her soul. Instinctively they knew each other's moves, rhythms, what buttons to push and what buttons not to push.

To top it off, they were so much alike—independent and entrepreneurial. They loved sunsets, scary movies,

Great Danes and even salsa dancing. She loved how he took charge in the bedroom but was comfortable enough in his masculinity to let her take the reins once in a while. Sure, they hadn't known each other long, but it felt like a lifetime.

And yet, they weren't meant to be.

Right now she had to choose between Dontrell, Tion and Evander. They were all nice guys. Any one of them had the potential to be a really good friend, boyfriend or even husband. As the show neared the final taping, with all three suitors scripted to present her with a ring, Jalila could honestly say that she didn't have any idea which man's proposal she would accept.

"I say you should take Tion," Fantasia suggested during a taped luncheon at Las Brisas. "He's smart and engaging. Plus, you never know, he might turn out to be the next Barack Obama."

"You think all black politicians nowadays are the next Obama," Martina said, sporting, unbelievably, her natural black hair color.

"I do not." Fantasia kicked her under the table.

"Ouch." Martina twisted her face. "Keep those hooves on your side of the table." She turned her attention back to Jalila. "I think you should go for Dontrell. He's got all those muscles bulging everywhere. Makes me wonder if he knows how to work the one muscle that really counts."

"Martina," Jalila snapped.

"What?"

"This isn't a cable show."

The cameraman chuckled.

Martina tossed the man a wink and then made a gesture with her hands indicating that he should give her a call.

Fantasia and Jalila just rolled their eyes at Martina's antics.

"Who are you feeling?" Fantasia asked Jalila.

Keenan. "Oh, I don't know. I think they're all really sweet guys."

"Sweet?" Martina swirled her wineglass. "What kind of answer is that? Either you're feeling these brothas or not. Hell, who knows? Maybe you'll have to do a season two."

Jalila and some of the TV crew groaned at that possibility.

"Aaaaaannnnd cut!" Wolfe yelled and then stepped from behind camera number one. "Can the crew keep it quiet?"

Everyone glanced around, feeling thoroughly reprimanded.

Much later, Jalila took Evander to her parents' place. This really wasn't a big deal since all the bachelors had gotten the chance to meet her mom and dad. Her father had walked around the house, puffing out his chest and drilling the men on everything from credit scores to criminal records. Dontrell had come clean that he'd gotten picked up for shoplifting when he was ten.

Of course, they, too, had an opinion about whom she should chose. Her father was pulling for Dontrell, her mother for Evander. Jalila silently wished her parents could've met one other bachelor.

Sidebar, camera one:

James swings an arm around Bettye. "We thought that all three gentlemen had something to offer. Of course, the decision really isn't up to us. We're going to support Jalila no matter who she chooses."

Bettye nods her head. "I still think this is a strange way to go about finding a potential mate, but who can keep up with what's hip nowadays?"

James frowns. "Do they still say *hip?*"

Bettye strokes her chin. "I think they do."

Sidebar, camera two:

A laughing Jalila rolls her eyes. "My parents are so cute. I know that they just want what's best for me." She lowers her gaze and seems lost in a memory. "I gotta tell you, this is a hard decision. I've learned a lot since being on this show. I've met some wonderful men. But you know, I think I've made my decision." She nods. "Everyone will have to tune into the finale."

Keenan felt as though he was sleepwalking through his sister's engagement party. Their parents had turned their house on wheels around and made it back in time to shower their only daughter with love and gifts. Keenan had opened up his home for the party. By his calculation his sister must have invited everyone in the Los Angeles and Beverly Hills area, but seeing his sister so happy and beaming on Jaheim's arm made handing over his platinum card worth it.

Yet, as the night wore on, he began feeling envious of his sister's happiness. Suddenly the idea of starting a whole new chapter in life with someone you loved seemed overwhelmingly beautiful and ideal.

He walked out of the house through the back door and was instantly accompanied by Chips. At least for now the dog had stopped giving him the cold shoulder. He walked around the grounds thinking about the direction he was going in his life. He thought about all the goals that he'd been working toward for so long and that had seemed perfectly fine a month ago. Now they all seemed empty—meaningless.

Success means nothing without someone you love to share it with. Now where had he heard that?

As Keenan walked, faint music from the party reached him, and his mind drifted to the last time he'd seen Jalila. The memory of her waltzing out of his office and thanking him so casually for serving her still stunned him. Yet it held up a mirror to all those one-night stands he'd had between his divorce and meeting Jalila. Essentially, hadn't he done the same thing?

Wasn't that her point?

Then, to top things off, she'd decided to continue with *Queen of Hearts*—effectively giving him the middle finger. Her decision did save A.M. Production, and he and Nitara were now on target for the three shows he had pitched to the network. Quite frankly, however, he would rather have taken the hit if it meant that he could win Jalila's heart.

"There you are."

Keenan looked up from his reverie and smiled when he saw his sister approaching. "Hey, you." He swung his arm around her shoulder. "What are you doing out here? The party is for you, remember?"

"I was looking for you." She leaned into his chest. "You disappeared on me."

He shrugged. "I just stepped out for a moment for some fresh air. I wasn't trying to escape, I promise."

"You don't have to escape—you don't even seem like you're really here."

Keenan's gaze fell to his feet as they walked. "Think you know me so well, do you?"

"Absolutely," she said confidently. "But I gotta tell you, I'm disappointed that you didn't tell me about you…and Jalila."

They walked a few feet before he said, "Who told you?"

"Nitara. She said that you told her that you loved her."

He gave her a sad laugh. "Well, that and a nickel will get me right where I am. Nowhere."

"Did you tell Jalila?"

"She's not interested in anything I have to say."

"How do you know?" she probed.

"Well, that part I'm not willing to share with my little sister." He tried to laugh again, but it just didn't sound right.

Keisha stopped walking. "Do you or do you not love this woman?"

"I do, but—"

"There is no *but*," she said. "You know, all my life I've looked up to you. You're smart, you're a go-getter." Keisha glanced around. "And you seem to do okay for yourself."

"If you're trying to stroke my ego it's working."

She smiled. "I just don't get why *now* you won't go after what you want."

"You're not listening," he said, shaking his head. "Jalila hates me."

"How do you know?"

"Trust me. I know."

Keisha was silent for a moment. "Women are complicated."

"Now *that* I've figured out all on my own."

"It's great to *know* that you're loved. It's great to *feel* that you're loved." She stared up into her brother's eyes. "But one thing we all need and crave is to *hear* that we're loved. The words mean so much." Tears shimmered in her eyes. "We act out when we think we're not valued. Some of us slash tires or break headlights to hear the words, and some of us give you a taste of your own medicine to make a point."

Suddenly it dawned in Keenan's eyes.

"If you love Jalila and you want any real chance with her, then you need to *tell* her."

Chapter 27

The Finale

The *Queen of Hearts* finale was being taped at the beautiful Hotel Oceana in Santa Barbara. The hotel, Jalila was told, had been selected for its lush romantic setting right off Butterfly Beach. The network was pulling out all the stops to make sure this was a memorable minivacation for Jalila, Martina and Fantasia.

Once Martina found out that everything was comped, she started packing up hotel robes, towel, shampoos—everything that wasn't nailed down. "What? It's free, ain't it?"

Jalila couldn't help but laugh while Fantasia pretended to be embarrassed.

"So, you're not going to give us even a little hint as

to who you're going to choose today?" Fantasia asked, giddy and excited.

"If I do, it'll ruin the surprise," Jalila said, lying under the sun in a cloud-white bikini while a three-man camera crew moved around them. "Besides, you know Martina can't hold water."

"Oh, that's cold," Martina said and returned to chugging down a super-size piña colada with a huge chunk of pineapple hanging on the side of the glass. "True. But cold."

Sidebar:

"Well, I guess I'm a little nervous," Dontrell says, chuckling. In the background is an incredible view of Butterfly Beach with its white sand and deep-blue water. "But I feel like we've made a connection. We've gotten extremely close over the past couple of weeks. I think she's feeling me."

Jalila returned to her hotel room to see that the hair-and-makeup team had arrived to work their magic. It was getting close to that time and Jalila was actually starting to get nervous.

"All I have to say is, whoever you pick, when you get married and have babies, I want to be the god-mother," Martina crowed.

Fantasia jabbed a hand onto her hip. "Well, I like your nerve."

Unfazed, Martina laughed. "Well, like the good preacher said, you gotta speak it and claim it."

Jalila choked on her appletini. "Since when did you start going to church?"

"Please, all the hell I raise six days a week, I gotta check in with the Lord and get a sprinkle of some of that holy water."

"I don't believe what I'm hearing," Fantasia deadpanned.

"Well, believe it. I'm covering all bets."

There was a knock at their door and Nitara stuck her head into the room. "Ladies? How's it going in here?"

"Fiiiinnnnneeee," they chorused back and then watched as the coproducer entered the room.

"I just wanted to tell you that everything is all set. We're going to beginning taping the ceremony at precisely six o'clock." She flashed a smile at Jalila sitting in the makeup chair. "Are you nervous?"

Jalila smiled. "A little."

"Well, don't be. Everything is going to be great. *You're* going to be great."

Jalila appreciated the encouragement but sipped down some more liquid courage nonetheless.

"Ladies," Nitara addressed Fantasia and Martina. "I need you two to come down with me to tape your predictions as to who Jalila will select and give your reasons why she should pick your choice."

"Humph! I know she better pick Mr. Muscle Man," Martina said. She was probably just a bit tipsy. "My girl needs a man who can give her a good workout on the regular." She released a loud cackle and held up one hand for a high five.

Fantasia and Jalila left her hanging.

"Oh, y'all gonna play me?"

"Looks like you're doing a pretty good job playing yourself," Fantasia mumbled.

Nitara laughed. "All right. C'mon, ladies."

Grumbling, Martina and Fantasia stood to leave. Each of them took a moment to give Jalila a hug.

"If you want, you can just whisper in my ear who you're going to choose. That way I don't look like an idiot downstairs," Martina whispered.

Jalila shook her head. "Nice try."

"Can't blame a girl for trying." Martina laughed, and then she followed Fantasia and Nitara out the door.

Once they were gone, Jalila's gaze shifted back to the large vanity mirror, and she stared at her reflection while the hairstylist buzzed around her head. *What the hell am I doing? Am I really ready to go through with this?*

Sidebar:

"Who me, nervous? Nah," Tion says with a laugh. He's standing in front of the same incredible view of Butterfly Beach. "I definitely feel that Jalila could be my Michelle Obama. I think we'll make a good team. We could build a great future together. 'Yes we can!'"

Jalila needed another drink, but held back because she didn't want to risk making a fool of herself if she got too tipsy. The hairstylist was now replaced by the makeup artist, and she, of course, was doing an incredible job in transforming her into someone ready for the small screen.

There was another knock at the door and Jalila

tempered her irritation at so many people drifting and out the room. "Come in," she shouted.

The door pushed open, and Jalila's eyes grew wide with surprise. "You," she whispered, dismayed.

Tenetria smiled. "Hello, I hope I didn't catch you at a bad time."

"You know what?" the makeup artist said. "I need to run and get my other makeup box from downstairs so I can work on your eyelashes."

Before Jalila could stop her, the woman raced out of the room.

Tenetria's and Jalila's eyes locked in the mirror.

"What do you want? Why are you here?"

"Actually," Tenetria began. "For the first time in my life I'm about to do something for someone other than myself."

Jalila was torn between bolting and wanting to scratch out the other woman's eyes. "I have nothing to say to you."

"No. I didn't think so. But I think in this case maybe I should do all the talking."

Sidebar:

"I have my fingers crossed, you know," Evander says. "Jalila is a wonderful woman and I think whoever she chooses is going to be a lucky SOB. I just hope it's me."

At precisely six o'clock, Jalila left her hotel room and was led downstairs by an intern to the taping of the grand finale. She walked like a zombie, her mind churning over Tenetria's confession.

Nothing happened.

Jalila felt sick to her stomach. Not only had the woman backed up Keenan's story about him not even being there that night, but she'd also confessed that when Jalila had caught them in Keenan's office, that was the first time they had seen each other since their divorce. And even then Keenan had spurned her advances.

Nothing happened.

"Oh, Lord, what have I done?" What did it say about her that she was so willing to think the worst of Keenan— that she didn't even give him a chance to explain?

And that day in his office! Jalila's legs wobbled.

"Ms. Goodwyn, are you all right?" the intern asked.

Jalila nodded, though it was clearly not the truth.

"Do you want to sit down?" The young woman looked concerned.

"I'm going to be all right." Jalila drew in a few deep breaths and tried her damnedest not to ruin her three-hour makeup job.

Just pull yourself together, she said to herself. She looked deceptively low-maintenance, dressed in a delicate peach summer dress that was both loose and formfitting while a pair of teardrop earring hung from each earlobe.

Nitara raced up to her. "Okay. This is how this is gonna work. We have three different alcove areas where each bachelor is waiting with a ring. Now remember, we've been through this, the ring is just symbolic. Focus groups suggest that the target audience prefers to believe that you're getting ready to ride off into the sunset.

"We'll take you to the first alcove, then the second— you get the picture. You all right?"

"Yeah, sure." Jalila was on the verge of crying. She had lost the best thing that had ever happened to her because of pride.

"All right. We're ready to roll."

"*Places everyone!*" the director yelled.

Jon Krammer stood at his mark before camera number one.

"Aaaaaaannnddd *action!*"

"Good evening, America. Welcome to the grand finale of *Queen of Hearts.* As you know I am your host, Jon Krammer…"

Jalila tuned out while Krammer recapped the past couple of weeks. Her mind continued to whirl as if she wasn't about to make a fool out of herself on national television.

Minutes later, she was directed to walk out to the first alcove where bachelor number one awaited his fate. Again, she found herself sort of sleepwalking, trying to form the words she would have to say to this kind man who'd spent the past few weeks trying in vain to woo her heart.

The honor went to a man who probably despised her.

Jalila walked around the bend, passing one camera and then coming toward another. Bachelor number one was waiting with his back toward her.

Jalila's heart pounded with the force of a jackhammer. She worried that when she opened her mouth that she would just begin sobbing.

However, when the bachelor turned, she stopped, confused and frozen in place. "Keenan."

He smiled. "Hello, Jalila."

There was no holding back. Tears leaped from her eyes and rolled down her face, undoubtedly ruining her makeup.

Keenan walked toward her with a smooth, confident gait, his eyes locked on her face. "I know that this may come as a surprise, but…" he knelt down on one knee "…we've been through a lot recently, but I want to put that all behind us now. I want us to move forward. I want us to have a real chance at love."

Jalila's hand flew to her mouth. She was trembling so badly, she thought she would fall down at any minute.

"I didn't follow the rules of this game. And maybe a lot of people watching this will wonder just how the producer of the show ended up asking for your hand, but…I just know that I can't live one more day without you in my life. You've taught me how to feel again. How to love."

He reached into his pocket and pulled out a ring box. "This isn't just a symbolic ring for the sake of the show," Keenan said. "I'm truly asking you, will you marry me?"

Jalila choked on sobs as she nodded and then threw her arms around his neck. "Yes…yes…yes."

Keenan whooped with joy, jumping up and swinging her around. "She said *yes!*"

The entire crew erupted with applause. From the

corner of Jalila's eyes, she even saw her girlfriends and parents cheering them on. It was absolutely the best day of her life.

Epilogue

Six months later, a grinning Jon Krammer sat in the center of a studio stage arranged with a ring of empty chairs around him. The audience was crammed into tight rows, excited and anxious to see the cast of the hit reality show *Queen of Hearts*. Unbeknownst to them, during the past six weeks the final edited version that made it to air had ended up being more about what happened behind the scenes than scripted reality.

A lot of the hidden-video footage that Nitara shot of Keenan and Jalila secretly dating, plus Keenan's vow to never fall in love, was edited into the show's episodes. It was all very risky, but the series that aired was more like a mini-soap opera than the typical reality show, and the results made *Queen of Hearts* the top-rated series for the network.

"Quiet on the set," the director, Bill Wolfe, yelled and the loud clamoring immediately stopped. "Places, everyone."

Jon Krammer flashed camera number one his blindingly white smile.

"Aaaannnnddd action!"

"Good evening, America. And welcome to 'Queen of Hearts: The Reunion Show.' I am your host, Jon Krammer."

The studio audience was cued to applaud while camera number two scanned the clapping, cheering crowd.

"This evening," Krammer continued, "we will be checking in with America's number one couple, Keenan and Jalila *Armstrong.*"

This time the applause was a thunderous reaction that needed no cueing from the assistant director.

"But first we need to bring out a few familiar faces. Our first guests were show favorites. One woman who had no problems speaking her mind and kept the viewers guessing what color her hair would be from week to week. Our other guest is a woman who encouraged our bachelorette to follow her heart every step of the way. Everyone, please welcome Martina Hudson and Fantasia Silver."

The two friends strolled out onto the stage, beaming at the warm reception. Martina was dressed in a tight, loud yellow dress. She had magenta-colored hair. Fantasia kept it simple, wearing a black A-line dress.

"Welcome, ladies," Krammer greeted them, and gestured for them to take seats. When the women were settled, he started right in. "First, ladies, as you know, the ratings for the series were through the roof. What everyone wants to know is how you feel about your girlfriend's choice?"

"I think it's great," Fantasia answered first. "I know during filming we didn't really get to know Keenan personally, but clearly he swept Jalila off her feet and won her heart. She's happy, and I, for one, am happy for her."

Krammer turned his bleached-white smile toward Martina. "And what about you? You'd made it clear that you preferred Dontrell Smith—even used some colorful language about how well his muscles worked."

Martina smacked her glossy lips. "All I can say is, my girl's loss is my gain."

"Wooooooo!" the crowd responded and then laughed at Martina's answer.

Krammer bobbed his head. "Yes, we found out that the show is responsible for another love match. Can you tell us about it?"

Martina beamed and then flashed the camera and audience her modest one-carat diamond ring. "Bam! How do you like me now?"

The studio cheered and Krammer climbed to his feet. "Everyone, please welcome Martina's fiancé, Dontrell Smith."

Dontrell strolled onto the stage, waving. When he approached Martina, he opened his arms and greeted her with a kiss that thrilled everyone. As he took a seat, Martina assured the audience, "Trust me, I found out that boo knows how to work all the right muscles."

The crowd laughed.

Krammer held up his hands. "Calm down. Remember this isn't cable." He turned his attention to the camera. "Next, we have via satellite another losing bachelor, Evander Taylor."

Directly behind the circle of chairs, Evander's image suddenly appeared on a large flat-screen monitor. Apparently, there was an Evander fan club in the audience that went wild when he appeared.

"Welcome, Evander. Sorry you couldn't join us in person this evening."

"Yeah, well. It's all good," Evander said, clearly a little miffed at the situation.

"The producers tell me that you were a little angry about the finale. Tell us about it."

"Would this be the same producer who married the woman we were all trying to date?" he asked sarcastically. He quickly realized how bitter and angry he sounded and tried to backtrack, putting a more positive spin on it. "It's cool, man…whatever. I've moved on. I wish Jalila the best. But as far as the producers of the show…" He shook his head. "I just don't appreciate them wasting my time like that."

Krammer grimaced, but he clearly enjoyed the drama and hammed it up for the cameras. Tion Johnson was much more good-natured when he walked onto the stage and was greeted with only mild applause.

"We have two bachelors who found their happy endings and one who's not too thrilled with the producers of the show," Krammer said to Tion. "How do you feel about the show's finale?"

Tion shrugged good-naturedly. "It was cool, I guess. After seeing the show and everything, clearly there wasn't a love connection between me and Jalila."

"Do you have any regrets?" Krammer grilled.

"Well…" He smiled sheepishly. "Maybe it wasn't such a good idea to take Jalila to the golf course on a first date."

The audience laughed.

Tion quickly filled everyone in on what was going on in his political career and ignored the fact that he was boring the heck out of the host.

"So are you seeing anyone?" Krammer asked when there was a break in Tion's lengthy monologue.

"I'm still out there dating, checking out my options. I don't have any regrets about being on the show. I genuinely wish Jalila and Keenan the best."

"That's very gracious of you." Krammer held out his hand and thanked Tion for coming on the show before cutting to commercial break. During the break, Martina, Fantasia and Dontrell moved to different chairs in anticipation of the stars of the show.

"And welcome back to the reunion show for *Queen of Hearts,*" Krammer announced. "Our next guests are the ones you all have been waiting for. They led America on a surprising journey, and displayed cunning in playing cat-and-mouse off-camera with their secret love affair. They have been married now for three months. Everyone please welcome Keenan and Jalila Armstrong."

The audience jumped to their feet with long, roaring applause. When Jalila and Keenan strolled onto the set arm in arm, a few whistles and shouts of their name could be heard from the audience. Behind camera number three, they saw Nitara giving them the thumbs up.

A nervous Jalila was overwhelmed by the response. She squeezed her husband's arm tight and was rewarded with a brief kiss on her temple. That only turned the crowd's applause into a near-frenzy.

Krammer directed the couple to their seats as the cast waited for the crowd to quiet down. It took a few minutes, but finally everyone returned to their seats.

"Wow," Krammer said. "That was quite a greeting."

"Yes, it was." Jalila beamed out at the crowd.

"Are you surprised by the response to the show?" Krammer asked.

"Absolutely," she answered. "In fact, I was surprised that Nitara, the other producer, even bothered to save the show. I thought once I'd accepted Keenan's proposal that everything would be scrapped and we would just go on with our lives." She glanced over at Keenan. "After all, I've found the one that I've been looking for all my life."

Keenan smiled. "That makes two of us." He leaned in and kissed her gently on the lips. The love radiating between them couldn't be denied, and the audience was swept away by what they saw.

Krammer looked reluctant to cut in. "We have a clip of you, Keenan, right after the famous proposal. Let's have a look."

On the screen behind them, a smiling Keenan stood before a camera with Butterfly Beach in the background.

"This is the happiest day of my life!" Keenan declared, glowing. "I can't tell you how hard I fought against falling in love with this amazing woman, but now that I've given in, I can't help but wonder why I bothered fighting in the first place." He shook his head as if privately admonishing himself. "I love her. I can't remember exactly when it happened but…I'm sure glad that it did. I'd like to say that I'm sorry to the other bachelors, but the truth is…I'm not. I'm walking away from here with a beautiful woman who has agreed to be my wife. I can proudly say that she is the queen of my heart."

Two months later…

In the middle of Grant Park, Jalila raced around Keenan, Cujo and Chips with her minicamcorder, getting absolutely no cooperation from any of them. "C'mon, guys. I want to post this on my YouTube channel."

Keenan laughed and then tossed the Frisbee that sent the dogs scrambling. "Don't you think your subscribers are a bit sick of us by now? I'm starting to feel as if we're still starring in our own reality show."

Jalila lowered the camera. "Please, you got off lucky."

"Lucky?" Keenan jabbed his hands onto his hips. "Did you forget about all that footage Nitara filmed of me creeping out of your window, flashing all my business to the world?"

Jalila lowered the camera and laughed so hard that she had tears running down her face. "Oh, please, she blurred that out."

"I'm so glad that I amuse you," Keenan said, rolling his eyes.

"Aww…" Jalila rushed over to him, wrapped her arms around him and planted a wet kiss on his cheek. "I didn't know that my baby's feelings were still hurt."

Keenan saw an opportunity to milk the situation and poked out his bottom lip. "Well, I didn't want to say anything."

Jalila tried to soothe his ego with a tender kiss. "How's that, Mr. Armstrong?"

"I don't know. I think I might need some physical healing, *Mrs.* Armstrong."

Cujo and Chips barked, demanding some attention of their own.

"Hey!" Keenan said. "Can't you see that I'm trying to make my move here?"

Jalila laughed. "Maybe they know a poser when they see one."

"Who, me?"

Jalila lifted her camcorder again and put her husband in the shot.

He rolled his eyes. "What are you trying to film now?"

"I just want to post on my channel your expression when you learn that you're going to be a father."

Keenan started to complain again—until he finally understood what Jalila was saying. His jaw dropped and his eyes widened. "I'm gonna be a what?"

A smile exploded across Jalila's face as she continued to record his reaction. "You're going to be a daddy."

Keenan let out a shout, swept Jalila off her feet and swung her around.

The dogs went into a barking frenzy.

Jalila's heart swelled with love as she enjoyed the second happiest day of her life. Finally she had achieved everything she'd ever wanted. Her Prince Charming, and soon a little prince or princess would enter the picture to fill the rest of their lives with more love. And as long as she had her camera, she was going to continue to share her newfound happiness with the world.

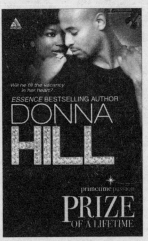

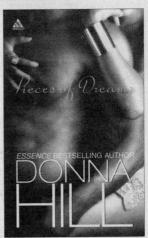

HOLLINGTON HOMECOMING

Where old friends reunite…
and new passions take flight.

Book #1 by Sandra Kitt
RSVP WITH LOVE
September 2009

Book #2 by Jacquelin Thomas
TEACH ME TONIGHT
October 2009

Book #3 by Pamela Yaye
PASSION OVERTIME
November 2009

Book #4 by Adrianne Byrd
TENDER TO HIS TOUCH
December 2009

Ten Years. Eight Grads. One weekend.
The homecoming of a lifetime.

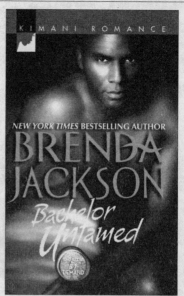

REQUEST YOUR FREE BOOKS!

2 FREE NOVELS
PLUS 2 FREE GIFTS!

KIMANI™
ROMANCE

Love's ultimate destination!

KROM09

HELP CELEBRATE
ARABESQUE'S
15TH ANNIVERSARY!

ARABESQUE®

2009 marks Arabesque's
15th anniversary!

Help us celebrate by telling us about your most special memories and moments with Arabesque books. Entries will be judged by the Arabesque Anniversary Committee based on which are the most touching and well written. Fifteen lucky winners will receive as a prize a full-grain leather duffel bag with the Arabesque anniversary logo.

How to Enter: To enter, hand-print (or type) on an 8 ½" x 11" plain piece of paper your full name, mailing address, telephone number and a description of your most special memories and moments with Arabesque books (in two hundred [200] words or less) and send it to "Arabesque 15th Anniversary Contest 20901"—in the U.S.: Kimani Press, 233 Broadway, Suite 1001, New York, NY 10279, or in Canada: 225 Duncan Mill Road, Don Mills, ON M3B 3K9. No other method of entry will be accepted. The contest begins on July 1, 2009, and ends on December 31, 2009. Entries must be postmarked by December 31, 2009, and received by January 8, 2010. A copy of these Official Rules is available online at www.myspace.com/kimanipress, or to obtain a copy of these Official Rules (prior to November 30, 2009), send a self-addressed, stamped envelope (postage not required from residents of VT) to "Arabesque 15th Anniversary Contest 20901 Rules," 225 Duncan Mill Road, Don Mills, ON M3B 3K9. Limit one (1) entry per person. If more than one (1) entry is received from the same person, only the first eligible entry submitted will be considered. By entering the contest, entrants agree to be bound by these Official Rules and the decisions of Harlequin Enterprises Limited (the "Sponsor"), which are final and binding.

NO PURCHASE NECESSARY. Open to legal residents of U.S. and Canada (except Quebec) who have reached the age of majority at time of entry. Void where prohibited by law. Approximate retail value of each prize: $131.00 (USD).

VISIT **WWW.MYSPACE.COM/KIMANIPRESS**
FOR THE COMPLETE OFFICIAL RULES

KP15ARACONTEST